I0706193

WINGO'S REDEMPTION

MIKE VANCE

DOS DOGS PRESS

Library of Congress Cataloging-in-Publication Data
Names: Vance, Mike 1959 – author
Title: Wingo's Redemption
Identifiers: LCCN TXu 2-442-717
ISBN (paperback) 978-1-965272-01-5
ISBN (hardback) 978-1-965272-02-2
ISBN (ebook) 978-1-965272-00-8

ALSO BY

Please enjoy these other titles by Mike Vance. They are available where books are sold and also at www.mikevancewriter.com

Non-Fiction

Undertold Texas Volume 1

Getting Away With Bloody Murder

Mud & Money: A Timeline of Houston History

Murder & Mayhem in Houston (with John Nova Lomax)

Houston Baseball: The Early Years, 1861-1961

Houston's Sporting Life

Stand-Up Stories: Tales from Behind the Microphone During Comedy's Golden Age

Brenham

Fiction

Wingo: The Remarkable Story of an Unremarkable Man

Wingo's Redemption

Zeke Gets Glasses. Jungleburgh Children's Reading Community (with John Swasey)

This is a work of fiction. Although its form is that of an autobiography, it is not one. All the names, characters, businesses, places, events and incidents in this book are either the product of the author's imagination or used in a fictitious manner. With the exception of public figures, any resemblance to actual persons, living or dead, or actual events is purely coincidental. The actions and words of public figures or businesses described in this book are completely fictitious and were created from the whole cloth of the author's imagination for the purposes of entertainment and humor. The opinions expressed are those of the characters and should not be confused with the author's. This is NOT a documentary. Anyone taking any part of this book as factual or real may wish to consider seeking help from a trained medical professional.

Printed in the United States of America

Interviewer's note: This is the conclusion of my interviews with Mr. Rube Wingo. Hopefully you have already read the first part. My intention is to provide the reader with a verbatim transcription of our visits, done when he was 116 years old. I recorded this second part of his life's stories over the course several weeks, and he rarely tired in his telling. With that breathy, drawling delivery, Mr. Wingo proved to be a consummate storyteller whether sharing a memory bawdy or sweet, and I hope that the reader will be as beguiled as I. It is certainly okay to laugh out loud since Mr. Wingo certainly sought my frequent acknowledgments that I was heartily amused. The words and the unique voice are his alone, and once the rhythm is acquired, they proved to be mesmerizing to me. Hopefully the reader will concur. Though his recollection of some events may appear to be a bit fanciful, his recall for baseball dates and statistics was astonishing.

CINCINNATI

Chapter One

Grief has a talent for unexpected visits. They're right when they say it's the little things. At first it was opening my eyes in the morning and realizing I didn't hear soft, off key humming from the kitchen or didn't catch the smell of buttered toast. Jenny made it in the oven broiler, you know. The feelings might come from what you found in a drawer or tucked between pages of a book. Most often it was the silence.

I know it's the dumbest bad song cliché there is, but I really did see her face everywhere I looked. There'd be a crowd of people waiting for the subway, and I'd catch a glimpse of Jenny, just out of reach. Most every place I passed had a memory associated with her. I never thought of myself as a wandering soul, but after just a few weeks, I'd convinced myself that it was time to move on. My old buddy Paul Flinkenberg had been there all along the way, stopping by the hospital or downing beers after the nuns booted me out. A couple of others stepped up, too, but I knew they'd all have to go back to their own lives quick enough. Who'd miss me in the end? You can rationalize all manner of bad decisions when you're carrying grief.

Everybody cautioned me not to do anything rash, of course, but the desire to just get the hell out of New York overwhelmed me. The bleakness of winter slush and the list of boys dying in the war certainly didn't help my mood. The Americans were stalled out in Italy. Our bombers were pounding the dog shit out of Germany but getting shot down at a clip that you were better off ignoring. Above it all, I didn't want to be the selfish bastard who wallowed in my own stink while the whole world was collectively going to hell.

You fret about whether you'd know anyone. You create your hijinks with those early running buddies, and they become your lifelong friends. But once you get older, you don't see them every day like you used to. I told myself I'd make new friends, but I had long ago learned the lesson that it's the friends of your youth who stick to your ribs. So that part was hard. I made up my mind.

Deciding where to go was not an easy pick, either. Once I'd decided on pulling up stakes, I started evaluating who might be able to get me another clubhouse or equipment job. Baseball was all I'd ever known, and my prospects at anything different than that were slimmer than Audrey Hepburn's capri pants. I weighed the pros and cons of various big league cities and some of the better Double A ones, those being the top minors. The West Coast had an allure, but it was expensive to get to and from there, and I wasn't exactly flush with jack. I'd heard good things about other places like Minneapolis or Milwaukee or Toronto, but I hate the cold. Kansas City was a nice town, but that was the Yankees farm club, so I scratched that right out. That team had already fired me once, and I reckoned at least one of us still held a grudge. A big league outfit would be harder to hook onto, plus the fact that three of them were right there in New York, the place I was in a hurry to vacate.

I've been having an internal debate with myself for 75 years as to whether or not I was completely decided on my destination when I dropped off my apartment key to the building super Dumitru, shook his hand, and carried my one big suitcase north on 7th Avenue. Even though it was colder than a popsicle on ice, I walked to save a little coin. The quality of my luggage had improved since I first laid eyes on Manhattan in 1922, as had the clothes inside of it, but there was still only the single piece I'd decided to take with me. And I planned to leave from the same giant of a building that had first welcomed me to New York.

Most long distance trains left Penn Station around dinner time. I took a deep breath and told the man behind the ticket cage to give me one for the Cincinnati Limited, a fancy new train in dark red with a spiffy yellow stripe. Aft of the regular cars were half a dozen rolling troop dorms taking young fellows on a journey to God knows where, and behind that were 10 more flat beds loaded with half-tracks. By the time I got down the platform to my car, I felt like I'd done walked to Ohio. Then I proceeded to settle into my seat and second guess myself for over 700 miles.

The fellow I knew best in Cincinnati was Waite Hoyt. He had been working radio for the Reds for two seasons, and though he was not what you'd call entrenched, he knew all the folks with the ball club. Now, he never did actually invite me, of course, but I'd convinced myself on the train ride that he would have if he'd thought about it. We weren't precisely running buddies, but we'd met with the Memphis Chicks and I'd took good care of him in the Yankee's clubhouse.

When the Limited reached her destination, I stepped down onto the platform at Union Terminal, bought myself a newspaper and a bottle of Coke, and asked the local operator to find me a number for Waite Hoyt. I'd last visited with him when he was with the Dodgers, his sixth team, and he pitched for a couple of them twice. It was around the first of May in 1938 on a day when he gave up a pair of doubles in the eighth and lost to us Giants at the Polo Grounds. About a week or two later, he and Heinie Manush each found a note in their lockers that they were being let go. That's like your girlfriend dumping you by text, ain't it?

He was surprised to hear from me, and it might be that he intended to be polite and let me go. When I explained that I was looking for a new city to call home on account of my wife passing away, he got real quiet.

"Rube, I am awfully sorry to hear that," he told me. And you could tell he meant it.

Technically, Waite worked for one of the radio stations, WKRC, not the Reds proper. Nevertheless, he asked me where I was and said he'd make a phone call. I'll bet it wasn't more than 20 minutes that the pay phone number I'd given him rang. For the second time in my life, that very nice man put in a word to get me a big league clubhouse job. Unlike in 1922, this time he was sober.

I was to report to the team offices, unimpressive little place such as it was, that day after lunch to speak to Warren Giles and Bill McKechnie. Giles was the team president, and he was as Midwestern as they come. Had been a lieutenant in France during WWI and had worked his way up through the minor leagues by being a smart and loyal baseball man. A straight arrow, as they say. He had married the great-granddaughter of John Deere in Moline, Illinois, and sadly, she had died suddenly in the summer of 1943, just a few months before my Jenny. Neither one of us ever spoke to the other about any of that, of course. That's not what men of different stations did. Still, I was almost certain that Waite had dropped a mention of my specific woes. I was hired.

With the war on, teams trained close to home. The Reds went right up the road to Bloomington, Indiana. It was my introduction to about half of the fellows. I'd met various of them through the years I was with the Giants or Yankees. Harry Gumbert had been a middle of the rotation pitcher for the Giants for six years, and his welcome probably smoothed the way as much as anything.

The star of the Reds in those days was Bucky Walters, the top thrower in the National League for the years just before and during the war. Hell of a hitter, too. He'd been an electrician for a time before signing to play ball, and I recollect that he ended up fixing the wiring on three or four lamps and a small chandelier at the Graham Hotel where they put us up. The night manager staked him to a little bar tab for his trouble. Bucky was coming off an appendectomy and had a big year in 1944, second best of his career. Nearly everybody had to keep his offseason trade to make ends meet, though. Even the best player on the squad.

All the spring baseball took place at the university there, so there was more than a bit of fraternizing betwixt the ballplayers and the coeds. Cute little sorority girls slipping in and out of that old hotel, up and down the fire escape and what have you at all hours. You could hear them trying not to squeal. At least they had functioning bedside light.

One fellow in camp with us was Chucho Ramos, an outfielder and first baseman from Venezuela. He ended up playing in about four games in May, but had a balky back, and that was the end of his big league career. He had been a top sprinter when he was younger, and had gone to their military academy. I found it fascinating that a body could be no more than a flyspeck in the Baseball

Encyclopedia up here in the States, but be a very famous player back home. He was only the second Venezuelan to play in the big leagues, you see. I imagine he played for well over a decade more down there in South America, and for years, aspiring ballplayers in Caracas or Maracaibo played in the Liga Chucho Ramos, just like some little bruiser in Scranton might play Pop Warner.

There was another rookie in camp that stands out, but in this case it wasn't due to baseball. Son, did you ever meet anyone who just seemed bred to be the butt of practical jokes? Bryson Baugh was just such a kid. He was a college boy who had pitched at William and Mary, so most of the guys wrote him off just for that alone. He had a middling fastball and lived on a big overhand curve. And this next part may confuse you, but he always smelled too clean. It just wasn't the odor of a ballplayer, and within a matter of hours after everyone's arrival in Bloomington, some fellows had determined that action must be taken.

Harry Gumbert let on to a few of the more high-spirited Reds that I had some chops as a creator of pranks, and one night a few of the veterans cornered me in a bar for suggestions. The one they latched onto was swapping his cologne out for pickle juice. We dumped the real stuff down the sink drain, keeping just enough to smear generously around the rim of the bottle. That Baugh kid wore it for the full five or six weeks until one day he noticed a seed floating around in there. By that time, he'd attracted a whole pack of Norwegian women. He never made it in the bigs, but from what I heard tell, he lived out his life as the happiest reindeer wrangler in Tromso. Sometimes things just work out.

Crosley Field was as big a change from Yankee Stadium and the Polo Grounds as Cincinnati was from New York. Like the city itself, Crosley was more small and intimate. It may have been a grand statement when it was new, but by 1944, the first thing you noticed was how close it was. Front row fans could damn near pick the pockets of the on-deck batter. The PA announcer was right by the end of the visitor's dugout, and any trip to the clubhouse meant gladhanding with the hoi polloi along the third base line. You were up close and personal at Crosley Field.

Perched just outside the turnstiles was Peanut Jim Shelton who spiffed up the neighborhood. He wore a top hat and bow tie and smoked cigars and sold hot peanuts that he'd bag up on the spot. He had him a fruit and nut stand on Liberty Avenue, but on game days Peanut Jim had him a coal-fired push cart. Young folks today will tell you it's part of a game day experience, but shit, hot peanuts taste good. I didn't realize eating had to be an experience.

The owner was Mr. Crosley, of course. He had gotten rich off of selling automobile parts through the mail, and then started manufacturing Crosley radios when that medium was still gumming pablum. By the 1930s, they made a whole bunch of stuff from oscillating fans to compact cars. You could pick up his radio station, WLW, in every corner of the U.S. east of the Rockies. If Ma Perkins scratched her armpit, folks in Tucumcari knew about it. Mr. Crosley was rolling in it.

I'd never seen the man, but I sure liked him. That was because of the employee discount we could sometimes finagle on Crosley products. I reckon it was after my second or third paycheck that I went and bought myself a record player and radio. That was a corker of a set, that radio. Streamlined and turquoise-colored with two knobs and a big dial over to the right hand side. It tuned in real nice, too.

The first place I lived was an attic room at 1020 Celestial Street in Mt. Adams. From my back window, I could see the ball yard. It was a blue collar neighborhood back then. Lots of Irish and Germans. A monastery was a block or two away, and it had a big stone wall around part of it. The fellows that lived there didn't mingle much, but I'd catch one or two of them sneaking a smoke as I walked past the gate, and we'd trade a head nod. I heard tell that in the 60s, Mt. Adams become the hippie part of Cincinnati with tie dye shops, hairy legged women, and ironic poets in coffeehouses. No word on if they sold my cousin's carved hogs.

The best part about the whole neighborhood, and the reason I never had a serious thought about living anywhere else, was the Mt. Adams Incline. The streetcar would drive out onto this platform and then a railway would carry the thing down the hill. It was slicker than olive oil snot. It was a tad disconcerting at first on account of you being perched several feet above the rails, but if you squinted, there was a certain Superman quality to the whole thing, flying slowly through the air like that. If it wasn't too crowded, I'd extend both arms out in front of me. The incline shut down in 1948, but I swear I never got tired of riding that thing while it lasted.

My dog Mango had moved with me. I'd named her that on account of her coat was just the color of that wonderful fruit when it got ripe. Turned out she was twice as sweet, though I didn't know it when I got her. She wandered up to me one day at the equipment shed out back at Yankee Stadium. Skinny and skittish. She'd had rocks throwed at her dozens of times, I imagine, but the hunger finally overrode the fear. We've all been there.

Mango'd come to Ohio with me from New York. She was one of my best pals for 13 years. Back in the Village, at nights, when my wife was fading and couldn't keep her eyes open, I'd chase Jenny off the couch and into bed. Then Mango would curl up in my lap, and we'd listen to the radio, just the two of us for hours. Big band music from the west coast. Best music that ever was. If you don't know that, son, you need to.

I think of Mango from time to time still, like I do with all my dogs. But it could be that, from this distance, her dying was the most memorable part of her life for me. There was a veterinarian in Cincinnati, Dr. Shook, who lived over on East Liberty Street. Old Mango had been sick. Some growths had popped up, and there was nothing anyone could do about it. I knew her time was coming for months. Then one night she couldn't get up to meet me when I came in the door. Tail wagging just a whisper. Grinning, but her breathing was labored like a fat man walking to a fourth-floor whore house. She tried to tell me it was okay at first, but I could see it in her eyes. At the back of those big black eyes, Mango told me it was time to go.

I wrapped her up in a towel, trying not to make her yelp since she was hurting. Then I flagged down a cab, and we woke up Doc Shook.

I held my sweet girl and talked to her while he give her two shots. Told her what a good girl she was. There was a thick white one that put her to sleep, then a thin looking one that just made her stop breathing. Her eyes never closed all the way, like she was still looking at me to let me know everything was all right when that was supposed to be my job all along. Above all, I couldn't help thinking of how much she'd rather just get up and go back home to play catch.

I thanked the doctor, paid him a few bucks and grabbed another taxi back to my place. The thing that made it so remarkable was that I sobbed like a baby the whole way home and kept crying like some big sap right through a bottle and a half of cheap-ass wine until I finally nodded off on the sofa.

The worst of it was when I woke up the next morning. Emptiness was every way I turned. There was no walk to be taken, no food bowl to fill, and no crunching noise to soothe me while I poked at my cereal. So, I just spent the hours staring and wiping tears. For days I'd lie in bed listening for her breath, her toenails clicking on the linoleum or a slurping at the water bowl. But they never come.

I had cried at my Jenny's death, you know, and my mama's. I was sad when I left New York and all that it had meant to me, but sometimes things build up without you knowing that it's so, and it just hits you bigger than you expect it will. Straw that broke the camel's back, as they say, and Mango was my straw. I loved her very much, but no more than all my other dogs, including this sweet boy in my lap right now, the little rascal. But Lord how I cried over losing her that night. Lord, how I cried.

I met Dummy Hoy during that first season in Cincinnati. He was among the old timers who used to come to the games at Crosley Field. The National League had give him a silver ticket signifying that he was welcome at any ballgame for free, and the man took advantage. He was north of 80 years old by the time I met him, but as spry as a puppy. If the weather was obliging, he'd walk to the ball yard.

His name come from the fact that he was deaf and mute. In his day, that meant people called you Dummy, and if anyone messed up and said his first name of William, by golly, he would correct them. He was a hell of a ball player at the end of the 1800s, especially for a petite fellow, and was important enough to his club that many of his teammates studied the hand signs a little bit to communicate with him.

I never learned to do that myself, but we had a hot dog vendor name of Dwayne Ivy who was deaf. He could tote that metal steamer with the best of them, but you sure as shit needed to grab his attention on the way up the aisle. He also had the most uncanny ability to give a customer a quick look over and determine mustard or ketchup and just the perfect ration of relish and onions. Never seen anything like it.

When things got slow in his section, he would sit and talk with Dummy Hoy, and once or twice, I got to join them when we had a ballgame called on account of rain. Dwayne, who could speak, would translate. The old man seemed to enjoy the conversations. Not for any great insights on my part, mind you, but I asked a lot of leading questions that ease the elderly into a good tale.

Mostly, though, it was thanks to my past acquaintance with Arlie Latham, an old ballplayer at whose delicatessen I had worked for two off-seasons straight. See, Hoy and Latham had been teammates in Cincinnati some 50 years prior, Hoy in the outfield and Latham at third. Bid McPhee and Buck Ewing was on that team with them. Charlie Comiskey, too, but they still weren't worth a goose turd. That might be a function of less than stellar pitching in an age when the ball was deader than grandpa's top hat.

There were two especially interesting fellows from that squad that Dummy reminisced about. One was a little outfielder called Bug Holliday. He had been ramping it up for a handful of seasons, knocked over 13 homers to lead the league twice, but then in 1894, he reached another gear. The Bug hit .376 with 123 RBIs. Then he had his appendix removed during the offseason, and never was better than a pinch hitter again. Got addicted to gambling on the horses, and died of gangrene in his leg barely after turning 40. Hoy judged it to be a crying shame, but there were those among the Reds of those days who swore that Bug's appendix possessed magical powers far beyond the little red sack of fluid that it was.

The other name that captured my fancy was that of Ice Box Chamberlain, a pitcher who had won 32 games once, but was also the first in baseball history to give up four home runs to the same batter in a single game. Hoy spun golden yarns about Ice Box's gambling and pool room hijinks including a doozer about him winning a diamond ring from some Irish bookie on a prize fight only to have the boxer he'd bet on steal the gem and abscond for parts unknown. It certainly seemed a tale straight out of Dickens.

Chapter Two

My local while I lived in Cincinnati, the neighborhood watering hole where I spent a good deal of my time, was a dark little place with a big jar of pickled eggs next to the cash register. It was named the Licky Dog. It was supposed to be the Lucky Dog, but the sign maker screwed up, and the original owner figured what the hell, a licky dog was more common anyway. I heard tell the fifty dollar discount he got on the sign was a real persuader, too.

It was more than memories I left behind in New York. What was left of my usual drinking buddies had been there, too. I made some good pals quick enough at the Licky. Do you know the difference between bar friends and regular friends? You can sit and expose every intimacy of your life with a bar buddy, buy rounds for each other and bare your soul, but chances are good that you have no idea what the inside of the other person's house looks like. It's 50/50 that you don't know their last names. Nothing wrong with that. It still provides for all your social needs. Eventually, you and ones closest to you start meeting up at a restaurant before you head to the bar. I'd leave tickets to a ball game here and there. That tavern was home plate for my social life in Cincy. It was a fine, dark, odiferous place.

I become especially tight with the guy who handled the vending machine route. He serviced jukeboxes, cigarette machines, and coin operated pool tables across Cincinnati, but the Licky was his hang out. He was a big, round Irishman who always had a smile on his face. Brody Byrne was his name. He was quick to buy a beer, though I never asked questions about why he always paid with nickels and dimes.

Since most of the places where he emptied the machines didn't open all that early, Brody had the mornings free. There were more than a handful of times we'd close down the bar then linger over a diner breakfast, swapping tall tales of previous lives. Once or twice, he even talked me into going to watch birds when the sun come up. He loved birds. That man could name every type of fowl that passed through the Midwest. It was amazing. We spotted hawks and bobwhites and a couple of colorful warblers that would put you in a good mood all day.

Brody had been seeing this plump but classy redheaded girl for three or four months. She always looked like she was slumming by coming to our little hole in the wall, but they had themselves a time, laughing it up, her springing for at least half the drinks and generally ending the evening back at his place. Once the deed had been done, she'd pack up and skedaddle. We told him he'd found a near perfect woman. We changed our minds after her husband showed up to drag her out of the Licky one night. He looked just as embarrassed as pissed off, and I suspect his main goal was to confirm his suspicions. The lack of eye contact from everyone would have done that for a smarter fellow, I reckon.

We didn't see her again, but Brody, for all of his protesting to the contrary, was down in the dumper. Then one night several weeks later, a paint and drywall man named Greg fessed up that he knew where this less than happy couple lived over by Bond Hill. He had applied two coats of burnt umber to their pergola. I allowed as how that sounded similar to what Brody had been doing to her back at his place.

That night, as the empties mounted, Brody decided that he needed to purge his heartbreak with a random act of stupidity, as he put it. About 2:30 that morning, four of us die hards located the house and decorated every shrub on their manicured lawn with the older contents of Brody's laundry basket. There were also two of three pairs of sheer and ample panties that the red head had left behind. We laughed for many a night picturing the early rising neighbors stepping out for their newspaper and milk bottles only to see the rhododendrons next door strewn with a dozen size 48 tighty whiteys. Brody said he needed new skivvies anyhow. I'm sure he paid for them with loose change.

I traveled with the team infrequently after I started working for the Reds, but when I went to Chicago, it was to the North Side. Still, I usually made sure to go spend time with Pearl. My first trip with my new ball club was late August of 1944. Understand, Jenny was my Juliet, but Pearl was my warm, soft blanket. We had known each other 25 years at that point. A quarter century. I could barely recollect the young kids we'd been when we first helped each other ease into adulthood.

I didn't have to tell Pearl how I felt about losing Jenny. She just knew. I reckoned she had undergone her own losses. Whoever the fellow was that she had been with those years before, she never had to hurry off home again. We spent a lot of time just being in each other's company, me and Pearl. Middle aged by that time. Or at least I thought it was middle age. I sure as hell didn't know I'd live to be a hundred and sixteen.

I had some odd emotions on that trip, if I can get all touchy feely for a second. Even while I was enjoying my evenings with Pearl, I found myself being guilty about how I left Jenny for a road trip one time long since passed. I'd been glad to get away, to get back on the road. It must have been in 1941. Me traveling was normal, but it was after we'd been together for a few years. Any married person who tells you they never longed for time alone is a goddamned liar. It didn't mean that I loved her one ounce less, but I suppose I missed the adventure of my occasional junkets with the club a bit more that day. In the hindsight of loss, it's easy to say you'd have done it all different, but skedaddling off to hobnob with the boys on the Giants was a complete no-brainer at the time. It just took three years for that kernel of guilt to pop, I reckon.

Of course, like always, I was obliged to work a full time job in the off season. The winter gig I found in Cincinnati in those early years was at the Hamilton Shop Rag Company, an outfit that manufactured little red wiping cloths of the sort that mechanics used on their hands while they shook their heads and told you that your whole transmission's shot. It was a vital part of the car repair industry.

Except for owners and the starriest of the stars, there wasn't a soul in baseball that didn't have to get a winter job of some sort. Most of the boys went back to their hometown and sold cars or insurance or worked in their daddy's service station. But me not having any kinfolks left by that time, I was obliged to stay where I was, so having a good old American factory job was a godsend.

My job was in the dye room. When the ladies in the edge sewing department got finished, they sent the rags along to us, and we assured that they come out of the vat a faded rose color. The management was very particular about it, too. They knew their customers. No gas pump jockey wanted to be wiping down your dipstick with something that was too cherry or ruby or garnet or jam. It was important that it be just the right shade to show oil wear. The sale of a quart of 30-weight depended on it.

The other fellow in the dying operation was Hank Woerther. He had been the head dye man there since 1906, when his boss had shown up to work with two snoots full, stumbled into the dye vat, and drowned. Hank said it turned the whole batch a sangria tint, and they was obliged to throw it all out. On the other hand, Hank told me that a simple garnish of orange truly made for a dashing open casket.

Being as how there was only the two of us in the dye room, I come on board as the assistant dye man, a step up since I was still a second assistant equipment man for the Reds. Old Woerther was a genial fellow. Had him a brushy grey moustache that was almost an exact match for his coveralls. He chewed Brown's Mule plug tobacco, and every so often, he'd aim a stream of juice at the vat. He claimed it softened the rags.

I'd figure you already know this, but it's funny. Whether there's a God or not, and I'm still not 100percent certain at age 116, one thing for sure is that life holds a damn interesting plan. Just when you think you know something, another thing comes along to remind you that you ain't all that damn smart in the first place.

What makes me think of that now is a vague picture of a kid named of Aaron Weckendecker. Big old pimply-faced first baseman that come to spring training in

March of 1946. His daddy had played minor league ball, and I reckon that counts for something. Now 1946, well, that was the year that the whole world was just trying to find its way back to normal, so it's almost as if nothing counted in the permanent record if it happened in 1946.

I was at that point in a man's life where you might be prone to feeling sorry for yourself. Sultan or hobo, you get to thinking that you're on the down side of the curve, stuck back of the alley cans, and it creeps over most every thought that comes into your pea shaped little head.

It's when you first notice that the shapely, unwrinkled girls can walk right past you and not be any more aware than a three-week old Chihuahua at the ballet. Hell, I still don't get the ballet, and I'm not a dog. Much.

So, Weckendecker was trying to make the big club, and we all knew it was a long shot. And let me tell you something, if a kid ain't gonna stick, you just learn to give him a wide berth. It's like how navy fellas are careful about not whistling on deck. You avoid the Jonahs. And poor old Aaron Weckendecker was surely all that.

The bad thing is that it's sort of what the professors on a club have called a self-fulfilling prophesy. If you treat some kid bad enough, ignore them like they were wearing a poison ivy suit, then what the hell do you expect? Their head ain't never going to be right for hitting a baseball.

Well, sir, one night young Aaron and me found ourselves standing together at the bar in Tampa, Florida. Little lounge of a place called the Bearded Lion.

Try as I might to ignore him, and that was my plan until I could sneak off, he was in a mood to start talking. What I found out was this here: Weckendecker was all of nineteen years old. Two years shy of legally having the rum and cola I was watching him drink. But there was more.

The boy had grown up in Eden Prairie, Minnesota and been a pure phenom, but then there's lots of nineteen-year olds with promise. Even Lyndon Johnson was good looking at one point. The thing is, though, not all of them find themselves at the bottom of a fox hole in Bastogne. Flat as you can get against the cold dirt and wanting to dig further, wishing your fingernails would grow like gardening spades.

Now, I got to say that I lived my life pretty sunny most every day, but here I was at that moment feeling a bit puny. See, it'd been one of those days where someone had jumped up one side of my not so skinny ass and climbed down the other. The kind of day where the toughest part of the toilet paper is the perforation. I try not to pay heed to those things. Like I told you about Babe Ruth, water off a duck's butt.

Not that it matters why, but I was feeling like the whole world thought I was dumber than an earthworm on pot.

And do you know what young Aaron said to me? He said, "You can't do that, Rube. Tomorrow is a different day."

Now Scarlet O'Hara told me that much back at the Capitol Theatre on Broadway in 1939, though I might not have heard it all that close cause I was in the balcony with my young wife at the time. And any fellow who ever touched latex in Elmira will know what that meant.

I hadn't even been talking to the boy, mind you, just listening, but in the middle of a silence, after sharing what was no doubt but a spoonful of the horrors he'd seen only 14 months before, the missing limbs, the exploded skulls, the hopeless sobs, and the blood curdling screams, young Aaron looked at me and noticed that I was blue.

Somehow what the boy said about tomorrow got through. In between the pity and the Hudepohl, it occurred to me what his day must have been like sometimes. Watching your good buddies calling for Mama and trying to stuff their guts back up inside of them is a mite different than seeing your pals slam a bat over the water bubbler 'cause they swung at a bad slider.

I guess it give me some perspective. At least for that night.

I don't need to tell you that young Weckendecker didn't make it past the first cut. I wish I could tell you what happened to him, that he become a doctor or a fireman or something and saved ten people's lives, but I'd be lying if I did. I never heard about him again. But his words sure slapped me in the head that night.

Weckendecker wasn't the only war veteran trying to make the big leagues in those days. There was guys who had left the Reds and every other ball club to go serve their country, and guys who was right on the lip of getting their big break when Uncle Sam called them up, and they was all home and trying to win back a spot on the roster. A hundred some odd ballplayers got killed fighting the Japs and Geris, but there was even more big league careers shot down by bad timing.

One kid comes to mind right off, a stocky little catcher name of Snouts Livermore. When the war came, he was about a year and half out of Oklahoma A&M and climbing his way through the minor leagues. He'd had him a sort of breakthrough second half at Wichita Falls in 1941, but before the next season started, the Army come calling.

I suppose he was a smart fellow for an Okie, of course that's relative, but they tossed him into Officers Candidate School, and he come out just in time to lead a pack of GIs into Morocco in November of 1942. The story was that he fought like a scalded lion across the desert, then up through Sicily and those stony mountains in Italy. He come home all sinewy and edgy but with one of the best throwing arms on any backstop I ever saw.

Trouble was that his mind wasn't all there. Boy had the flashbacks. Periodically during a game he'd run to the stands, snatch something out of a fan's hands and fire it toward second base. Didn't matter what it was, beer bottle, hot dog weiner, chicken leg, Snouts would holler "Nazi Bastards!" and zip it down to poor Bobby Adams when he'd least expect it.

Things got real ugly the Sunday afternoon we had a tinned food drive, and Livermore lobbed more than three dozen of them into right field. A little trivia for you, that's where we get the old baseball saying "can of corn".

The last straw for the boy come one evening when a particularly fluffy soprana from the Opera was performing the National Anthem, the fat lady singing as it were. Just as she was fixing to shatter glass with "rockets' red glare," Snouts leaped from the dugout, screamed "INCOMING!" at the top of his lungs and threw her to the turf. He didn't get suspended or nothing, and we all thought it was damned funny. The trouble was that her pointy breastplate punctured his lung. Poor old Snouts Livermore.

Of all the other sad ballplayer war stories, the only one I know that ever come close to Snouts was a Navy vet the Indians signed. One day Dutch Meyer ripped a hellacious fart in the clubhouse, and this poor schmo started hollering, "DIVE. DIVE!"

Chapter Three

That winter, I went back down to Cuba. Sam Estill, my childhood buddy from Lee County, had given me a call, saying he had a man drop out on him. It sounded like something fun to do, and I imagined it lifting me the final way out of my two year funk. I was hooked on with Cienfuegos, the Elefantes, as a clubhouse and equipment fellow and jack of all trades, same jobs as I'd done two decades prior. That means elephants, by the by. Elefantes.

It may have been a mite more mixed than my first trip to the island, but a body still couldn't miss the divide between Black Cubans and Whites. Every baseball team was buzzing with a different feel, though, knowing that Jackie Robinson had been playing Triple A ball up in Montreal. Even more exciting was that he'd be coming right to Havana that spring. They might have denied it, but there was not a dark-skinned player in the country who didn't see it all as a sliver of hope shining through the new crack in the door. Who didn't want to reach the bigs?

It was a fascinating place to stay, Cienfuegos. A really pretty town on this blue bay lined with palm trees and colonial buildings. Once you got off the main drags, the streets were narrow and a little mysterious. There was a man who sold coffee by the cup from a suitcase near our hotel. There were lottery tickets everywhere just like Harlem in the 20s.

I liked Cienfuegos, despite a few things that would put you a tad off balance. There was an old lady who fed the neighborhood cats. That don't sound scary, but you didn't see it happening. It was an alarming spectacle. There were seemingly hundreds of them, and they began to gather about half an hour before the big daily event. They'd be hunkered in doorways, beneath bushes and on top of stone walls. There were cats under and on top of cars lining the street, and good luck to anyone's upholstery.

It would be easy to say the woman had a witchy quality, but that was not the half of it. She could see, I think, but it's possible she could only see cats. She'd look right through you if you tried say good morning, which I did exactly twice. She would yell variations on the word gatos and call some of those strays by names she'd given them. It was a high-pitched caterwauling, which I reckon is an appropriate word except that noise come from her. Then she'd pour pans of food scraps into big piles on the street. The cats would swarm it like ants. Big, flea-ridden, furry ants. The image of it would keep you awake.

Havana was the happening spot, of course, and we seemed to play most of our games up there since they had multiple teams in the league. The place was crawling with tourists, the war being over. People looking for gambling and music, hookers and sun, and watching them was satisfying entertainment. To this day, I recollect spying a pale yellow, two-piece bathing outfit filled by the most tan and shapely senorita in all of Cuba, and she was walking a matching poodle. The full-sized kind, dyed the same pale yellow.

There were some good players on the Elefantes, and a few great ones. Lefty Tiant, the father, Alejandro Crespo and the legendary Martin Dihigo, the immortal, who was also our manager. He was 41 that year, but every Cuban still considered him the best ballplayer who ever lived.

My occasional running buddy was Max Manning, a pitcher who was about 28 years old and hitting his peak. He was coming off a year with the Newark Eagles that ended with them winning the Negro World Series, and had followed that up barnstorming with Satchel Paige's team against the Bob Feller All-Stars. It was his first time playing in Cuba, and having someone who had been through the island season before was comforting, I reckon.

Manning was one of the most interesting fellows I met in baseball. His family had left mud-poor Mississippi to move to New Jersey, and he had such success as a high schooler that Max Bishop, who was scouting for the Detroit Tigers, offered him a contract sight unseen without realizing Manning was Black. Once that fact become known, the Tigers, a particularly racist organization at the time, tripped over their own shoes rescinding the deal. He had been a truck driver in France, and then picked right up as a star again in Newark. Sam Estill had told me I was going to like Max, and that was true.

During our off time, the American peloteros damn near drank the island dry of Cerveza Tropical. In spite of living on the edge that was the league's financial instability, there was a raw love of the game, and it was fun to be a part of it. Any minor trouble that took place was swept under the mangrove tree on account of the government being very fond of baseball. Some of the Cuban players, like Dihigo, were much less fond of the government. One off day, the whole team was invited to tour a rum distillery, and we each left with souvenir bottles. Woe betide the fair damsels of Cienfuegos that evening.

We finished third that season, and though our club was not involved in it, the Lions of Havana and the Almendares Scorpions, my old ball club from 1925, had a hellacious pennant race that year. Almendares swept a series from the Leones to end the season, with Max Lanier throwing two complete games out of the three. He did it in front of an overflow crowd and a certain number of Dodgers brass since they took over Gran Stadium for their spring training before the champagne was dry.

I'd love to tell you some romantic tale about catching the last DC-9 out of Havana with Fredo Corleone as the rebels bayoneted fat sugar barons, but that would be a damned lie. That winter marked my last time in Cuba. I'd always meant to go back, but never did. It wouldn't have been the same anyway. The next year, the Cuban League signed an agreement with the majors to be all legitimate. Like most else that gets respectable, the fun melts away like an August sno-cone.

Coming out of spring training in 1947 we played our way north from Florida in a group of four teams. We'd stop and match up in a pair of five inning double headers. It was us, the Tigers, Pirates and Red Sox. The last stop on the barn-storming tour was in Louisville where we played an honest to goodness, complete double header before boarding our separate trains and heading off to start the year. Day before that was Nashville, Tennessee, and the start of a story I think you're gonna like.

Hank Greenberg was with the Pirates that year, which would prove to be the final one of that man's great career. He missed all of three seasons and half of two others serving in the war, you see. One of the guys who really went for the duration. Lord only knows what kind of numbers he would've put up with all that extra time. The other fellow like that, of course, was Ted Williams, the greatest hitter who ever lived, and he figures into this here story, too.

I don't know if you know this, but Greenberg was the first $100,000 player in big league ball. Yes siree, he sure was. He'd been living the Hollywood life style for some time being a big handsome ball player, but when he got that last big contract, he went out and bought himself the prettiest Lincoln convertible that you ever did see. It was long and curvy. A deep royal blue with red leather interior and enough chrome to choke a rap singer. He bought it down in Florida and talked one of the minor leaguers, a journeyman backstop name of Bud Tate, into driving it from town to town while he rode the train in comfort.

We got to the Union Depot in Nashville to catch the evening L&N north to our last stop. We had played the Red Sox in the first half of that double-header, and as it happened, Ted Williams had tried to squeeze in some quickie before departure. I can only surmise that it was a talented young lady, because the Splinter missed the train. He could see it pulling out of the station when his cab dropped him off, but it was gone. Then he spots Bud Tate idling next to the curb where he had just dropped Greenberg. Williams hailed him.

"Hey, Tate. I missed my god damned train. Drive me to Louisville."

It was a statement, as opposed to a question, and as Ted tossed his duffle into the back seat, he quickly determined that Bud Tate was drunker than a sack of chimpanzees. For all his famous chippiness, Ted didn't drink, so he announced that he was going to drive. That was fine with Bud. As soon as that big Lincoln started rocking down the road, Tate fell into a nap, but woke up around Bowling Green, Kentucky, and started pulling on a bottle while swapping tales with his newly appointed driver.

About 20 miles north of town there on Highway 31W is Mammoth Cave National Park. It's the longest cave in the world, did you know that? Over 400 miles of passages in that sucker, but at 9:30 P.M., every one of them is closed. Still, the highway signs leading into Cave City and Park City and Horse Cave sure did pique the fancy of those two ballplayers. By the time they got to the turnoff, they had agreed that mere technicalities such as operating hours were not going to stop them from seeing one of the nation's wonders.

The chain on the parking lot didn't deter them. New Lincoln convertibles did just fine across a lawn. Now, it would help if you understood Ted Williams and Bud Tate. They were both intrepid outdoorsmen. Ted later become known as one of the top sport fishermen in the world, and Bud Tate, having grown up outside of Crockett, Texas, knew his way around the backwoods better than a bobcat. So, when they got out of the car and slowly began to realize that breaking into the world's biggest cave might not be the swiftest notion they ever concocted, neither man was going to be the first to blink. Not that blinking would have helped since the inside of those caves was darker than the dirt in an earthworm's bathtub.

You've probably read about Ted Williams and his famous eyesight, and at first, as they descended that staircase into the mouth of the crevice, they both felt their eyes adjusting. Ted even voiced that confidence out loud. Not forty yards past the opening was a string of very dim little blubs.

"Hell, they leave the lights on all night, this is better than I expected."

"Could be better in my book, I left my bourbon in the glove box."

"Well, we'd best not get trapped in here then without your most needed supply."

That brought a brave laugh.

They could feel the path dropping deeper into the ground, but the scenery was giving the two men goosebumps. Little underground springs dropping delicate waterfalls. Calcium and mineral deposits grown into every shape and color. As they come to the end of the bulbs, they felt certain that they'd find more light at the end of the darkness, and it was no doubt going to be the most breathtaking part.

They intended to only venture a little ways down a black turn in hopes of finding one of the big cavernous underground cathedrals where surely the Parks Service had a few more bulbs burning all night, but macho competitiveness made them keep walking a tad farther than logic dictated. Their steps got shorter and the pace slower. They were just trying to keep to the center of the path by feel, but still, neither man would fess up to a possible mistake. By the time they turned to backtrack, they had passed Lord knows how many side tunnels, so they kept going and hoped for the best. Ted, who was a rather legendary cusser, turned up the heat.

"Well, fuck. I think we're lost, Bud. Son of a bitch, we may miss the goddamned game tomorrow. I can't see shit, and I need my sleep."

"Nah. We'll be good."

"How the hell do you figure that? We've been wandering down some blind path for 20 fucking minutes. Ow. Goddamnit."

Ted had smacked his shin on something low and really hard.

"Shuffle your feet and stick your arms out."

The reply was sudden flapping and fluttering and more hollering from Ted.

"Son of a bitch. Goddamnit. Fucking bats.""

"They're harmless. And they eat mosquitoes."

"I'd slap the shit out of you, if I could see where you are."

Bud Tate chuckled at that, then he promptly pinballed his noggin off three or four stalactites and knocked himself plumb woozy. Not only did his confidence wane, but he started seeing visions.

"Shit, Ted, I think I just saw Floyd Collins."

"Who the fuck is Floyd Collins?"

"The fellow who died in this cave 20 years ago."

"Did he leave his bourbon in the glove box, too?"

"He starved to death, you skinny son of a bitch."

"No, whimpering. There's a flashlight beam up ahead."

Sure enough, the night duty guard had spotted the Lincoln in the parking lot, and had come to investigate. Midnight interlopers were not as infrequent as the fellows imagined. The guard, however, a man of about 70 years, was already drunker than Bud. He slurred out this Barney Fife-like question.

"Who goes there?"

"Teddy Fucking Ball Game."

Now, the baseball hero of Kentucky was Pee Wee Reese, but there wasn't a fan alive who wouldn't recognize Ted Williams, though randomly finding him in a cave while you're liquored up was a mite disconcerting. Nevertheless, the old man led those two spelunking ballplayers back out of Mammoth Cave and saw them to the Lincoln. As a grudging thank you, Bud handed him the remainder of his pint of bourbon. When the guard's relief shift showed up at dawn the next day and woke him up, that old man started weaving a disjointed tale of finding Ted Williams inside the cave and leading him to safety. Amazingly the Parks people let him keep his job.

There's more books been written about that 1947 Dodgers season than anything I know of, and it changed the country, to be sure. But I feel obliged to share a story or two all the same.

The Dodgers played their first 15 games that year without ever leaving New York. Their first road trip was that famous one down to Philadelphia where Ben Chapman showed the whole world his bunghole, and it looked just like his soul. I'd known Chapman from the Yankees, of course, so I was not surprised by him. He's sort of cornered the market on bad press related to Jackie's debut, but there are a couple or three other fellows who deserve to have their names run through the mud, too.

You'll also remember Herb Pennock from back in my Yankees days. He's the one who scolded me for keeping company in Chicago with my Black friend Pearl. Well, sir, by 1947, he was the general manager of those same Phillies. Herb come from just outside there, and despite pitching all those years for the hated New Yorkers, he managed to retain his popularity back home. The scribes called him the Squire of Kennett Square, after the little burgh he come from.

That brings me to a bone I want to pick. Nothing personal, but you writers have done ruined the historic record to end all get out. Every book I've ever seen about the old time Yankees will tell you that Pennock's nickname was the Squire of Kennett Square, but fact is that's just what one of the beat boys put in his column one day when he had inches to fill. A nickname, boy, is what people call you. Ain't nobody ever had a nickname that was four or five words long. Wild Horse of the Osage or The Commerce Comet is what some crazy scribbler wrote. A ballplayer's nickname is, invariably, something like Smitty, Pussy, Horse Breath, or Boob. It might be the difference between Paul Gallico and Redd Foxx, but it ain't the truth. Unless Squire is a synonym for Grand Dragon.

Pennock picked up the phone a day or two before that road infamous trip and told Branch Rickey that the Phillies weren't going to play if the Dodgers brought that "n-word" down with them. He called Jackie every racial slur you could think of, though I'm sure he did it in a squirelike fashion without ever dislodging that stick up his ass. Herb dropped dead in a hotel lobby about a year after that. I like to think his heart stopped as it finally dawned on him that almost all the cooks and kitchen help who had been preparing his meals in Philadelphia were Black.

The very next out of town stop for Jackie and the Dodgers that year was in Cincy. Two games in the middle of May. We took both of them in spite of some shaky throwing by Vander Meer and thanks to a real gem by Blackwell. At Crosley Field, it was less the Reds players and more the fans who were intent on hating. The hollering from the stands was something awful. We had nigh on a full house that first game, but the next day only six thousand something showed up. I reckon folks of that mind set couldn't afford tickets two days in a row.

Lots of people say that Pee Wee Reese walked over and put his arm around Jackie during that first game in Cincinnati, but I don't believe it was so. Jackie played first base, so Reese would've had a long walk. If you listen to what Jackie said years later, it happened one day in Boston in 1948 after Eddie Stanky had been traded to the Braves and was letting his ugly side out.

As bad as the Phillies players had been, it might have been even worse with the damn Cardinals. Enos Slaughter deliberately spiked Jackie early in the year, and that no-hitting tool Garagiola was still spiking Jackie in September. The only difference was that by then, Jackie was established enough that his next time up, he got in Joe's face and reminded him just what a limp-bat no talent he was. Stealing money, that bastard.

I didn't meet Jack Robinson in 1947. My work was in the Reds clubhouse, and there wasn't much truck with the other team.

Chapter Four

Here's something for you. I'd like to set the record straight on a matter that has become a schoolboy cliche. They say there's no such thing as bad sex. Well, I don't know who they is, but they must have been one of those Ottoman eunuchs. My first time trying to get back in the saddle after my sweet Jenny passed is a prime example. At least my first time stateside.

It was 1948. It had been just over four years, not counting some rum-fueled hijinks in Cuba, and I figured it had been long enough. Though Willy might jump to attention on his own now and then, my mind hadn't been in it. Every time I found myself checking out some woman's backside, I'd feel guilty. And I've always been an ass man, along with a leg man, and an eye man who was also damn partial to a woman's mouth, her smile and good hair. Oh, and tits. I like tits.

Anyhoo, I was out at the Licky Dog having two or ten cold ones after my shift ended at Hamilton's, and Bird, the bartender, slid an extra beer in front of me.

"I still have three-fourths of this one," I told him. "You're not quitting, are you?"

"No, that dame at the end of the bar bought this for you."

He smirked at me and gave his head a shake.

I looked down toward the end of the bar and saw this little woman waving at me. Try as I might, I couldn't place her. It never occurred to me that a complete stranger would buy me a beverage. If it had happened before, it had been some cigar-chomper in a green plaid sport coat who was trying to get the low down on how some pitcher's arm was holding up. And I didn't even recall that.

Well, sir, this little lady sidled down to where I was perched and grabbed the stool next to me. She wasn't what you'd call a classic beauty, but she was cute enough in a Cub Scout den mother sort of way. Her hair was bouncy and her eyes bright and brown. Her smile reminded me of a border collie that figured it was time to play Frisbee. She was also a giggler.

I started to introduce myself, but it turned out that she already knew who I was. She was there to talk baseball, said she played on a softball team and was a pretty crack third baseman. Or woman.

Well, knowing that, whatever thoughts I briefly entertained about her being interested in the likes of me went flying out the window. Back in those days, softball player was durn near synonymous for being a girl's girl. You could have used the basest slang for lesbian, and I won't, and it wouldn't have been any worse to most folks than saying softball player. My lips to Babylon, I'm not judging anybody on what they do in their free time. I'm just relating the thought process and lack of enlightenment in the late 1940s. Whatever shyness and anxiety I might have worked myself into was plumb gone once I heard softball player. I figured the only come on I'd be getting was "do you have a sister?"

We talked about Raffensberger's dealing with men on base and how Virgil Stallcup might have developed a hitch in his swing. I told her a story about how Ted Kluszewski once left his bare ass print on the top of Johnny Neun's birthday cake, and she giggled in all the appropriate places.

After about beer number eleven she pulled a wiffle ball out of her car trunk, and we had batting practice right there in the smack middle of the deserted street. By that time, I might have been giggling myself, who knows. I was having fun.

The long and short of it was that once we started kissing, it sure didn't seem like she preferred girls at all. Her biceps said one thing, but her tongue definitely said another. And I'd had plenty of beer to dull my nerves. We was back at my little apartment by one or one thirty.

Now that was another story. I never lived in anyplace very fancy, and my little place in Cincinnati wasn't exactly designed for entertaining. The dining table legs was cut down from a batting cage the team had replaced the previous spring. I did have some nice clubhouse signage that I'd brought home to dress the walls, though honestly, I hoped she'd forego spitting even without the reminder.

She yanked off her knickers as soon as I shut the front door, but once we got under the covers, things ground to halt like a donkey cart on the Santa Monica Freeway. Not to be indelicate, but the crux of the matter was that I couldn't get her to touch my johnson. All the groping was going on according to form earlier, but the most she was giving my little rascal was to poke at him with one finger like she was trying to determine if a garden lizard was going to bite her.

In hindsight, it probably didn't help that I was still calling her "ma'am", but I just didn't think I knew her that well. I do admit now that "ma'am" is not what you want to yell out in the throes of passion.

Now, I have never in my life forced a woman into something she didn't want to do. Even for a minute. That's not the way a man behaves. But when I'd decided this wasn't her thing and moved back to my side of the bed, she'd pull me close again and kiss me harder. It was frustrating, and eventually, it was time to pull the chute.

I'm not saying it wasn't my fault, too, you understand. In fact, after what seemed to me like an hour or two of standing at attention, the little soldier sat down. Even she noticed it, though likely only because the blanket got slack.

"What's wrong?" she asked me, acting like she was just about ready.

"Well, ma'am, what I'd tell you is that dicks are like dogs. They smell fear."

If it's possible to go lower than the bottom of the hill, that's what happened to our once good evening. Between my long time riding the sexual pine and her no doubt having to overcome the faulty assumptions of the day, it was not to be. A giggler to the end, she tittered the whole time she got dressed and halfway to the car. I got less than two hours of sleep before I had to be back at the factory. And let me assure you that dog tired, humiliated, and still a little bit horny is one rough combination. Rougher when you're 47 years old.

Now I notice you looking squeamish now and again during that story, but the fact is that old folks still enjoy the idea of sex whether you youngsters want to think about it or not, and that's the whole point of me sharing that story. You'll also notice that I said the idea of sex.

When you get old, and for your sake, I hope you will, it'll suddenly occur to you one day that young people assume that a person of your years shouldn't notice the opposite sex. Hell, the truth is that you might even appreciate it more in the abstract cause you know you won't be touching it. It's not you being a dirty old man at all, you just have good eyesight and a healthy appreciation of a fine looking woman. God's greatest work of art, that is.

Let me ask you something. Do you know who the biggest liar in the world is? A mirror. By the time you reach your 60s, or even your 50s, you look into that mirror knowing that you're perfectly capable of running the fastest race, building the tallest bridge, or wooing the prettiest woman. And all it shows you in return is a broken down old man.

The groundskeeper at Crosley was an institution named Matty Schwab. Around baseball, he was more venerable than Connie Mack's piles. Started maintaining things for the Reds in 1903 when his daddy retired from the job after 20 years. His one brother worked for the Dodgers and his son for the Giants. They probably had fescue pubic hair, for all I know. Never saw him in the shower.

I was always taken with groundskeeepers since I had that job, among other duties, for the Chicks. Hehe. I said doody. Anyhoo, half of what you see on ballfields today come from old Matty Schwab. He added underground drainage and made sure he put down new infield sod every season. It was the green shade of your dreams, and the sweet smell before a game was better than morning biscuits. He was always throwing seed in the outfield. Prior to him, some diamonds looked like a tired preschool teacher come August, but Matty, he perked things up fine.

He was a fair man, too. Matty didn't cheat as much as the other teams. You recall me saying about the head man in Memphis beefing up the chalk lines, well, half of the groundsmen in the majors had some trick they used to help their team. The Indians literally moved the fences back before they played the Yankees. Seattle lengthened the batter's boxes to let the hitter move up. Atlanta, Detroit, and Wrigley would water down the infield to slow bunts. Candlestick Park was such a wetland in front of home plate they had government frogs. The White Sox sculpted the infield to help or hurt the opposition's best hitter. It was famous the kinds of grass cutting tricks they tried during DiMaggio's streak.

Every writer who's ever covered baseball has tried to explain a hitting streak. The kind of times when batters say the ball looks like a melon floating in there. Sometimes, though, there ain't no explanation. I guess if you watch the video for days on end, you'll think you see that a flexor tightened up and brought your elbow in half an inch or some such shit, but then again maybe not. All I know is that when a hitter is going good, the birds sing more, the sun shines brighter on your shoulder, and the girls at the bar put out like rodents. Of course, that last one is probably self-fulfilling.

The flip side is when a good, big league batter can't buy a hit with a sack of dollars. Put it on the screws, and it lines right to an infield glove. You feel like that cartoon character with the rain cloud hooked directly above your noggin.

Everybody who ever played went through these ups and downs. In July 1949, Ramon Standard, a good looking rookie call up, got on just such a bad streak. By the end of two weeks, he was beside himself. It had got into his head. After one especially embarrassing trip to the plate, swinging at dirt and watching pot roast down the middle, Ewell Blackwell sidled over to him and handed him the ugliest looking bat you ever saw. The thing had no taper to it whatsoever. It looked like a 40 ounce newel post, the kind of thing you'd buy from the hardware man.

Ewell told young Ramon that it had worked for him. The kid had been a good hitter for average all through the minors, and he did it using a light piece of maple that he controlled like a drum major's baton. But he was desperate. I'll be damned if he didn't try that hideous looking bat of Blackwell's and get a hit his next time up. In the seventh, he come up again, and rapped a liner over short that brought him standing up into second. The look on his face was surprised and elated all at the same time, like finding a twenty in your pants pocket.

I'd love to tell you that it turned him around and paved the way for a successful career. Fact was, though, that he followed that day up by going 0 for August, and ended the season back at Syracuse. I think he had a year or two more in the Senators organization, or maybe it was Pittsburgh. Probably both. He just wasn't good enough for major league pitching. The most important lesson out of that whole thing is that pitchers don't know a goddamned thing about hitting. Long live the DH.

During the off season, heading into winter of 1949, Virgil Stallcup invited one of our newest call ups to come down to his hometown in South Carolina and go bird hunting. Virgil was in his mid-20s, and he had palled around with this kid back in the Piedmont League. The fellow was named Grant Younger, and though he was the same age as Virgil, he was late getting his chance at the bigs.

Younger was a big toe-headed kid. Horrible deformity. He went through stocking caps by the dozen, but that's neither here nor there. Anyway, Red, which is what we all called Stallcup, had him a little house just big enough for him and the missus, so Younger was going be sleeping up the road a piece at Stallcup's widowed mother's place. Red met the boy at the railway station in Greenville, and their first stop was to meet mother Stallcup and drop his duffle bag.

The way I heard the story a dozen or more times is that Mrs. Stallcup was a fine Methodist woman who thought the best of everybody, at least to their faces. When they arrived, the sweet lady was just finishing the white icing on a spice cake.

"This is for my friend Ida Mellwood from my Bible study," she told them. "She loves spice cake on a rung just below Jesus, and the Lord has blessed her with capacity to enjoy it. Tomorrow is her birthday, and the ladies are having a potluck at Marjorie Thorn's house over across the hollow. I have to get an early start of it since the walk is about 90 minutes, but I promise Mr. Younger here that I will have the stove lit and a full breakfast warming by 4:00 A.M.. Do you like country ham, Mr. Younger?"

"Yes, ma'am."

"Well, there will be ham and gravy and as many cat head biscuits as you can eat."

"Please don't go to no trouble for me, ma'am."

Virgil assured him that that was just his mama's way.

Well, sir, the two boys went into town that night and proceeded to get drunker than West Virginia possums. I'm sure that keeping the farm truck on the dirt tracks back home was quite the challenge, but thankfully they made it. How mother Stallcup didn't wake up from the commotion, I can't tell you. When she come in to light the wood stove the next morning, her first clue that something was amiss was likely Grant Younger's trousers which were draped half over the back of her late husband's parlor chair.

The old lady continued into the kitchen where she found a mostly naked journeyman infielder sprawled out flat on his back on the linoleum floor holding the window curtains and covered in spice cake. He had come home high and hungry, you see. Not knowing the drawer arrangement, he didn't put in much effort to investigate. He attacked Ida Mellwood's cake with his bare hands, polishing off fully 60percent of it before he realized he needed a napkin. Not readily finding one of those either, he started using his shirt tail before beginning to wipe his face on the frilly little kitchen curtains. When the rod broke, he keeled over backwards and come to rest on the floor holding the drapes across his chest and with the rest of his body smeared with frosting.

I reckon Mrs. Stallcup was rather speechless to find that nice boy Mr. Younger in such a state of debauchery. The sack of quails and one grouse they bagged that afternoon may have assuaged her feelings a little bit. I'm sure it didn't help explain to poor Ida why she had no birthday cake, though.

My old friend from the Giants, Heinie Groh, was back in Cincinnati. He was working as a cashier out at the horse track. River Downs they called it. We would meet every so often. Sometimes, I'd go out to catch a race or two on off days before we'd adjourn to a tavern on the byway. I was younger than most of the oldsters who frequented the horses, still it always made me smile being in my mid-40s and having people call you young man. There were a couple of fellows whose legs were so spindly, they'd ask me to walk to the windows and place their bets.

It was an education, watching all those gamblers. They were men who couldn't help themselves. Every losing streak is bound to end sometime, of course, but these fellows were ever convinced that it was the next race. An odd mix of unreasonable optimism and deep self-loathing. A few spent the winters in Florida so they could keep betting when River Downs was out of season.

Heinie pointed out one loud gentleman in particular as we were walking out one day.

"Next time you're out here, grab a beer and watch that feller," he told me. "He is quite the show, that one."

Heinie was not lying. This old guy might look mild-mannered, bespectacled and mousy, but when the bell rang, he would holler and jump and urge his nag onward as if the horse was his only child. Every damn race was the same. If it had been my track, I'd have been running side action on when the little man stroked out.

One day he was particularly vexed. He has lost every race, when in the sixth, his place horse had just enough of a stumble at the finish line to drop from second to third. He let out a primal yell and tumped over a tall table with a huge heave of his arms. Discarded wrappers and empty cups flew to the winds. Without pausing for breath, he started yelling, "Police! Police!"

Eventually a track manager come running up, and about 30 seconds behind him was a red-faced, retired copper who was sucking wind to the point he couldn't get a word out. If he had been one of the horses, they'd have shipped him to the glue factory.

"Sir, what happened?" the manager asked. No doubt he recognized one of his regular bettors.

"I was minding my own business," the little fellow told him in a voice like a cornered Wally Cox. "Then some hooligan ran by and knocked over this table. I had just returned from the concession with my lunch, and now it is lost." He gestured very broadly to the litter.

The flatfoot was still wheezing, but managed a cursory look around. It was the track man who answered him.

"Oh my. We'll be happy to replace your meal. What had you ordered?"

"Four chili dogs and two Hudephol's." He never batted a lash. I reckon his thought process was that free food would make him two races closer to breaking even.

Lots of folks still recollected Heinie as a ballplayer in those days, and he had his share of gents who wanted to tell him about a great play he made at the hot corner, as if he didn't know himself. What they really wanted was to recapture a moment of the long ago and shake hands with a hero. Those hands that were so gnarled from fielding with a raggedy ass glove that they kept him out of WWI.

Chapter Five

I still considered myself a young buck in the 1940s. Lots of life laying out in front of me. When the new decade come, though, I would catch myself thinking about things. You look confused, but you have to understand that at that time of history, the middle of the 20th century, most men were not what the hippies would classify as in touch with our feelings.

I'd spent nigh on seven years thinking about Jenny, but memories slip away, or parts of them do. Leastways until something pokes you in the backside and brings them to the forefront again. At that point in time, I often found myself thinking of hugs. Jenny gave the greatest hugs. It's a simple, stupid sounding thing, ain't it, but there was love in them that I'd not felt since.

I had to admit to myself that I was lonely. The off seasons were especially rough, and as much as the Licky was more my first home than my second, I had days when I began to figure I wanted more. It was nothing I dwelled on. I was sleeping fine. I just got a bit restless some days was all.

It just so happened that one of our young pitchers was due to get married around that time. He was a gangly right hander name of Harry Hickey. His bride was the spunky and weak-chinned daughter of an overall magnate. Her daddy supplied work clothes to factories on both sides of river, all the way down to Louisville. She was the middle of three girls – April, Mae, and June. There is no accounting for what parents will make their children suffer in the name of cuteness.

The whole team went to the wedding. Once word got out that Mae's folks had money, nobody wanted to miss the chance at top shelf whiskey and roast beef.

Eddie Erautt was the best man. Both him and Hickey was from out west, and though Erautt stuck around the Show for several years, they were both that same kind of hard luck, hard thrower who had been an All-Star in the minors but never seemed to bring it all together once they got upstairs.

Harry and Mae scheduled the wedding for a Wednesday in April. Back then Cincinnati always got the opening day, so the Cubs came to town for one game on a Tuesday, then we didn't play again until we opened up in Pittsburgh that Friday. So, the Wednesday wedding was not only an off day, but they even got a half day honeymoon since the train for Pittsburgh didn't chug out until Thursday night.

It was a fine ceremony. The boys from the ball club passed their flasks around both before and after the vows. The happy couple marched out of the church underneath a canopy of raised bats, as was often the fashion at a ballplayer's wedding. It was a nice afternoon, and then we all adjourned to a rented ballroom at the Netherland Plaza Hotel. Young Harry Hickey was no one special to me, but the whole thing hit home.

I've been to funerals, although I don't like to go and will do anything to avoid them, where I barely knew the fellow but I ended up sniffling like a telenovela actress. Funerals are a fine time for unexpected purges of emotions, I guess you'd call them, so why not a wedding reception? At least that one was. I'm not saying I cried, no sir, not at all, but I did feel up the mother of an ugly bridesmaid in a hotel coat check closet. She had hands big as dinner plate chargers, and it does make me tear up a mite when I recollect that. Hands like that will make a fellow feel right inadequate.

The end result of all that involuntary introspection was that I vowed to give dating a chance. I'm not saying I was fixing to join some church social club, but the memories of the softball player was pretty well worn away. I opened the door just a tiny crack.

People talk about things coming to you when you let down your walls and invite the world in, or some such bull dookey. I don't buy a minute of it, and whoever said that probably smells like patchouli. But a few weeks after that, I first met Dorothy Robichek.

Her friends called her Dot, and she worked in the bookkeeping department at Kahn's Meat Packing Plant. When it came to beauty, my initial impression of her was that she was tolerable. I reckon she felt the same way about me. She had a happy face and a disarming manner.

Kahn's was a sponsor of the Reds, you see, and periodically, lucky employees got a ticket to the ball game and a behind the scenes tour. By that, I mean a ball club flunky walked them onto the field, past the third base dugout all the way to left field where they pointed at the clubhouse doors before dropping them off at a concession stand so they could start spending money on hot dogs and Burger brand beer.

It's not like they got to root around in Johnny Wyrostek's locker or anything, but it made them feel special. I'd long since learned to pay them no mind, the looky-loos from Gatchett Plymouth or some tire company or sporting goods supply. Normally, I didn't even notice them, but that Thursday evening I'd stopped to shoot the shit with Matty Schwab while he was tinkering with a mower. Dot Robichek ambled over to me big as you please and struck up a conversation like she was my long lost neighbor. Her handful of workmates had gone off and left her there down the foul line, but she didn't seem overly concerned about it.

After about five minutes, she stuck out a hand.

"My name's Dot, and I hope you don't mind me chewing your ear off. I was trying to ditch my coworkers from Kahn's Meats, and I'll tell you straight out that you're the first decent-looking fellow I've seen in five weeks who don't smell like canned ham."

I heard Matty snort out a laugh from someplace underneath the mower blades.

I'll be damned if she didn't ask me out for beers after the ballgame, and I plumb surprised myself by saying yes. The ball team took a shellacking from the Braves that night, but I found myself looking forward to meeting this pushy woman and wondering if she'd still be there by the time I got my work done after the game.

She was indeed. We closed down the lounge at 2:30 that next morning. I recollect asking Jenny to forgive me when I got back to my little apartment, though I can't say why. In spite of whatever lingering guilt there was, Dot and I kept seeing each other. Drinks here and there. Dinner a time or two.

Just after the first time Dot and me did the nasty, which took a couple of months to build up to, she rolled over on her back, let out the biggest sigh in Ohio history, and quoted the famous slogan from her employer's hot dog package.

"That, sir, was the Weiner the World Awaited," she told me.

Made me laugh out loud, at least until I started wondering how many previous fellows she went through perfecting her timing and delivery.

I'll tell you a thing that never changes is that most ballplayers, after they hang up the spikes, still miss the game until they day they die. You'll always have the old players looking for an excuse to pop around the ball yard from time to time. Some like talking to the youngsters, though except for the great ones, two thirds of the new players wouldn't know the oldtimers from a Siberian pimple.

One of the all-time greatest Reds was Edd Roush. Yes, sir. He was a gooder. Used to talk about place hitting, though many folks will swear that is not a thing. Roush was not a big man, but he swung a 48-ounce bat. Weighed more than a Chihuahua, only longer. He said by using that heavy bat and a half swing, he could put the ball into the outfield wherever he damned well desired. Maybe he could, or maybe that's just some old dude rambling about times that never was, but Edd Roush won him two batting titles and had a lifetime .323 average.

When I was with the club, he was long since out of ball and was living down in Bradenton, Florida. Every spring, we'd get a visit or four from Edd Roush. One time, I got to shooting the breeze with him about the 1919 World Series, and the old man sure enough had strong opinions. There was not a whisker of a doubt that the Cincinnatis were a better team than the Chicago Sox that year, whether they were black sox or white. Heinie Groh agreed with him too. They was fond of pointing out that the Reds won eight more games and totally run away with the

National League that season. The pitching staff was the best the team ever had in the long history of the club, too.

I think one of those same years I'm recalling marked the short season of Petey Flannery. What a bittersweet tale that is.

The kid was a right-handed pitcher with a decent menu of stuff. He'd worked his way up through Muncie and Tyler, Texas, Charleston, West Virginia, then had him a big year at Tulsa in the Texas League. Won 11 games, and topped that off by looking as sharp as any pitcher in spring camp.

He'd never played at the top level of the minors, so the club sent him down for a final touch of seasoning, but three weeks into the campaign, he got the call. He debuted against the Phils at Shibe Park. Most players will admit how nervous they are at first their big league game. There's no shame in being scared of a thing as long as you overcome it.

Young Flannery, on the other hand, looked as unflappable as a petting zoo sloth when he was warming up. He took the hill and promptly struck out Eddie Waitkus on four pitches, the last one being a swinging 59-foot slider. He got Ashburn on a groundout to Red Stallcup, then Dick Sisler lined the first fastball straight to Big Klu. Three up, three down. Flannery looked all straight-faced. He headed back to the dugout with a mile long stare, and the instant he crossed the chalk line, he blew about two days of clubhouse buffet all over his shoes.

He settled into a pretty good rhythm after that. Those Phillies were a good hitting ball club, and he held them to six hits and three walks. Sewell pinch hit for him in the seventh, but he left with a 5 -2 lead and got the win. After a lot of glad handing and a hot shower, Flannery went to dinner with a couple of the other youngsters on the club. Adcock was one of them. I know the two of them had played together at Tulsa.

Philadelphia fans are somewhat famous for being a particular brand of dick-weed. I'm sure you know that. Throwing batteries at players. Butt humping Santa Claus on the Thanksgiving float. So, it's not surprising that an unreasonably happy opposing player out celebrating in a Philly bar didn't sit well with the locals. Sure enough, taunting turned to puffery then to fisticuffs. Adcock claimed he got in a couple of doozies, but Flannery slipped in a puddle of suds on the linoleum floor, and this hairy-backed Phillies fan landed square on top of him. It dislocated his right shoulder something awful. He went on the DL and never made it back to the show again. It would take a pretty optimistic soul to not have regrets about that one.

The ball club had a big change in 1951. Warren Giles who had been our general manager, and most importantly from where I sat, was the guy who have given me a job, left to become the president of the National League. Gabe Paul moved up to take his place.

Here's a little story about friendship and, I guess you'd call them mentors. It also goes to show what a small world baseball is, and how it'll serve you right if you develop a reputation for being friendly and primarily honest.

Warren Giles got discharged from the service after the First World War and was living in Moline, Illinois where he talked himself into running the local team, the Plowboys in the Three-I League. First move he made was to hire Earl Mack, Connie Mack's boy, as manager. That got him a winning team and then a better job at St. Joe, Missouri where he pulled a thorn out of Branch Rickey's paw when Rickey was running the Cardinals organization. On account of him impressing Rickey, Giles got promoted to run the Rochester Red Wings, and it was there that he, in turn, promoted a teenaged batboy who was fresh off being called Gabie Paul, to be the ticket salesman.

Paul had started being a batboy when he was ten, and the Red Wings manager was George Stallings who had won the World Series with the Miracle Braves of 1914. Stallings taught that little kid Paul to deaden the baseballs by putting them in the freezer.

Anyway, when Warren Giles got hired to run the Cincinnati Reds in 1936, he brung his protégé Gabe Paul along to be the traveling secretary and PR man. He was the club's vice president when Giles took the league job, and Gabe Paul become head man. He liked to trade ballplayers, but I can't rightly say he was all that great at it. I heard a writer say something along the lines of Gabe Paul being affable enough to pass as competent, and I reckon that just about hits the mark.

The best trade he ever made was with his old mentor Branch Rickey when that man was running the Pirates. Gus Bell was one of Pittsburgh's best hitters, but Rickey, who could squeeze a nickel until the Indian screamed, saw Gus Bell's wife throw away a diaper rather than wash it, and Rickey got it through his head that Gus Bell must lack character to be that wasteful. Gus Bell become a Cincinnati Red. It wasn't long after that when somebody finally told Branch Rickey about disposable diapers.

I kept seeing Dot Robichek during those days. We were having a grand time, us middle agers. I won't say we were sweethearts. We had thrown out words like casual and uncommitted till our toes curled, but I can't say I was seeing anybody else, either.

In August 1951, the club went on a long road trip, and it was my turn to go along. We rotated so the second and third man didn't travel on all the road trips. Whoever stayed at home did things like see to the home uniforms and catch up on some mending. In those days, a uniform was still expected to last for a good while. If you ever forgot that, some pencil neck from the general offices would be happy to remind you.

One night over some post-game cocktails, Dot tossed out the idea of meeting me for an overnight on the road. She allowed as how she hadn't been on a getaway since she and her ex-husband spent a weekend at Cedar Point in Sandusky back in 1940. In fact, she said it had been another nail in her marriage's carcass when the old man proved too weak-kneed to take a second turn on the Cyclone.

We talked through the schedule, and did some calculating of her savings, and decided she could just about take the Metropolitan to St. Louis in August and have enough money to treat us to a steak dinner. I, in turn, would cover the rest, score her a ticket to the Saturday ballgame, and get us a hotel room.

Almost all of the National League clubs stayed at the Chase Plaza Hotel in St. Louis in those days. You may have read about it because they stayed segregated for years after Jackie Robinson and the rest broke into the majors. Finally, they let Black players stay in the hotel but refused to let them use the main dining, the fancy swimming pool, or go to a show on the rooftop garden. Hank Aaron told the story that even after all that was supposedly put behind them, the only rooms he ever got at the Chase overlooked a brick wall or the alley where they banged the kitchen garbage cans.

Normally, on a road trip, every man roomed with someone else. Ball clubs before free agency where tighter than Dick's hat band. If players were two to a room, they'd have been happy to put equipment men in an air shaft tent, if they hotel would've let them. The cheapest room rate at the Chase, which was the fanciest hotel in town, was about six bucks a night, if I recollect.

Now, the most important fellow when a ball team leaves town is the traveling secretary. The hotel wants to keep in the good graces of outfits like a big league operation that rents 40 rooms several nights a year, and a smart traveling secretary is not above calling in a few favors, as long as he likes you. That's how I was able to secure a private room that Friday and Saturday night for just two smackers. It might not have been the presidential suite, but it wasn't the maid's closet, either. Dot was mightily impressed.

The Saturday ball game that night was close, but the Reds got the short stick. Max Lanier threw a two hitter at us. The only two knocks being singles by Kluszewski. There was nothing to pack up since we had a Sunday game, so once I got a couple of hampers into the big clubhouse washing machine, off we went for our second night on the town.

True to her word, Dot had treated us to a steak on Friday right after her late train arrived, so that next night, we went into the Chase Club. It was the best entertainment spot in St. Louis, and Lena Horne was booked that weekend. In spite of any connections I might have had to the Cincinnati Reds, the maître d' gave us the once over and promptly motioned us to a fine table overlooking the swinging kitchen door. Given the fact that we managed to nurse a beer and a Manhattan through an entire 45-minute final set from the Horne, I'll compliment the old boy on his ability to assess his customers.

The kitchen service was winding down, and given the prices, we figured a splurge for room service was our best bet. After doing the math, we ordered a ham sandwich, a BLT, and a bowl of potato salad. Set me back two dollars. We decided to forego the side of mayonnaise since that would have run us another two bits. I'm not trying to overly dwell on our penny-pinching, but in the days before credit cards, those were the kind of decisions a body had to make.

It didn't stop our fun, though, and Dot got the titters when she saw that even a ham sandwich and a BLT were delivered underneath fine stainless steel covers. Hopefully putting aside any lovemaking that might have transpired, I'm not sure if those high-class plate covers weren't the highlight of her trip.

Being the red-blooded American gent that I am, as soon as we finished our second go around in the sack, I nodded off to sleep. No doubt that I shut my eyes with pride that I'd done my manly duty and then some. Dot, though, must have thought I'd wake up and rally. She killed time by scribbling out a couple of postcards from the desk drawer then perusing a brochure of things to do even though she'd be catching the B&O back to Cincinnati the next morning.

Just before she gave up on my abilities, she decided to set the tray of dirty room service dishes back out into the hall. She had been amused by that practice and the various unshined men's shoes sitting beside the doors on our floor.

It was two o'clock in the morning at least, so she probably thought nothing about opening a hotel room door naked. It was only long enough to slide the tray out there anyway. But as she reached a little farther than planned, she heard the door shut and lock behind her.

In hindsight, I can understand her dilemma at that moment. Here she was stranded in a potentially busy and high-end hotel corridor with her own end completely exposed to all who might pass by. And that's saying nothing of her coochie and everything else. You might think at first blush that she'd want to pound loudly on the door so I would let her in, but then you run the risk of the guests in adjoining rooms coming out to see about all the hubbub that had roused them from slumber.

She started with soft knocking, but by this time, she could hear me snoring through the door. At least that's how the story went in the retelling. Gradually she got louder with her thumping. That was soon accompanied by her whispering "Wingo" with ever increasing volume. For my part, I vaguely remember dreaming about Dorothy Gale and a loose house shutter banging in a tornado. By the time I woke up enough to realize where I was and let her in, Dot was laughing uncontrollably at the pure absurdity of the situation. And I swear to you I heard at least four other hotel room doors click shut right along with ours. We called it the old lady floor show at the Chase.

Chapter Six

When I was new to the big leagues, all the way up to when I was married to Jenny, it was normal to spend time away from the ball yard with players from the club. Oh, you do that on the road because you probably don't know anybody else. That's just your natural drinking partner out of self-preservation. I'm talking about times when we were playing at home. Sure, we all had our circle of close friends, and mine was generally not connected to baseball, but occasions still came up where you found yourself with some group of ballplayers out tripping the night fantastic, as the hippies said.

It felt like the thing to do. I was socializing with people close to my age. By the time I got to the Reds, though, I was a good decade older than most any player on the squad. More than that for most. What did those young fellows want to be hanging out with an old man for?

There were a few times it came to pass, of course, and not to give anything away, but that remained the case until I retired. Even after that, though that was probably more akin to either a research project or being kind to your grandma's cat.

No, sir, my time with the Reds marked a change in that if I was to be included in any activities outside of the business of baseball, it was more likely to be with coaches than players. I'd known Tony Cuccinello when he popped in with the Giants for half a year in 1940. When he signed on as a coach for Cincinnati back in the '49 season, we'd shoot the shit every once in a great while. He had three younguns at home to occupy most of his time, but once in an Irish Monday, we'd knock back a few.

Cooch was what folks called a good baseball man. Infielder. Smart. He retired once at the start of the war to manage in Jersey City, but ended up coming back and damn near won a batting title in his last year, though he didn't get it. Everybody thought he was washed up by then. He was 37 and never had fully come back from having his knee all busted up by Dick Bartell. When the White Sox, ...that's where he was playing, when they realized at the start of September '45 that Cooch chasing a batting title might put a few more fannies in the bleachers, Jimmy Dykes was forced to pencil him in most every game even though Cooch was a mite worn down. He hadn't been playing every day for most of the season, so he needed the at bats just to qualify.

It come down to the last game of the year. With a week to go, it looked like Cooch had it all in the bag over Snuffy Stirnweiss of the Yankees, but after a big doubleheader at Fenway, the ChiSox had five days off. Stirnweiss wasn't going to catch him, but Cooch run out of gas, and Stirnweiss went six for ten in the last two games and took the title by less than a ten thousandth of a point. Ain't that a kick in the shorts way to end a career.

Well, one night, must've been the first week after the end of the '51 season, I was packing the last of the clubhouse away and Cooch stopped by the park for some reason. He certainly didn't have to be there, but habits are tough to break. We made a plan to go out to dinner. He said his oldest boy was now big enough to where he might be trusted to babysit, so he was to bring along the missus, and I'd grab Dot. It would be a hoot as they used to say up thereabouts.

Now, you probably already sussed out that Tony Cuccinello was Italian, and so was his wife, Clara, a little woman from Indianapolis. I knew for a fact, on account of Tony had bragged about her to everyone in the clubhouse, that Clara was a regular wizard with the old country recipes. He was not always a talkative fellow, but if his mood was right, Cooch would wax on about a cannelloni like an opera writer about elephants.

No matter what they were having every night at home, Cooch and Clara wanted to go to Scotti's for dinner. It was a Southern Italian joint that had been around Cincinnati since way before I come to town. It was a busman's holiday, if you asked me, but since I loved Italian food better than a kitten in milk gravy, I heartily approved.

Cooch was a small man in stature, but he loved to eat. Back in Lee County, Arkansas when I was a youngster, I'd shovel that third helping of supper into my belly, and my old daddy would remark that I must have a hollow leg. Same joke every time. That come to mind watching Tony Cuccinello. He could put it away.

He took charge of the ordering, and we proceeded to work through a helping of capicola and provolone, two baskets of bread, and a couple plates of olive oil. Most of that disappeared down Tony, but I tried my damnedest to keep up. Always a little competitive, you understand. Three of us went for the veal dishes, but Dot wanted sausage and spaghetti.

I'm telling you what we had for a reason. We was all chatting to beat the band when the waiter set our plates down, and Dot grabbed up her fork in one hand and her knife in the other. Out of nowhere, like a bat swooping for a mosquito, Concetta Scoleri, one of the owners, come running out to the table with a big wooden meat tenderizer in one hand. I noticed bloody remnants of what I hoped was not a customer. She was waving the thing at my date. May have been a coincidence, she might have just happened to be holding that behemoth at the time, but Dot opted not to ask any questions. The old lady was yelling in broken English for the whole dining room to hear.

"No cutta your spaghetti! You grown woman!"

Now, I was inclined to agree with Mrs. Scoleri. All those good Italians I'd come to know back in New York, Bingo Tavarozzi being top of the list, would have skinned someone alive if they'd seen such a display. Dot very quietly lowered her table knife and flashed Mrs. Scoleri a big smile.

"I was so caught up with the good wine that I almost forgot what I was about to eat. It sure smells delicious."

For good measure, she tossed in another smile at the end. The old lady threw Dot a touch of the evil eye, but I reckon she bought it. No punches were thrown or anything.

I had a brief recollection of Tony Lazzeri telling me a story about walking out in the middle of a date with some Anglo girl when she cut her spaghetti. In my more impetuous days, that might have flashed to me as a viable option, but I was too invested in Dot. I like to think I was wiser by that time of my life, plus she handled the situation smoother than a glass alderman.

Once the third bottle of wine showed up, all four of us was laughing and having such a fine night out that even me and Cooch splitting the check didn't hurt too much. We piled back into Dot's car and headed to drop off the Cucinellos. As we pulled onto their street, we all at once spotted two Cincinnati Police cars sitting in front of their house. One had his lights still turning, and there was the expected passel of neighbors standing out on their little lawns. Several of them were sporting loose-tied bathrobes without possessing the good sense to knot them a little tighter. The sight of one old boy made my veal do a backflip.

When we looked closer, we could see that the coppers weren't just at Cooch's house, there was two of them coming out of the next door neighbor's place, too. A few more were standing in the yard, and that's never a good sign. The front windows of both houses were all lit up like Christmas, and about the time Dot pulled to the curb, we saw that a pickup truck with a horse trailer was blocking the whole street coming from the other direction.

Cooch brushed by some disinterested boy in a uniform who was loitering by his stoop and made a quick perusal of the front room. His two youngest plus a couple of extra kiddos were all packed together on the couch looking like they'd been grilled under hot lights and just fessed up to taking the Lindbergh baby. There was a large quilt draped over the dining table and some bits of broken lamp scattered against the wall. The dented lampshade was propped up on the quilt like a cheap centerpiece. A Ward Bond-looking police sergeant was standing there, and when he heard us come in, he turned around and pushed up the brim of his hat.

"Mr. Cuccinello?"

For a second I thought he might ask Tony for an autograph, but he just stuck out his hand.

"I understand you folks had an evening out."

The sarge had a wee bit of smirk on his lips, but the four of us were still a mite slack-jawed. I don't recollect us answering.

"The Morgans next door are evidently away for the weekend, and their boy Melvin, an enterprising lad from what we could gather, invited the entire neighborhood full of children for a party."

He paused just long enough for Clara to get her voice back.

"They call him Trippy. He's Melvin the third. He's trouble, that one."

"Yes, ma'am. I'll need to show you just how much. Your older boy is still over there. The little ones here were just playing in their fort. They didn't cause no trouble. The only reason I even come into your house was that they had The Little Red Hen record playing so loud we could hear it from the street when we pulled up. Now if you folks would just follow me."

Like the saying goes, Dot and I had no dog in this hunt, but this was sounding better than Hollywood. We were going to keep watching the train wreck until somebody stopped us.

Just as we got to the Morgan's front door, which was standing wide open, the sergeant threw out his arm and said, "Make way for the donkeys."

Yes, sir. You heard right. Two rather shabby looking fellows come through the doorway and down the Morgan's front steps leading little jackasses, one after the other. As soon as they were clear, the sergeant restarted his story.

"Best guess is that Melvin... the third... opened up his parents' liquor cabinet about 10:30 this morning. Things went downhill from there as you might imagine. By late afternoon, Melvin or one of his cohorts decided to pilfer two of the riding animals from a carnival that is set up in the Albers Grocery parking lot. Somebody had the bright idea that they should probably hide the animals in the upstairs bathroom lest they get pinched. That was the term young Melvin used. They didn't plan on one of the donkeys turning on the bathtub faucet."

Sure enough, the rug in the entry way was squishy as all get out. The policeman pointed to about a dozen 13 or 14-year olds standing in the kitchen like ponies in a corral. Two others were in arm chairs passed out colder than icebox pie. The sergeant pointed to a mountain of soaking towels at the bottom of the stairs. However sopping they were, the downstairs hardwoods still held almost enough water to ski on.

"I'll give this to them," Sarge said. "Once they sobered up and realized the mess they'd caused, they at least tried to clean up. I'd wager some of those bath towels are yours. As to what shorted out the toaster and started that little fire, well, that's anybody's guess. And word is the cat will be just fine. Hair grows back."

The law and the various parents sorted the whole mess out. My memory tells me that there were no repercussions for any of Cooch's little angels, but I imagine various houses in that neighborhood heard some high volume discussions that night and the next. I'm fairly certain those hijinks didn't mark the start of anyone's life of crime, but that tale was being retold for the next 50 years, I can promise you that. And the number of burros probably got bigger every time.

I reckon I sowed my oats plenty of times or dropped my barley or cracked the old hazelnuts, but as I was surveying that havoc, and about the time another piece of loose plaster dropped from the Morgan's living room ceiling, I was sure thanking my stars that I didn't have any kiddos of my own to deal with. I know Jenny and me had talked about a baby, but looking at a scene like that will sure put those notions off their feed.

Out in front of the house, Cooch shook my hand and gave me a serious look as he told us good night.

"That was fun. Let's never do it again."

I reckon he was joking, but we never did. Luke Sewell, our manager, got fired halfway into the next season, and Cooch went along with him. As the saying goes – that's baseball.

I liked Cincinnati, but there were a few things that baffled me. One was that some people who lived there couldn't pronounce the name. They'd say Cincin-nat-uh, like it had an a on the end of it. I've heard jackholes do the same thing with Missouri. I'm rarely a grumpy sort, but there were moments I wanted to thump their ears. I might not be Noel Coward, but I can read.

Another thing that lots of folks will tell you was an abomination was Cincinnati chili. That one, I grew to appreciate right quick, though. I have heard since that a Greek fellow come up with the idea back in the Twenties on account of none of the Germans in town would eat his Greek food. Somehow, though, I managed to avoid it until a different Greek fellow opened Skyline diner way out in Price's Hill. I'm sure it was not invented for this reason, but it was a good pre-drinking meal. Very absorbent. Some of the Reds swore by it, though they were not exactly gourmands.

I've mentioned before that ballplayers are just big kids, and sometimes that means they can carry on like six-year olds and think it's the funniest durn thing in the world. Danny Griesbaum was one of the part-time hitting instructors. Grew up in one of them old neighborhoods in Chicago, and longed to be a magician when he was a kid. There was some old Russian man who run a little magic shop down the street from Danny, and as a youngster, that's where he spent all of his spare time and change.

I mean all the spare time that wasn't on the ball lot. See, Danny was a big guy with eyes like coal and a huge head of curly black hair. He was stronger than the other boys his age, and that enabled him to hit a baseball a country mile, as they used to say, though since he lived in Chicago, I reckon they said something different.

For all that power, Danny never could learn to hit for average, and his minor league career topped out with the Class B Yakima Pippins in 1937. He was 32 years old, married with a little boy. I think Danny's life might have crested then, too. He bounced around the lower minors and worked selling whatever caught his eye during the off season, until his wife passed away just prior to the war. His little boy went to live with an aunt someplace. I don't think they talked much. As for Danny, he reacquainted himself with magic and clowning around as a way to keep some joy in his life.

Baseball's like a small town, and it wasn't hard for various clubs to scare up enough money to throw some nice fellow like Danny a part time job. To know him was a pleasure, but you always had the idea that he was a lonely man.

He was popular with the Cincinnatis in the early 50s. He didn't travel with the team, but if he happened to be around after a loss, he was liable to brighten the mood by producing a six-foot long handkerchief or pulling a bird out of his pants. And no, that's not a euphemism. Though Danny being so big and hairy, I sure felt sorry for the dove.

Danny and me shared a love for practical jokes, too. One of his favorites was this contraption where he could pull out a pocket watch and his whole trouser rig would fall to his ankles. No skivvies or nothing. And Danny was such a big goof that he'd drop them in the middle of the street or the train station. Didn't matter where. The guys would whoop it up every time. Never got old.

Well one night, four or six of us was dodging in and out of the bars around Fountain Square. We'd just hit the sidewalk in front of the Mill, headed toward the next joint, when we hear this screaming from like three feet behind us.

"My dick! My dick! Oh, my God! I've lost my dick!"

The lot us of spun around expecting the worst. Big Danny's pants was around his ankles, and he had his knees locked together and his manhood tucked back between his legs. The guys from the team fell over. Johnny Wyrostek hit the ground laughing. Even some bystanders started yukking it up.

All of a sudden, Danny Griesbaum's eyes got big and round, looking just beyond us.

"Hello officer," he said

We all whirled around the other direction, still guffawing, and sure enough, there was this uniformed policeman with that veteran's look on his face.

"What the hell are you doing?"

"Sorry officer, my zipper broke."

I thought Willie Ramsdell was gonna bust a gut. Tears was flowing. The copper eventually started shaking his head and told Danny to pull his pants back up. We was with the Reds, so we could get away with anything there was to get away with. It turns out that policeman was a fellow named Frankie Moretelli. He turned out to be a good buddy of half the team over the next few years. We even got him a job doing security over to Crosley Field.

I was still seeing Dot at the start of 1952. Things had been swimming along. She was easy to be with and understanding. Her, with her day job, and me working night games, there were times we didn't get together with each other for a week or two at a time, but I never heard the woman complain even once.

The off season was a different story. I'd moved on from the shop rag factory and got myself an extra job as a shoe and check-in man at the Mergard's Bowling Lanes. After all of those years in a baseball clubhouse, I knew my way around sports equipment. Handing out pairs of shoes and polishing the balls on a rack was something I could do in my sleep. As long as I told a ribald story to Bobby Massuci, the manager, now and again, everything was golden.

One Saturday toward the end of February, I had the day off. Dot asked me to go along on an errand or two and make a day of it. It was something we had done a dozen times before, but this time she said we'd be stopping to see her mother. We could just pop by there for a few minutes, then we could go out for pastrami sandwiches, her treat. There must be some kind of ancient animal instinct that makes the hair stand up on a male human's neck when his girl suggests meeting her parents. Like when a hound sees a rabbit. Stupidly, I shrugged it off and said yes.

My first impression was that Dot's mother was a naturally angry woman which couldn't be farther from Dot than a butterfly from a potato. She opened the front door, scowled out a greeting, produced a one-note cigarette cough, then turned so we would follow. Dot gave me a weak smile as we plodded along behind her.

The house was as typical a Midwestern mom house as you could have found in 1952. Sunlight was kept to a minimum by pleated gold drapes, but I could still see a collection of snow globes on the recessed chotchke shelves as we followed the old lady through the living room. There was flocked wallpaper, an oval braided rug sitting on top of the yellow linoleum floor, and lace doilies on what I presumed was every flat surface. That may or may not have included the cats, of which there were at least three.

Though the felines were perched on the sofa and chairs, us mere humans might not have been allowed there, at least that was my thought as we went through the swinging panel door into the kitchen. To merely say that room was pink would be to do it a grave injustice. The porcelain sink and the matching formica countertops brought to mind the remedy for a meal of old sardines, and the curtains, the wallpaper, and the several dishtowels were each a different pattern of bold blossoms and tiny green leaves. The stepped down gold metal cannisters on the counter offered the only relief from the pinkness. And it was all viewed through a haze of Pall Mall smoke.

Mama Robichek turned down the radio soap opera and sat in her favorite chair. There was no mistaking it since a large glass ashtray took up the whole corner to the right of her Niagara Falls placemat. Dot and I took our seats and began to poke at the offered fare – celery sticks topped with pimento cheese. The entire experience felt like an outdated edition of Better Homes and Gardens... if Mickey Spillane decided to write for them.

The first fifteen minutes of the visit did not require me in the least. Dot and her mama caught each other up on the various transgressions made by cousins and neighbors. There was talk of putting more seed in the bird feeder and of moving a paving stone underneath the side hose bib. It lulled me into thinking this whole drop-in would be painless. Then, just as my daydreaming got the better of me, I noticed that things had gotten very quiet.

I offered Dot a handsome smile, even if I had not a snail's guess as to what I'd missed, then I turned my smile back toward Mama Robichek. Her bottom lip was sticking out further than the top one, her nostrils were a tad flared, and the overall expression made me think that a strong whiff of cat pee had penetrated her cigarette smoke.

"Baseball."

It was a statement. A lone word really, but my answer escaped involuntarily.

"Yes, ma'am."

She let go another big sniff.

"What do you think you're going to end up doing with your life?"

"Well, ma'am, I'm 51 years old, so I reckon this might be it."

"Hmmph"

I had seen that noise spelled out in books plenty of times, but I think Dot's mama might have been the first person I ever heard enunciate it so perfectly.

My sense is that it was downhill from there, but I've purged part of that specific memory. Suffice it to say that Dot, being empathetic, made her excuses and we were on our way after just three celery sticks – what I'd gauge to be about 20 minutes total.

Well, sir, the worst part of it, the part that blindsided me, happened after we were back in the front seat of Dot's car. It was a 1940 Ford Standard Coupe, if you were wondering about that. Lyon Blue. Anyway, I got in, and Dot patted the seat next to her and wiggled her eyebrows a little, asking me to get closer. I slid across the broadcloth and shocked her lips with one of those hellacious static electricity kisses. That should have been an omen.

"Sweetie..."

She give things a long pause after that word, and still I wasn't picking up on the cartoon piano that was hoisted above my noggin.

"It could be that my mama is right. I've never been more comfortable with a man. Maybe we should be thinking about settling down."

"Weren't you comfortable when you picked out your husband?"

It just slipped out, and I'm pretty sure in hindsight that it wasn't the best way to keep the conversation moving forward. To her credit, Dot laughed.

"That was a different me back then."

I may have been getting smarter already cause I kept my mouth shut after that one.

"What do you say, Wingo? Let's get married. Let's take the plunge."

She gave me a peck on my stunned cheek and ruffled my hair. My mouth opened again when it likely should not have.

"It might be more attractive if you didn't make it sound like us falling to our deaths."

She put the car in gear, and there wasn't a whole mess of conversation between there and the pastrami. Halfway through the sandwich, though, I thought things were back to normal. Dot was laughing. We kept on with the afternoon. Picked up new socks. She grabbed a bicycle basket from Western Auto. We even bought two gingerbread men from a little bakery. They gave us a couple of pennies off on account of one man having a misshaped foot.

As I've said before, I've always been a tad slow on the uptake. When she pulled up in front of my apartment, I gave Dot a kiss and told her that I'd see her tomorrow. We were due to go out for dinner. But before I could open the car door, she grabbed my hand.

"Wingo, I think maybe we need to take a little break. That way we can both figure out what we want."

She meant that I could come around to figuring the same as her, but I wasn't smart enough to understand that.

"I want to keep doing what we have been. I care about you, and we're having a good time."

She mustered a weak smile.

"Then I need to figure out what I want."

I know full well that Dot didn't shove me out of her car, but once I was standing there on the cold sidewalk, I'll be damned if I could recollect getting out on my own volition.

After two years of reinforcing to each other that we were just having fun, the rules were changed on me right there on the bench seat of that navy blue Ford. It had been nine years that my shining light had been gone, but I just couldn't see jumping into another marriage, and that's what it felt like. Jumping in. It's like hitting a fastball – timing is everything. In some other year, maybe I would've seen my way clear to settle down with Dot Robichek. She was a fine woman, and we might well have been a happy couple with a backyard grill, but my whole life would sure be a damn site different than what it turned out to be. Hell, I might never have come close to seeing 116 years on this Earth. I probably would've choked to death on a klobasnik.

Chapter Seven

The 1952 season was not a great one for the Cincinnatis. It was just as underachieving as 1951 had been, and the same as 1953 would shake out, too. I mentioned that the club fired Luke Sewell in July. Earl Bruckner, another one of our coaches, managed for a week, then they brought in Rogers Hornsby.

Now, I'd not spent a great deal of time around Hornsby in his prime. Except for 1922 when I was a wide-eyed kid at the Polo Grounds, drooling over every new event, I just didn't see much of him. When folks was calling him as good a right-handed hitter as ever played, he was in the National League, and I was working for the Yankees. We faced him in the Series in 1926, and though his Cardinals ended up winning, it sure as shit wasn't anything to do with Hornsby. That whole seven games, he couldn't hit the water if he peed over the side of the canoe. We faced him often when he moved over to the St. Louis Browns, but by then he wasn't but a whisper of the player he'd once been.

Of course, just because an athlete is a genius in uniform, there is no guarantee that he is any great shakes as a human being. Look at Cobb. For all the terrible and possibly exaggerated things that have been written about Ty Cobb, you could make the case that he was a better person than Hornsby by a whisker and that Hornsby was a better hitter by the same thin margin. Ask me tomorrow, and I might have a different answer.

Rogers Hornsby earned better than a half a million dollars as a ballplayer, did you know that? He gambled most of it away on the horses, running with good looking brunettes, and whatever else rich people waste their dough on. He never drank or smoked, but maybe he should have tried it. Might have drowned that bug up his ass. When his boy got killed in a plane crash, Hornsby's ex-wife wouldn't even let him come to the funeral.

He'd been unable to find a job in organized ball until the Yankees organization hired him to manage the Beaumont Roughnecks in 1949. He didn't make any friends among the players, but it earned him a job with the Browns. He was back in the big leagues, if you can say that about the Browns. When he got fired from St. Louis after just 51 games, the players were so happy that they bought a trophy for the team owner.

Everybody with the Reds knew the man's reputation before he got there, of course. His whole career as a manager, he had made pitching changes from the top step of the dugout. Didn't even have the respect and generosity to walk out to the mound. The week of that announcement, as we waited for Hornsby to arrive, may have been when I learned the word trepidation.

One good thing come out of it, though. Luke Sewell had brought in Ben Chapman to coach third base at the start of '52. That was the jackhole who had given Robinson such a vile measure of shit the year he broke into the league. Even all these years removed from it, I don't want to repeat the things Chapman hollered at Jackie Robinson. Lower than animals Chapman was. You know that wasn't the first time that man showed the world what a bigot he was. Back in the 30s, when Hitler was first rounding up the Jews, Ben Chapman would scream names at the Jewish fans and give Nazi salutes to the bleachers, even in his own ballpark. He had fist fights with umpires, opposing players, teammates, and his own manager. If I ever sat down to make a list of the worst humans I ever run across in the game of baseball, Ben Chapman would be on it.

The good news I'm talking about is that right before Hornsby come in, Chapman quit. He found out that Hornsby liked to be in the third base coaches box his own damn self. We laughed in the clubhouse that old Ben was just afraid that the new skipper could outmiserable him. Most of us were plenty happy to see the back of that guy, but it's the old admonition – be careful what you wish for.

I found myself on a short three-game trip to Chicago right after Independence Day in '52. Dot and me had been called off for several months by then. I'd confined my social life to whatever opportunities wandered into the Licky. I was no more than an old and mostly uninterested lion with one eye open for any lame zebras that might near the watering hole. I knew I'd made the right decision with Dot, but there was still a certain amount of licking my wounds, I guess.

Well, when they assigned me to make the trip up to Wrigley for those games, I called Pearl. I hadn't talked to her for about three years. Most of that time I was seeing Dot, and I didn't reckon it was seemly. We had visited even while I was married to Jenny, though nothing happened between us, of course. I'm not sure why I'd treated my time with Dot any different, but I did.

When Pearl heard my voice on the telephone that evening, she didn't say anything. The silence lasted so long that I thought we'd been cut off. But when I said her name the second time, she softly offered that she was there. She had a busy weekend, she told me, but after some coaxing, Pearl agreed to meet me for dinner.

Like most men, I reckon I'm not always the most perceptive creature, but it was clear from the time we said hello that Pearl was unhappy with me. She gave a half-hearted hug then shoved out of it after a second or two. Her eye contact was worse than a cat trying to avoid a pill. Still, she was not prone to be shy with me, and she soon got to the point in a quiet, firm voice.

"Wingo, I haven't heard from you in better than three years. And I know that's how things have sometimes been between us, but after all this time, I think I deserve better, don't you?"

I tell you, son, you've never seen more genuine eyes. They were full of sadness and hurt and what I took to be 25 years of frustration. I realized later that it was a lifetime worth.

"Yes, Pearl. I suspect you do."

All I could manage was a little croak of a whisper as I added to that.

"It's just that all those years ago, when I asked you for more, you said we had no future because of, well, because of me being White."

I'll emphasize that women don't much like hearing I told you so, even if they was the ones doing the telling. A lesser person might have raised her voice or whizzed her tea glass past my ear, but Pearl just let loose a little sigh and cast her eyes downward for a minute.

"Honey, I don't need you to remind me of my skin color. There's others enough who do that most every day."

We sat at the table without saying anything. I was afraid to move. The waitress broke the spell by bringing a basket of rolls. Pearl stared at me and took me by the hands.

"I suspect you did the best you could."

It wasn't a very lively conversation the rest of the meal, and we skipped any drinks or nightclubs. When I walked her back to her place, Pearl told me she was tired. I didn't see her on Sunday because we had a doubleheader. Day games only at Wrigley Field, you know. After that, it was the train back to Cincinnati. I did make a point to call more often, at least for the next couple of years.

The Reds officially changed their name to the Redlegs in 1953 because of McCarthy and the House Un-American Activities numbskulls. They claimed to be after spies, but netted store clerks and screenwriters. It reminded me of my good friend Izzy Levy. He would have been a goner right off, and just for wanting to make the world a better place for the little man. The whole thing was nothing but third-rate politicians metaphorically hollering "Look at me!"

I thought Redlegs was the stupidest thing I'd ever heard in my life. Tailgunner Joe my ass. He was a no account drunk. News moved slow in the Midwest sometimes, I suspect. The whole loyalty and red-baiting had been going on for six years before the name change. It reminded me of the school kids back in Lee County who would make shit up to get attention. Few of them ever amounted to squat.

The ball club never had anyone accused of being commies, of course. It was just that some pencil dick in the front office decided to take a few crackpot letters to heart. The story that bubbled up in my head was one that my daddy told me during my early years in Memphis. He had a step cousin from a couple counties over, the kind you knew about but only saw once or twice in your life. They had a name, of course, but you generally referred to them as "Uncle Cecil's wife's boy, Jimmy." Like it was one word. Daddy didn't recollect much about him other than he was quick with a joke, liked his beer, and had a prominent dimple in his left cheek when he smiled.

The Jimmy in question was brung up on the same Farm Union stories I was, but with him, it become a calling. When he was in his 20s, Jimmy headed out west and, eventually, hooked on as an organizer for the Wobblies, the IWW. He ended up in Goldfield, Nevada, a magically named place where surely there were fortunes strewn like dandelions. The miners had already joined up with the Wobblies, who wanted all workers, skilled and unskilled, to be part of one big union. Jimmy's job was to organize bartenders and newsboys and barbers and faro dealers, the townsfolk, in other words. There was such a demand for laborers that the Wobblies didn't even try to negotiate. They just posted the new wages on a bulletin board for the owners to see,

Like I learned by watching Izzy Levy on Coney Island, Utopia rarely lasts more than a few months. It wasn't long before the Wobblies, hopped up on success, started ordering the restaurants to turn away workers from other unions, and the whole thing disintegrated from there. It wasn't violence that got them, though. The rich mine owners, using bullshit stories, talked their way into getting federal troops sent out, and the very first day the soldiers arrived, newly backed by Army protection, the owners chopped wages. By that time, there was enough discord that the grand experiment fluttered away like a wounded moth.

Jimmy bounced around, avoiding most of the violence that followed the Wobblies, gaining the occasional blow from a 2x4, or a scar from a rifle butt. The Great War changed all that. The union strongly opposed the war and kept urging their members to strike for better pay. As far as public opinion went, it was a miscalculation, to say the least. In 1917, the government raided every IWW office in America, and the army attacked more than three dozen strike sites calling them insurrections. Jimmy, above a pool room on the wrong side of downtown Billings and no doubt shouting about worker's rights, was shot three times by a scared, apple-cheeked private newly recruited from some idyllic town like Calistoga or Eau Claire.

I never met step cousin Jimmy. Never even knew his second name for certain, but that's who popped into my head when I heard that some pea brain in the Reds front office thought it would be a good idea to change the team name in defense of American values.

I knew a very wise baseball manager who got fired and said that sometimes the players just get tired of seeing the same old face at the end of the dugout. Maybe that had been the case with the last two months of 1952 because we rallied enough to go a couple games north of .500 the rest of the way. It was good enough to finish sixth out of eight, mostly because the poor Pirates were about as woeful a bunch of ballplayers as I ever did see. A couple of the more optimistic folks in the Reds front office expected that Hornsby might at least lead the club into the top half of the National League in '53. Since we only had one pitcher who could throw a full 60 feet, and we were slower than three legged turtles, a lot of us just couldn't see it.

Son, I was watching one of those nature programs the other night, and they were following a passel of capybaras around South America. Cute little buggers, but they're apt to stare at some unseen object for hours at a time. The Marlon Perkins wannabe hitched up his utility pants and asked his guide just what the capybara was thinking about, and the fellow answered "nothing." Didn't consider the question for even a second. He just knew that aside from biting grass, there was not a thought to be had inside that rodent's noggin. It was emptier than the priest house when the nuns shower.

And that's what Rogers Hornsby was like. He knew baseball, though he might not have been a patient teacher of it. Hell, he was almost 60 years old and could still put on a better batting cage show than anyone on our club save maybe Kluszewski or Gus Bell on a very good day. He would sit and talk baseball with anyone who came around, or I should say talk at people about baseball. Any other subject, though, and he was just like that damn capybara.

We was in St. Louis early in 1953. We had seven games called on account of rain or snow that first month, and all our illustrious manager knew to do was come down from his room and sit in the lobby. He didn't read. He just stared at the walls imagining hanging curve balls from 30 years prior.

I had traveled with them that road trip, and I happened to pass by Hornsby lecturing one of the hotel bellboys from a wing back chair. Skinny, nervous looking fellow who was afraid to move lest the old man stand up and slug him one.

"They're home run happy!"

That's what I heard Hornsby telling the kid as I strolled past. Really getting himself worked up, he was.

"They ain't willing to work to overcome their weaknesses. They're happy to stand in the box and just guess what a pitcher is going to throw. You need to know what you want to do with the pitch. You! That's your pitch. You work it to wherever you want it to go. Inside, outside. Opposite field. I'd step into the box and feel downright sorry for the pitcher."

The bellboy was thinking about making a break for it. Maybe he could outrun Hornsby, but instead he asked a question.

"Do you think this rain might cost us the game tomorrow?"

Hornsby narrowed his eyes down to little slits. His face betrayed that he wanted to make a growling noise, but no sound come out. He just got up without a word and moved to a chair on the other side of the lobby. It was baseball or nothing. Not even the weather.

The Reds were still an all-White ball club that year. Nino Escalera had come to spring training, but he got sent down well before we broke camp. It had been six years since Jackie Robinson's first game with the Dodgers, but as of Opening Day 1953, only six teams had Black players – the Dodgers, Indians, Browns, Giants, Braves, and White Sox. From time to time, I'd think of sweet Pearl or my old pal

Herbie, and reflect that I was losing all faith that we would ever see a real integrated league.

I don't reckon Hornsby or Gabe Paul were all fired up to have Black players, or they would've done it. Hornsby had managed Satchel Paige with the Browns, though I'm not sure he liked it. For what it's worth, he also mouthed off about Jews to our GM without realizing that Gabe Paul was Jewish - the son of refugees who fled the damned Cossacks, in fact. Hornsby might have known that if he ever bothered talking to anyone.

That's what did our famous manager in, really. Hornsby never had a meal with his fellow coaches. If he spoke to the sportswriters it was to call them second-guessing sons of bitches. If he shared a full sentence with a player it was usually something like "I can spit further than you can hit" or "You're throwing wilder than a shit house rat."

At one point, Gabe Paul suggested that the club find some old hand of a pitcher who might teach these young fellows on the Reds a thing or two. Hornsby tossed that notion aside and said that a ballplayer needed to learn to hard way. The team fired him with eight games to go, saying that the new breed of baseball players needed to be coddled a little more and just wouldn't respond to a manager who was hopelessly wedded to the past. Makes me chuckle a little. That was better than seven decades ago, and you could probably find the same quote from last September.

Chapter Eight

I've not really talked a great deal about my job with the team, about the things I did every day. That's because it was boring as shit. The head man would get the glory of hobnobbing with the Louisville Slugger folks, so most of my time was spent hauling bats, repairing gloves, doing laundry, picking up towels, running the occasional errand, and trying to make life better for the ballplayers. Back in Memphis, I was a jack of all trades, handling the groundskeeping, equipment, stadium maintenance, running in whatever direction they pointed me.

Big leagues teams had more help, of course, but even then, we were not far removed from the days when the clubhouse man was also expected to be the trainer. Even in my day, if the doc said come hold this third baseman down while I shave his groin, you muscled up and averted your eyes. That was the cause of the incident that got me run off from the Yankees, remember.

As I've told you, I got to travel a good deal when I lived in New York to help with the equipment and be the general road gopher. Those were good times, since the local club was usually responsible for keeping the locker room tidy. It was a small break from barehanding dirty skivvies.

By the time I was nearing my first decade with the Reds, my road trips had gotten less frequent. I'd earned a little seniority. The rotation we'd worked with was still in play, but it was unevenly applied. If there was a particular trip I wanted to make, I could generally pick my spots.

At the end of May in 1954, the team had a three-day road trip to Wrigley Field. It was a scheduling quirk, I reckon. We were off on Thursday, played the weekend versus the Cubs, then didn't go again till Wednesday when the Phillies come to

Cincinnati. It looked like a fine opportunity for a free trip to see my friend Pearl. They had no lights, so the ballgames were in the afternoon, and my nights were free, if she could spare me some time. She seemed to be completely over her small fit of pique from two years prior.

We had never been picky about what we did together. It's not like she expected me to take her to fancy places, though I'd tried a few times. Friday night we had a restaurant dinner and a few drinks at a nice nightclub on State Street near Garfield Avenue over toward Pearl's neighborhood. It was the first time I'd seen Joe Williams sing, and he was the real deal, man. The billing went to the Red Saunders Orchestra, and they were swell, but it was clear that Williams was the star. He had him a baritone smoother than his shiny tuxedo jacket. We stayed for two full sets before she let on that she was getting sleepy. We were not the youngsters we once were, you know. I tucked her into a taxi and grabbed another one back north to our team hotel.

For that Saturday morning, Pearl suggested we go to the art museum. I'd never been there, though I appreciate art when I remember to be around it. It sounded like a fine idea. I met her out front at opening time. I recollect that she had on a navy blue dress with white petunia flowers scattered across it, and a bright white hat. As usual, my clothes felt a little shabby.

A good painting can sure put you of a mind for reminiscing, can't it? I remember telling her that the weak-chinned woman in American Gothic was the spitting image of Albert Spurles' mother back in Lee County. Being around her as a youngster, you feared that a stiff breeze would just curl her up in a corner. We saw the Edward Hopper canvas of the late night folks in the diner. It gave me memories of drunk dining with Paul and Eddie back in New York, but I didn't say anything about that one.

Otherwise, we strolled amongst the paintings, and caught each other up on our lives. I didn't really have much to impart beyond the latest hijinks at the Licky.

One of their most famous paintings is the gigantic French one made up of all the dots. Covers a whole big wall, that one does. It's people enjoying the park on a Sunday afternoon. It put Pearl in mind of Sundays when she took her boy to

Jackson Park to watch the sailboats and soak up the sunshine while they laid on the grass. They would get corn dogs from a greasy spoon on 57th Street, though none of the Frenchies in the picture were eating weiners.

She had never told me much at all about her son, but that painting opened the barn door. He had saved up and taken two years of study at Chicago Teachers College, but then he got drafted into the Korean War. After that he had bopped around from job to job, trying to find his footing. He had finally got hired on at Montgomery Wards, and she was hopeful that he had found something stable. She worried about him and didn't want his tendency to be restless and angry to hurt his prospects. Pearl figured that Korea had not done her boy any favors.

We went to lunch before I had to get back to Wrigley. Howie Pollet befuddled our lineup that afternoon. Scattered four hits, as they say. Pearl cooked me dinner at her place afterwards. First time I'd been at her apartment in many a year.

Sunday was a doubleheader, so I had to go straight to the ball yard after a quick goodbye. I know both games were humdingers. We split with them. The second game we had a pitcher going named Corky Valentine, and he got the W. He was part of our rotation that entire season, but ended up back in the minors by the next year. I run into him years later when he was working as a cop at Fulton County Stadium. He had been 24 or so on that day at Wrigley. One of the many reminders at how fleeting success can really be, ain't it? I still recall the grin he had on the train ride home.

Negroes were still a concerning subject to small-minded people, and there seemed to be a never-ending shitload of those. The things that you shouldn't have to worry about at all in a perfect world sure do come up a lot in America. True history tells you all the secrets of life, and you ignore it at your own peril.

You recollect what I told you about Jackie Robinson and how things just flat stalled out. Baseball was a funny place. See it had plumb near been the leader in finally allowing the races to mingle, but it didn't happen all even-like. For every hump they got over in Brooklyn, there was a mountain in Boston, and there sure as shooting were a few rugged hills in Cincinnati.

It wasn't until 1954 that a couple of players of color wore the Reds uniform. They debuted back to back in the same game, they did. Seventh inning in Milwaukee. Nino Escalera hit for Andy Semminick, and then Chuck Harmon in the pitcher's spot. A couple of utility players more or less, neither one of them would make much difference player-wise, but they were the pioneers. Harmon had been a college basketball player, and both he and Escalera would go on to be baseball scouts. Did you know Harmon worked as a basketball scout, too. For the Indiana Pacers. Yep. How 'bout that?

They didn't go through near the hell in the big leagues as some of the first ones, but I heard tell of some pretty toasty crevices they had to crawl through down in Tulsa before they got the call up. The two of them got kicked out a cab together on account of it being a Whites only cab. Even in a world of crazy, that's up there, ain't it? Like their blackness was going to rub off on the taxi cab seat and then attach itself to some fat White lady's ass.

There was some heckling up in Cincy. Lots of it, and vile. It was a yankee town but not by much. There was no doubt some degrading situations they had to endure. Harmon often told me that finding a restaurant where he could enjoy a good meal was damn near an impossibility. The saving grace was that the Reds team didn't really have themselves a Dixie Walker. The boys held their tongues for the most part, but I likewise never once heard of a White Reds player socializing with a Black one throughout the time I stayed there.

What smoothed the humps out of the road for the Redlegs was getting from a Black player to a star player who just happened to be Black. My theory is that the reason Brooklyn took to Jackie so quick was because he was good. There were more than a few liberals up there who felt it was high time to end the segregation, but truth was that most run of the mill New Yorkers didn't cotton to Black folks any more than a South Georgia well digger did. The fact was that from day one, Jackie Robinson was the most exciting player on that team. He was liable to smack a double, steal a base, or make a diving stop at any second. He let the folks who might have had a little of that hate start seeing Dodger blue instead of black, like they say.

For us in Cincinnati, the fellow who won over the public was Frank Robinson. That kid was a hitting machine in 1956. He had two hits and a walk in his first big league game.

Yes, sir. Robinson convinced most of the Reds fans, if not to forget their prejudice, at least to drop it a few notches down their priority list. But that wouldn't be the end of the trouble for the Black players around the leagues.

The Licky was my main haunt for the whole time I was in Cincinnati. Like every kind of watering hole in any country you go to, save some place like Saudi Arabia where you get beheaded for ordering a double, the Licky had lots of real characters. Some of them almost lived their entire adult lives in that joint, but others just migrated through like a drunk goose. You might get a glad-handing fellow who'd show up one night spinning a tale of moving to town and just when you figured he was becoming one of the regulars, he disappeared like a gnat fart in the wind.

Blah Blah Benny was an in-betweener. He was a fixture at that bar for, oh, I reckon three or four years in the middle 1950s. Then one day he quit coming in. None of us ever saw him again. It's not that he died. We would've known if that happened. A tavern rumor mill is as strong as it gets. You don't miss much gossip about what a bar regular is up to because everyone is always walking past the other one's house right as an embarrassing decision is trying to sneak out the side door at dawn. Sometimes you spot another boozer in a grocery aisle and try your best not to make eye contact. You don't want that youngun in the cart basket to start asking questions about where daddy gets off to every night. No, Benny must've moved away. At least that's what I prefer to think.

I can see in your face that you have a question about how somebody could come by the nickname of Blah Blah Benny. I know you hear people say blah blah to signify somebody rambling on about a given subject, but son, this fellow Benny would reach a point in his drinking schedule that he would forget words. Not like an old person grasping for a single, long forgotten name, mind you. Benny would forget all of them. He'd start a sentence, and about four words into the thing, he'd start saying blah blah blah blah until he figured his entire thought had been adequately conveyed. He had a low bass of a voice that give his blahs a touch of Everett Dirksen gravitas. It was something to behold.

There is no doubting that Benny had a serious drinking problem, but he was also a house painter by trade, and I don't reckon those five gallon buckets of flat white in an unventilated six by ten room was doing him any favors either.

None of that ever stopped him from carrying on as if he was right in the midst of your conversation. If the gang was all laughing at something, Blah Blah Benny would be yukking it up with the rest of you. If something bad happened, Benny would arch his eyebrows knowingly, nod slowly and wave his hand in a little circle, then cast his eyes toward his shoes.

What reminded me of Blah Blah Benny was a lively discussion from July 1955. The club was at the tail end of a long road trip – Pittsburgh, Brooklyn, Philly, and New York. This gangly right hander name of Jim Hearn with the Giants took a no-hitter against us into the ninth inning at the Polo Grounds, and Chuck Harmon was the one who broke it up. He come off the bench to do it, too. His pinch single was the only hit we got that day.

I was at home for that trip, and about seven or eight of us listened to the game on radio sitting at the bar at the Licky. When it was over a lively discussion started about why Harmon didn't get to play more. They were always after me for the inside scoop.

"Wingo, what's the scuttlebutt? Is Birdie afraid to play Harmon because he's colored? He's a better hitter than Palys. He ought to be in there."

"Birdie seems like an okay fellow. Knows his baseball. I don't want to speculate on what he does."

Somebody else jumped in.

"He had Milt Smith out there at third, and Smith couldn't hit if my grandmother was pitching underhand. And my grandmother's dead."

Benny started his low rumble, pointing his finger like a manager after an umpire.

"Blah blah blah .250! Blah blah! Damn it!"

Benny cocked an eyebrow to underscore his point. Brody Byrne didn't miss a beat.

"You're goddamned right, Benny! He sure as shit should be."

All of us had learned to decipher the code.

Now, Benny never started out an evening in blah blah mode. If you happened to get to the bar right when he got off the job, old Benny was as sharp as the next guy. His road to blah blah was a short one, though. The paint and Pabst generally come into synergy about 45 minutes in.

It was an awful sad tale, the story of Benny's life. I don't know if he was always a man of low ambitions, but he was married for years and had a daughter. He was never able to beat the drink, though, and he knew it. He was one of those who needed to teetotal. There was no such thing as just a little for Benny.

In the years that I knew him, his wife was remarried and living across the river in Covington. He seemed to have let that memory go, but his daughter was another story. Catch him about one and a half beers in, and Benny was more likely than not to show you the picture of his girl. It was probably from junior high school, but it was the one he carried in his wallet. Frayed around the edges from being pulled out so much and thinner than Alabama ice. It was one of the few times that Benny would look you right in the eye. He didn't have much in the way of teeth, but he flashed those at you.

"She works at a bank now. A teller. Doing real good. I tried to go see her, but..."

That's when his eyes would drop to the bar and his right hand would throw a dismissive wave.

"Blah blah blah."

And Benny's words would be gone for the night.

Rocky Bridges had his best year in 1955. Did you ever know him? A knock-about infielder with a prickly crew cut who could stuff as much chaw into his cheek as most anybody in the bigs. He managed in the minors for another 30-some odd years after he quit playing, and he could tell a good joke. It was hard not to like Rocky, though I don't know of anyone who tried. He played tough, but he knew he ought to be having fun since with his talent every day up at the show was a gift. At least, that's how I interpreted his outlook.

Rocky had been born at Refugio, Texas, a couple hours south of where we are now, but he grew up in California. He had a cousin of his who was a goat farmer outside Temecula in the days before that place was trendy, and this old boy, name of Ernest Bigelow, had once auditioned to be on You Bet Your Life. He didn't make it, but he spent the rest of his life under the impression that he was in show business.

In August of '55, Ernest, who went by Specs, loaded a 3-year old LaMancha goat named Eula Fay into a 16 year old DeSoto Deluxe and come to visit his famous ballplayer kin. Specs was sort of stubby and non-descript, and Eula Fay was mostly black but had cream colored stripes that ran from her mouth up over her eyes. Like all LaManchas, and most respectable gophers, Eula Fay had virtually no ears.

You remember that cop I mentioned, Frankie Moretelli? He was working the player's gate at Crosley when he was approached by a squat, bespectacled gent walking a slick-headed goat on a rope. One of them, the fellow or the goat, began to spin a tale about surprising his cousin who was an infielder for the Reds. It didn't even take reaching the end of the story before Frankie did what any other level brained person would do. He let them in just to see what would happen.

It was early, still a couple hours before first pitch, so I figure the late arriving players got the biggest shock, walking into the clubhouse to find a goat chomping on their striped socks. With some heartfelt persuasion, Gus Bell and Stan Palys talked Specs into letting them take Eula Fay for a snack on the field. Before they let her through the tunnel into the outfield, they slipped a groundskeeper's shirt on her. Sadly, nobody was there to snap a picture. We all thought it was high comedy, but Matty Schwartz threw such a conniption that it woke Birdie Tebbets, who had been napping in the manager's office. The Reds were a really young club that year, so Birdie already felt like he needed to keep the guys on a tight leash. He tongue-lashed everybody so hard that we lost to the Pirates, and that was not an easy task that season. Eula Fay and Specs got the unceremonious heave ho from the home clubhouse and were forced to watch the whole debacle from the right field stands. Luckily, I kept plenty of extra socks.

Chapter Nine

There was a young Black player in camp in '56 – Wally Pink. I suppose somebody thought that was a funny name back in the slavery times, and this whole family got stuck with it. To make matters worse, Wally run faster than scalded lightning and had acquired the nickname of Rabbit. Rabbit Pink. But there you have it.

Now Rabbit was a second base prospect. His daddy had played on the Prairie View A&M college team back in the 1920s and bounced around the lower rungs of the Negro Leagues, and Rabbit had followed his footsteps to the college team, too.

Another thing about Rabbit Pink. That kid loved blues and jazz music more than a crisp strip of bacon. He had him a cherry red transistor radio, a Zenith, I believe it was. Slicker than goose shit, that little radio, and he always had the thing tuned to the closest rhythm and blues station he could find. Now it wasn't like today where your satellite radio or your durn cell phone can bring you 5,000 choices. Nope, back in those days you took what the DJ and the record companies bribing him told you you'd take.

I reckon Rabbit thought I was pulling his leg at first when I told him how much I enjoyed his music. More than one White man in those days, if they talked to a Black man much at all, would shine them on a little. They thought leading someone on, or downright ridiculing him, was hysterical tomfoolery. It built up an understandable reluctance to take whitey at his word.

Eventually, I convinced Rabbit I was on the up and up. See, his locker in Tampa was right around the corner from my stool. All the players would drop their shoes in front of my stool for me to polish up, so when the spring games and workouts was over, I'd be buffing toes and popping a rag, and Rabbit would be taking his sweet time getting dressed and listening to the latest music. It was an eye-opening thing for me, and led me down a path of seeking out radio stations that most White folks might not have knew were even on the dial. Old Rabbit didn't head north with us, but he and I had many the toe tap and good conversation that spring.

Cincinnati had a fellow spinning records on WCIN name of Buggs Scruggs. The number of White folks in Cincinnati listening to R&B music in 1956 could have held their convention in a Porta-John. "This is Buggs Scruggs, the man with the plugs, back on the scene with my record machine." And then he'd blast you with some James Brown or Platters or Lavern Baker or Otis Rush. *You Know I Love You Baby*. I think that might have been the one that got me hooked. It took me back to Memphis, snoot sandwiches, and my long ago friend Herbie. The only reason I knew Otis Rush was thanks to Rabbit's little red radio.

I loved Ray Charles. If you can have a love affair with music, man, for me it'd be Ray Charles and Aretha Franklin. If those two ever had a baby, Lordy me. You know, Ray had two number one R&B songs in 1956. The first one was *Drown in my Own Tears*, and it would break your heart. You felt Ray's pain with that sweet wailing and punctuating saxophone. There was a touch of those girl harmonies at the end, but he was still holding auditions for the Raelettes, sometimes every night. His second big hit that year was *Mary Ann* about one of his side ladies. Sort of a Latin swingy thing.

Ray come to town that August while the team was on the road, and me and Brody Byrne went to see him. We were sitting way toward the back, but Brody spotted his boss from the jukebox company coming out of the can. Turns out that Atlantic Records had seen fit to buy a few cocktails for those who might help them sell some records. They had a nice big table to one side of the stage, and Brody's boss took it upon himself to make room for us. A radio station owner and his wife had already bailed before Ray even come on, so there we were.

The record company dude took it all in stride. He clearly enjoyed having an expense account, and all he heard was that Brody was in the jukebox business and that I was with the Reds. From that moment forward, it was free drinks and knowing smiles. I was the proverbial pig in slop.

Our host's name was Barry something, and I would classify him as a first rate nocturnal engineer. He was clearly made to schmooze. I could almost picture him as a kindergartner wearing Vitalis and putting a chubby little arm around the kid next to him. The longer the evening went on, the more I began thinking that it was a no brainer that we'd be going backstage to hobnob with Ray Charles. When the stage fellow had led Ray away from the piano after the last song, Slick Barry pumped everyone's hands and slapped our backs, then he got this conspiratorial look on his face. As if this wasn't what he did every show.

"They normally don't like this, but would you guys like to come backstage and tell Ray hello?"

Ray had four hit records by then, but he was no superstar. Still, I was looking forward to saying thanks. Barry led Brody and me, a record store owner and his missus, and a radio newsman down a hallway and parked us by this table of booze. He and two DJs disappeared further into the bowels of cinder block. A quick scotch and a half later, he come back to take us to Ray.

I'd seen a lot of drunk ballplayers. In some cases, I guess ballplaying drunks would be more to the point. But some of the backstage folks that night was pickled like a ten year old gherkin. I didn't snap to it the time, but it was clearly a mix of the hooch and the heroin. They were in various stages of recline, and you could have gotten a close shave using the reflection from their glassy eyes.

Ray was smiling and real mellow. Warm handshakes all around. But I couldn't take my eyes off of the bare hind end of some gal who I assume was one of the backup singers, though I never saw her face to be sure. Her dress was pulled up around her waist, and she was draped over a big speaker case like yesterday's housecoat. Nice round butt pointed in our general direction. Every time anyone passed by her, they'd give her a hearty spank on the bottom. She rewarded them with a wiggle and a low moan. I'll be damned if I caught a blessed thing anyone was talking about.

After about three or four minutes of visiting and peek sneaking, Barry said he's catch us on the flip side and led us to the door. I felt a little sad for those musicians and their addictions, not to mention that young lady's proctologist. At the same time, all Brody and I could think of was getting back to the Licky for a few beers before last call. But man, was that some good show.

Of course, like I told you before, the story of 1956 was Frank Robinson. Just 20 years old, and he won Rookie of the Year. He made the jump straight from A ball to the bigs and pounded 38 home runs. Frank was not one to take even a little shit from anybody. He had spent the last two years in the Sally League playing at Columbia, South Carolina. You would reckon that was hell for a young Black ballplayer in the 1950s, but Frank said the worst year he ever had of it was in the Class C Pioneer League.

That's where he started when he was 17. Ogden, Utah. It was part of the Mormon religion that Blacks were inferior. Written right into their bible from what I could gather. If that ain't a steaming pile to dump on a 17-year old urban kiddo dropped alone into the middle of Cletus Town. He said there wasn't a place in that backwards little burg that he could get served food. They wouldn't let him see a movie. Nothing. He spent the whole season in his room, letting the resentment fester, I imagine, but also putting that energy into every inning on the ballfield.

When he got to Cincinnati, he lit a fire under some of the other guys. Right behind him was Wally Post and Kluszewski. Bell and Ed Bailey not far after them. The club set the new record for home runs in a season. What's more is that we were winning games. Our pitching wasn't great shakes, though Brooks Lawrence who come over from St. Louis won 13 straight to start the season. That meant that both the Reds' best hitter and their best pitcher were Black. You had to think some of those rednecks who'd been heckling poor Chuck Harmon was biting their tongues to the point of bleeding in 1956.

We were in the pennant race. The year before, we didn't even top .500, but with a week to go in that '56 season, the Reds climbed to just a game and a half out of first place. The trouble was that the two teams atop us, the Dodgers and Braves, well, they wasn't losing any games either.

For yours truly, it was sneaking up on 20 years since I'd been part of a pennant winning ball club. Twenty years. I kind of forgot that winning was exciting. Even assistant clubhouse men might get a little extra spring in their step. We sure hadn't had players digging for any extra in September in Cincinnati since I'd been there. Even a single year before. September was the month a player lined up their winter job, their barnstorming, and said farewell to their sidepiece.

That season of 1956 wasn't without troubles. Middle of September, Brooks Lawrence was sitting on 19 wins. Birdie never give him another start. Lawrence told everybody who'd listen that was on account of his skin color. He believed deep down in his heart that Tebbets didn't want a Black pitcher to become a 20-game winner on his watch. He had moved Lawrence into relief.

Now, you've listened to me sit in this chair and ramble on for weeks, and you know that I won't truck that kind of hatred and race baiting, at least not in silence. I may have evolved over the years, but I like to think I was always more open than most. Thing is I can't say I heard Tebbetts pop off about Black players. He was no Ben Chapman or even Hornsby or Stanky or Slaughter or any of those other toxic bastards. But I can't sit here and deny a pattern of behavior, either.

Birdie had a say in bringing Chuck Harmon up in the first place, but there's no doubt that he should've played him more once he got there. Same went for George Crowe. Frank Robinson, for one, had mostly good things to say about Birdie, but I got no other reason a manager would pull his best starter from the rotation in the middle of a pennant race. If you ask me, Birdie was not a hateful man, but he was indifferent. Like a lot of folks, if he'd taken the time to cross the street, he might've done a world more good.

In Spring Training of 1957, there was a little episode of the sort that ballplayers find absolutely hysterical but that will make a Junior Leaguer blanch and seek a damp towel for her forehead. Though the boy involved in the affair sure would've welcomed a damp towel his own self.

I got to Tampa a few days early that year. Didn't really have much else to do around Cincinnati, so I caught the train down south.

We had a big hitting ball club again that year. Frank Robinson was back, Post, Bell, Bailey. George Crowe was fighting for the first base job that spring because Kluszewski, who had been piling on some poundage, had it finally catch up with him. Klu was younger than Crowe, but his back was hurting him. That ain't surprising when your training regimen is Budweiser and German Chocolate Cake. Crowe had been with us the year before, but Birdie didn't play him much. Interesting fellow, Crowe. He'd played NBA basketball and Negro League baseball before he come to the National League. It was the last season for Big Klu, though we didn't know that at the time.

There was the usual gaggle of youngsters trying to move up, the most notable of which that year was Curt Flood and Chico Cardenas, a skinny Cuban teenager who would turn into a real solid ballplayer. Everybody was looking to make a name for himself, and boy Heidi, is that exactly what happened to Bucky Klingheimer.

Klingheimer was a gangly pitcher from upstate New York. He'd had a little success with the High Point Toms, enough to get him to Tampa. I don't reckon that much of anybody suspected Bucky was going to stick, but stranger things have happened. For Bucky's end, which would come to be an unfortunate turn of phrase, he was a game fellow. He run and threw as hard as he could. Not that the veterans and him would be exchanging Christmas cards, but they showed him a half cup of respect.

About ten days in, some of the younger boys went for a night on the town in Ybor City, the Cuban district. They'd heard the stories of fun to be had in the form of beer, tequila, and loose women. I heard later that, in addition to the suds and assorted high balls, Klingheimer had also consumed a big plate of ropa vieja, two roasted quails, a triple helping of black beans, and might have got ahold of a bad plantain.

When the culprits showed up the next morning, Tebbets figured he'd better send a message. One whiff and a glance at these boys was enough to alert all those present that these fellows was someplace between still drunk and wickedly hungover. A six-year old nun could've sensed the previous night's hijinks.

Birdie starts to yelling.

"You no good sons of bitches! Don't even bother walking to the cage. Nobody's taking cuts until they've run five laps around the whole goddamned complex. Now get going!"

There was a chorus of groans, then off they went. You know the saying "like a herd of turtles?" Son, a red eared slider would've looked like Usain Bolt next to that group. They were stumbling and huffing, and by the time they was twenty feet past first base, their durn shoes had filled up with sweat.

They all made the first time around, though everybody but Cardenas was looking more than a mite jelly-legged. It was so painful, yet you just couldn't turn away, and on account of that, it felt like the whole ball club and every one of 75 folks in the bleachers was focused on them stumbly runners. They was a wobbly knot jogging from right field toward center when all of a sudden, Bucky Klingheimer stopped and stood up straight as Jehovah's bookkeeper. His eyes were wide where you could see the whites all the way around, and he turned direct toward home plate.

It's hard to describe the boy's gait. It was a trot, I reckon, but with his legs above the knee held as tight together as he could muster. From there down, it was like the little scissor kicks you do in a swimming pool, and every third step was a hop, as if his spikes were possessed by the ghost of Tinkerbell.

Batting practice ground to a halt. The whole team had their collective jaws dangling. As he floated past the shortstop, you begun to hear people oohing and aahing, but not in a good way. To simply say that Bucky Klingheimer had shit his pants would be a disservice. It was more like an ongoing seismic event.

Unfortunately for the Redlegs fans in attendance, the wind was blowing in that day. As he neared the foul line. High pitched squeals of "Haw" started to dot the grandstand. It was like 20 or 30 Bob Wills had showed up.

There was an old man named of Darrold who never missed a ball game in Tampa, least that's what I like to believe. The odd thing about that story is that old Darrold was blind. He'd lost his eyesight after getting a bad dose of poison gas in WWI. Every game day, spring training or Tampa Smokers minor league, didn't matter, he would grab his white cane and walk from his house a few blocks away. He had him a regular seat right behind the bench.

Tebbets had been standing there gabbing with the man, a pretty regular occurrence during workouts. As Bucky went prancing by them on his way to God knows where, Darrold stuck his nose in the air like a hound dog on a windy day.

"My smeller ain't what it once was on account of the mustard gas, but I swear, Birdie, you got a dead possum under this here grandstand. Maybe two of 'em, and they are some stinky sons of bitches."

About June of 1957, a utility infielder we had named Roy Spiller got kicked out of his house. His wife of less than a year had found lipstick on his clothes, matchbooks in his coat pocket, love notes in the chester drawers, or some such nonsense that told a damning story. Roy told the team that his plan was to sleep in the back seat of his 1956 Oldsmobile Super 88 until his wife changed her mind.

Roy had spent a large portion of the previous year's salary on that ride. It was his pride and joy, and somewhat of a wedding present to himself. I recollect some of the older guys questioning the wisdom of that purchase only weeks before getting hitched when he could have put it into a down payment on a home. Roy's answer was, "You can sleep in your car, but you can't drive no house."

So, one year after that prescient bon mot, all his possessions were crammed into the trunk of that car. At least it was a hot looking ride, two-toned with black on the bottom and the trunk and cherry red everywhere else. He had even installed this louvered shade on the back glass and a deluxe eight tube signal-seeking radio.

He had imagined that things would blow over in a day or two, but that was not what come to pass. After about a week or ten days of fruitless begging, Roy initiated Plan B. That consisted of trying to get laid every night so he didn't have to sleep in his back seat. When we went on the road, he had a hotel, but when we come home, he would hit a rotation of the three or four busiest nightclubs in the Queen City. At 9:00 P.M., he was searching for good looking women that might like to cozy up to a big league ballplayer. But by 12:30, Roy was slobbering all over any willing chippie with a pulse and an apartment key.

Of course, he didn't volunteer all this information willingly. The team found out after Roy struck out three nights in a row in late July. He had been parked at the players' parking lot, snoozing it off in the back seat of the Olds. What he didn't take into account was the slant of the morning sun. By the third day, the left side of his face had four very pronounced streaks of sunburn from those fancy louvers on the rear window. It give him the appearance of a tiger with insomnia. That's when the whole sordid story come tumbling out.

Some of the boys took great pity on Roy and a small committee was formed to go plead with his wife. In the end, she agreed to give him another chance. I can't swear that he walked the straight path for the rest of his life, but last I heard, Roy had him a coaching job at a small college someplace and was still married. I do believe, though, that he removed the louvers from his back glass.

I'd be a sorry storyteller if I left this one out. The All-Star game brouhaha of 1957. The game was to be at Sportsman's Park that year, and Gabe Paul, or somebody in the front office decided to really go all out to get the Cincinnati players into the All-Star Game. All they had to do was talk the local fans in to stuffing the ballot boxes. It was all legal within the rules, so Gabe figured why the hell not.

The newspaper sponsor was the Cincinnati Times-Star. That's who it worked, one of the local rags in every big league town printed up ballots, then folks filled them out and mailed them in. Or I reckon they could drop them in the newspaper's lobby in a big barrel. The main attraction to the newspaper was that it upped their sales.

Well, the Times-Star took things a step further. They printed the ballots with the Reds players already filled in on the National League side. Then Burger Beer joined the act and ran off their own ballots that got distributed to every bar and tavern in the city and beyond, and I can promise you, son, that's an assload of taverns. I recollect at the Licky that Bird, the bartender, would make every customer fill out at least three ballots every time they ordered a new beer. No telling how many 1957 All-Star ballots had a ring from being first used as a coaster.

Waite Hoyt was pumping the voting campaign during the games, of course. One of the radio promoters loved the Reds, so the stations he worked for were reminding people for weeks. Schools started assigning ballots to be filled out as homework. There were no such thing as official ones, so the kids just wrote up their ballots using a Number 2 pencil on Big Chief paper. Hairdressers, pizza joints, dog groomers, shit, I wouldn't be surprised to hear about some hooker who had a stack of ballots on her bedside table.

I'm not sure the league even counted them all. Cincinnati sent in more All-Star ballots than the rest of the league combined, and every one of them voted for eight Reds. Ford Frick, who was still stooging as National League president and hadn't yet gone on to stooge for all the rest of the owners, overruled the fans. He was an old PR man, so he should have understood the absurd beauty of the thing more than anybody. But he kicked Post, Bell, and Crowe off the All-Star teams and replaced them with Mays, Musial, and Aaron. You sure can't argue with the quality, but it always felt a mite random. He did see to it that the guys he removed got the same bag of trinkets as the rest of the players. I'm sure that key ring was always a great comfort to Wally Post.

On top of that, Frick decided that the fans would no longer vote for the All-Star teams. Cincinnati was the kid who threw the spitball and ruined it for the entire rest of the class.

Chapter Ten

Gabe Paul called me up in late January 1958 to tell me that he needed me to go to minor league spring training that year instead of the big league camp. In all my time in baseball, I'd never had to do that, and I took it pretty hard. It felt like a demotion. You see, there were no spring training complexes with a dozen diamonds and tourist attractions. The big league squad went one place and everyone expected to play in the minor leagues went to another.

The grand scheme for the Reds minor leaguers that spring was the brainchild of Dick King, the scout who was in charge of the Southwest and Mexico. I say scout, because that was his title, but deep down he was a promoter, a dreamer and a huckster, and he saw a bit of the future, I reckon. His idea was to send all the minor league squads to Laredo, Texas and let them play their training games all across Northern Mexico, to build the Reds brand and bring in some income.

Bill McKechnie, Jr. was originally supposed to be in charge down there, but ultimately, it fell to Tal Smith, a deep-voiced Duke University boy who was a full two months into his baseball career. So, in late February 1958, we packed up and headed to the border to provide minor league training for twelve clubs and hundreds of players. They worked a cheap deal on the old Mercy Hospital, a recently abandoned building, and moved us in. Dick King, whose real name was Karabatsos or some other Greek pastry, had not only secured the place, but even hand painted the hallway light globes with baseball stitches. They did everything they could to make us feel welcome.

The club had rented furniture hauled in, and that supplemented the odd medical equipment. The hospital folks had left a few stocked closets, so players rode in wheelchairs and some of the loonier ones had races down the hall wearing backless gowns and trying to hold a vinyl LP in their buttcrack.

They had Mexican food cooked by a local man named Lupito who ran the dining hall, and that was a happening in itself. Shoot, they hadn't even invented ballpark nachos yet. This stuff was completely new for most of the boys, and the gastric effects ran the gamut. Some fellows lost 15 pounds. On the other end, I recall one kid from Smoot, Wyoming who ate so much chile con queso that he didn't shit for over two weeks. I suspect he was happy to get back to our Geneva, New York club in April.

The workouts and position drills went fine, but once the exhibitions started, it was trying to conduct an orchestra with cooked spaghetti. Every day there were teams spread out in little towns all over Tamaulipas, Nuevo Leon, and Coahuila. Everyone was wearing Seattle or Nashville uniforms no matter who they played for. It was just shy of chaos. Bags and pillowcases full of pesos showed up every so often and got dumped onto Tal Smith's hotel bed. Nobody but the cook could even tell the money apart.

I saw my good buddy Paul Flinkenberg about every year or two in those days. He traveled on business still, and we talked on the phone and agreed that this had the stench of adventure written all over it. He showed up on the train from San Antonio about halfway through, and we retold the tales until his dying day.

They were shorthanded, so nobody thought twice about sending me out to handle games. I used the little Spanish I'd picked up in Cuba, but there was a good deal of pointing and hoping. You always feel much more confident in a foreign language until the words hit the road. Some of the confusion was local custom, and some was my pronunciation. I'm not sure which of those led to the difficulty when I tried to order three cabrito tacos in what turned out to be a cantina run by hookers, but judging by the owner's impassivity, I was not the first to make that specific request.

Fans in Mexico were a hoot and a half, singing songs, banging drums, and dressing up in costumes. They sold all manner of things in the grandstands. Two of our infielders had to buy their own gloves back in Monclova.

For me personally, one of the bigger happenings was right across the border in Nuevo Laredo. It ain't like it is today with all the drug gangs and violence. We was most likely as safe south of the river as north, but being paranoid gringos, we had gotten into the habit of dividing the gate receipts amongst two or three of us. The theory was that if something happened to one sack of money, we wouldn't lose the whole enchilada, as it were. That night I had a third of the total gate stuffed down the front of my trousers. To the curious locals, I looked tall, hairy, pregnant, and jingly.

Paul and I and a young reliever name of Willie Guisto stopped for a late supper on our way back to the border. Normally, we wouldn't be hanging out with the club's youngsters, but the poor kid was damn near begging, he was so hungry. He was all right, if a little green and very naïve. His whole family were lumberjacks from Shingletown, California. Heard tell that included his sister. The equipment truck dropped the three of us off about five blocks from the bridge. We found this open air spot that had pork tacos, posole, and beers that were barely south of lukewarm.

It was likely the cerveza talking, because a couple hours later, when the restaurant told us they were closing at midnight, our goal quickly became to find an open bar. We wandered around for a mite before we spied a knot of jovial folks outside a likely looking door, so we ambled inside, ordered a round of Carta Blancas, and helped ourselves to an empty table.

There was a floor show underway, and as our eyes become accustomed to what had seemed like pitch darkness, we sipped and guzzled and watched the gal gyrating and flirting to a jukebox with a bad hum. She looked like a Carmen Miranda luggage decal that got badly plumped up in the rain. Now, at some point earlier, I'd passed the money bag to Willie. It had been down my pants for over two hours, and it had really started to bind me. We agreed it was only fair. Willie still had it when he excused himself for the little boy's room.

"There's only three women in this whole joint," Paul pointed out. "This chunky dancer and two on guy's laps back there."

"Well, it is half past midnight. Not the time for any respectable lady to be in a honky tonk."

All of a sudden, Willie Guisto stumbled out of the darkness at just shy of a full run. He was still tucking his pecker into his fly, and his eyes were round as cookie dough.

"It's boy boys!" He was whispering at a volume more suited for a helicopter. "Men are making out with other men, and Lord knows what those noises in the stall meant."

And with that, Willie sprinted out the door. I sat there perplexed for about 15 or 20 seconds, wondering why any of that should be a dealbreaker. After all, they were still selling beer, weren't they? Then it dawned on me that the game proceeds were my responsibility, and they were stuffed down the front of Willie's pants. I leapt to my feet and ran after him. Paul was slightly delayed in the guzzling of his Carta Blanca.

Luckily, Willie picked the right direction to run in, but he still had about seven unlit blocks to go, dead drunk, and imagining he was being chased by who knows what evil demons. Even from a block back, I could hear coins clanging the pavement as they worked their way out through his zipper. Trying to scoop them up allowed Paul to catch up with me, but we were losing Willie.

I have not a clue how they heard about it or where they come from, but by the time we got halfway to the border, a whole pack of kids had joined the chase, and they were all between us and our bag of money. During the daytime, these little urchins sold Chiclets, but at midnight, they were more than happy to simply chase rolling centavos on the sidewalks. Of course, the longer Willie kept running, the looser the knot on that bag. It was dark, but we could just make out darting little blurs and hear squeals and jingles.

When Willie Guisto hit the bridge, the customs officers asked what he had to declare. Soaked in sweat and out of breath, he still managed to yell out, "God damn it, his tongue was down another man's throat!"

Me and Paul managed to talk the guard into letting us all back across. Dropping the name of the ball club helped. In the process, we got the money sack retied.

Two things proved to be my saving grace: the paper money was all still there, and the peso was trading at about 300 to 1. Even with everything that fell through Willie's wee hole, I only had to pony up about the cost of a spaghetti chili plate back in Cincinnati. I could have kept my mouth closed, I reckon, but I am an honest man. And I'm sure there were some happy little boys in Nuevo Laredo that night, too.

The club never did try another experiment like that, but I must say it still brings a smile to my eyes. Did you know that Tal Smith and Dave Bristol both had kids born while we were down there? They had to hear about it all through the lone payphone that was left working inside that abandoned hospital. That whole deal was sure something.

That was the first year we made a trip out to Los Angeles. It was big doings being in LA and San Francisco that season, two of the most exotic locales the old U.S. of A. had to offer. Most of the players had visions of spending the night waist deep in starlets.

For me, I took the chance to look up Raymond Chandler and some of my old Hollywood friends to see if they wanted tickets to the ball game. Playing at LA Coliseum with all those seats, the club's traveling secretary passed the word that we could get all of the freebies we wanted. I'd come to love Chandler's writing by then, plus I felt sort of a personal stake, but he was pretty much a drunk by that turn, battling depression and living down in La Jolla. Not much money in that, I reckon.

Bob Meusel come out to the first game as my guest, so I wasn't totally shut out. It was June the 3rd. We won the game 8 to 3. I'd like to say we blasted them, but we scored those 8 runs, all earned, on just five hits. It had to be the strangest line of Sandy Koufax's career. No hits, six walks and five earned runs in two and two thirds innings. Koufax led the league in wild pitches that year, if it tells you anything. But maybe they were distracted. That was election day in Los Angeles, and voters barely approved the money to dispossess a few hundred families and build Dodger Stadium.

I was disappointed about Chandler, but there was no shortage of stars hanging around the ballpark. I spotted Danny Kaye, Buddy Rogers, Mervyn Leroy, and Gene Autry in the stands during that series. Burt Lancaster shook hands with the fellow beside me. It almost reminded me of the heyday in New York with the Babe. I'll share this part of the story since the lady has long since gone on to her great reward, but I come close to having my most famous boudoir adventure on that trip to L.A in 1958. I almost banged Joan Bennett.

It happened that after the Wednesday game where Podres shut us out, I was nursing a drink or five at the Biltmore Hotel bar. Now seeing faces you recognized was not uncommon there, but that night was the one and only time I was rendered speechless by celebrity. There was a table in the corner occupied by Humphrey Bogart, Lauren Bacall, Joan Bennett and two older fellows whose faces I couldn't have picked out from a Burmese rock collection.

I probably watched them talk for close to half an hour, trying to think of some clever way to interrupt their conversation. That was a hurdle that never stopped me before, of course, but this was Humphrey Bogart. The best grizzled tough guy or put upon detective that ever walked under the lights. Before I could think of anything snappy, they were doing the hugs and handshakes and headed for the exit. I was crestfallen, I reckon you'd call it, until I realized that Joan Bennett had brought her full highball glass to the bar and plopped down on the stool right next to mine. Hot ziggedy.

The bartender slid a fresh cocktail napkin under her glass and freshened it up without even asking. Silently, I thanked him.

"I sure would have liked to shake Humphrey Bogart's hand," I told her. "It was thrilling just to be in the same bar with him. Of course, you're better looking. I've had the hots for you since Bulldog Drummond."

For some reason she found that funny, and our conversation was off to the races. It turns out their little meeting was for a left-wing political committee, and they was all in cahoots to promote equality. Even with the red baiting behind them, there was so much to be done. She was so charged up about Blacks and farm workers that I couldn't hold back. I told her the whole story of Izzy Levy in Spain, and she countered that Ernest Hemingway had a little dick. She liked my stories about me and Herbie in Memphis, and I liked that she wasn't afraid to say the word dick. The whole time, the bartender never failed in keeping us well oiled.

You may find it hard to believe, but after about half an hour of our heads pressed together saving the world, I had ceased to think of her as a movie star at all. She was just an interesting lady named Joan, and I was beginning to imagine that I had a shot with her. Though the whiskey and cigarettes had not done wonders for her breath, she was getting mighty touchy. Her hand had been on my thigh so long that it felt like a heat tattoo.

"I'm in no shape to be driving," she finally told me. "I don't even know your name, but I'm going to ask you if we can adjourn to your room."

"Uh..."

She put her finger to my lips to shush me, though I doubt if any more words were forthcoming.

"I don't want to know. Anonymity has its moments."

"Well, I hate to bring this up, but you're wearing a wedding ring, Miss Bennett."

"Pshaw. My husband and I haven't lived together since he shot my agent in the crotch over a little afternoon delight."

"Uh..."

I was becoming a one-word pony, but that previous sentence was a verbal cold shower if I ever heard one.

Mentally, I was doing the math. Bedding a movie star versus the risk of being shot in the crotch. Finally, I made the manly choice. I excused myself for the loo. There were only the two items in my brain, but I stood there at the urinal and kept batting them back and forth until I reached a decision. The good side of the ledger was a sure thing. She'd already asked me, for crying out loud. And the scary side was remote. I didn't even bother asking advice from the attendant, just dropped him a nickel for the towel.

Well, sir, strolling back across those plush carpets to the bar felt like tangoing on a trampoline. That is until I saw her and the bartender clearing the doors to the lobby, headed for the taxi stand with his hand on her butt cheek bigger than you please. I reckon you'd have needed a chisel to get my chin off my chest. My whole mind had been wiped clean.

"Don't take it too hard buddy."

It took a second, but I snapped out of my fog and realized the other bartender was standing in front of me, hooking his thumb toward the lobby.

"It's an art form. He always ends up with the older actresses. I think he nailed Eve Arden last Thursday."

I had met Officer Frankie Moretelli back in 1951 when Danny Griesbaum lost his pecker, and I'd seen him pretty regular since then. Now, it's not like he was there for every home game, but along in early fall of 1958, as the season was winding down, we noticed that he wasn't working any security at all. When we asked one of the other flatfoots, the fellow hemmed and hawed but finally told us Frankie had got the lung cancer real bad.

Walt Dropo and I went out to see him. He lived in a duplex. Just him and his dog, a Weimaraner named Barkio. His strength was gone by that time. No way he could've walked a beat. He'd been trying to work through it for years, I suspect. It's one of those things where in hindsight you can recollect a body having a smoker's cough or even their eyes having that watery look. They waved it off, and you focused on your own life and just give it a passing notion. Frankie would sit on his front porch every day. Other cop buddies would stop by to have a beer. He felt at peace with it, he said.

By January, when the worst of winter had the town by the short hairs, Frankie couldn't take Barkio for walks anymore. A kid from two houses down come to get the big lug of a dog three times a day. It was too cold to sit on the porch, so visitors dwindled. I went by one time that month and found him and the hound curled up together on a green love seat that might have been velvet at one time.

Had a chenille bed spread laid over the both of them. Talking much set him to coughing, and after an hour or so, I was low on stories, so I said my goodbye.

It was less than a week after that when some neighborhood thug snatched Barkio with the idea of selling him. Dumbass didn't realize that a three-foot tall, 120 pound dog stands out like a diamond in vomit. It was barely a day before some Samaritan recognized him and brought him and the culprit back to officer Frankie's place no doubt intending that the lad would get a stern talking to. The next thing we knew about it was what we saw in the *Enquirer*.

Frankie held the hoodlum there, lecturing him between coughs. Speculation was that he may have had the criminal tied to a chair when the neighbor boy come to check on his buddy Barkio and take him for his walk. Once the two of them were a good distance down the block, well, I reckon Frankie figured this was as good a time as any. Somehow, in his weakened condition, he got the dognapper into the kitchen where he pulled out his service revolver and shot the little bastard in the knee. Neighbors was trying to figure out what the noise was, but nobody come running. Frankie turned on the stove gas, let it go for a bit and then lit a match. Blasted the both of them into several pieces. From what I heard later, Barkio lived the rest of his time with that kid who walked him, but oftentimes, he still wanted to go sniff around his old duplex. You don't jack with a man's dog.

Ball club-wise, we went down to spring training in 1959 with a little bit of hope. Our two biggest additions from the year prior would be with us for a full season in '59. That was Don Newcombe, who is in the Hall of Fame today, and a 20-year old youngster named Vada Pinson. He was a doozer.

I liked Pinson from the get go. He had been born in Memphis, though he didn't recollect a whole lot about it since his folks had moved away when he was seven. Nonetheless, it made him solid in my estimation. The other thing, the part that was even better, was that Vada Pinson was a hell of a trumpet player. He'd brought it with him to Tampa, and I would coax him to drag it out and play. I'm not saying he was Satchmo or Roy Eldridge, but he could play a soulful version of "Someone to Watch Over Me" that wouldn't embarrass nobody.

Pinson had grown up in Oakland, California. Same high school as Frank Robinson and Curt Flood and Bill Russell of the Celtics. He was strong, graceful and fast as a shot of 151. He flowed around those bases like water. His daddy had worked the docks, and Vada had got all muscled up helping out the old man. He didn't try for home runs, mind you, but sometimes that short swing of his couldn't help itself.

It might not jump out at you today, but once again, that meant that the three most exciting players on the Cincinnati team were Black. Negroes, as people of color were still known then. The difference from three years prior was that by 1959 the Civil Rights movement that you saw on TV news was starting to percolate, and while things had made some baby steps in big league ballparks, down in Florida where we trained, there was nothing of the sort.

You finally had every big league team integrated by that year. Boston was the last, but it still wasn't run of the mill. See, the whole Jackie Robinson thing had done wore a might thin by that time, and though the number of Black ballplayers by team was still pretty small, those fellows had started to move beyond just being happy to be there. They figured they'd earned some respect. That spring, a part of that was being able to stay and eat with their teammates.

The White guys on the club stayed in a nice hotel, but the Robinsons and Pinsons, well, they had to find a family to rent out a room. Now, home cooking as opposed to a hotel coffee shop sounds like a bonus, but if you're just reckoning who was getting the best biscuits and gravy, well, you're missing the point entirely.

There was another bit of excitement round the Cincinnati club that year. It was on account of a journeyman lefthander name of Don Rudolph, or I should say on account of his wife. The Reds acquired Rudolph from the White Sox at the start of May. The Sox coveted Del Ennis, and the Redlegs, well, I always wondered if somebody in the front office was just feeling a little randy.

See, Mrs. Don Rudolph was a famous burlesque dancer, a stripper. Her stage name was Patti Waggin. Nowadays people still use the word stripper, but what they really mean is a dancer wearing glitter and a little g-string and flexing her coochie in somebody's face for dollar bills. But back in the 50s, folks would've been outraged by all that. What with the Commie scare, they didn't want even a glimpse of anything pink.

Tough as it is to fathom, your burlesque dancers were legitimate performers. They put on a show. A strip tease. They started with clothes and feathers and fans and danced around to the big finish. They belonged to a union, for crying out loud, though where they kept their cards is anyone's guess. A few of them toured the country and become household names like Sally Rand and Gypsy Rose Lee. Hell, Gypsy Rose even recited a funny, high-brow poem while she undressed. Patti Waggin was famous almost like that, and since she was often around the ball club, it caused a bit of a sensation.

Mainly it was the beat writers all competing who could come up with the best snide pun whenever Rudolph took the hill. They referred to the poor man as Patti Waggin's husband, and frequently said that his curves weren't as good as his wife's or that he took something off that one. Rudolph was the fastest worker in the league, and those scribes wrote that it was because he was in such a hurry to get home to the missus. Opposing players and fans on the road would yell about Don giving his wife the high, hard one or ask if he used the rosin bag at home. For the most part, he let them slide, but once or twice I saw him stick a fastball in somebody's ribs. Ballplayers are famous and mostly athletic, and they've always attracted the lookers. There was two dozen young wives and girlfriends as cute as Patti, but the fact that theatres advertised her getting naked shot all decorum clean out the window.

She was a nice girl, Patti was. Loved her husband and for some reason reckoned that he was suddenly going to find his stuff and become a real top of the rotation fellow. Maybe she knew pasties a lot better than she knew a two-seamer, but she was all right.

In mid-October of 1959, about two weeks after the season ended, I got notice that Pearl had passed away. I hadn't seen her in a few years, not since the weekend we went to the art museum, but it still made me awful low. When you're close to somebody but they slip from the front of your mind, the mere flutter of a gnat's wing can be enough to bring it all back to you. Whatever was between Pearl and me sat no more than an egg glaze beneath the surface.

After I got the phone call about Pearl, I'd get little flashes of memory for weeks: us laughing about something, the old strawberry print drapes that hung in her kitchen, her smell, or the touch of her skin. I'd be smack in the middle of doing something, anything, when a little bit of Pearl would insert itself into my thoughts. One night, maybe two, three in the morning, Pearl's sweet potato pie woke me from a sound sleep. To be specific, it was the taste of that pie as I found it on her lips over forty years previous. Sweet, savory, precious. I didn't get no more sleep that night.

It wasn't too long after she passed, I got a knock on my door one afternoon. I opened it to see a young Black fellow. He was muscular, about my size, and he didn't look none too pleased.

"You Mr. Wingo?"

"Yes. I suppose I am," I answered, trying to figure out if I owed anybody money.

He didn't extend a hand, so I did it myself. He stared at my mitt for a minute or two then took it, slow-like, with what seemed more than a little bit of reluctance. At that point the lively conversation ground to its first halt. I would come to find out that would be a pattern.

"What can I do for you?" I was still hoping the answer didn't involve my writing a check.

"My name is Felix Rogers," he said. "And my mama asked me to come up here to see you."

Now this fellow was maybe 30 or 35 years old, so it wasn't like he was there to sell candy bars or a subscription to Grit, so the idea that his mama had sent him around to my door wasn't making a great deal of sense. Like I told you, Cincinnati might have been up north, but just barely. The neighborhood where my little apartment was located didn't have too many Blacks living in it in 1960, so I was scrambling to picture just who his mama was.

"Your mama?"

"Yep. I sure as hell wouldn't be here otherwise."

"All right. Then I s'pose you'd best come inside."

We sat down at the kitchen table. It was one of those yellow formica ones with a chrome band around it. Some of the color was worn thin where my elbows sat. You remember those? No, I reckon you're too young.

That table's on my mind on account of I can conjure up the picture of that meeting now as if it wasn't ten minutes past. Up to that point he had kept his eyes locked on mine, defiant I'd say, though I still didn't know why. Now, though, he took to staring a hole in that yellow formica. I had me a set of copper-looking salt and pepper shakers, and Mr. Felix Rogers slid those toward him without saying a word. He twisted them in his left hand so that they orbited one another about three times, then he pushed them back to where they had been and put his gaze back on me.

"My mama was Pearl Hawkins in Chicago. It was her strong wish that I come see you and bring you this. I've traveled from Houston, Texas to honor her wish." He pulled an envelope out from his jacket pocket and shoved it at me.

"So, you're Pearl's boy," I said, holding the letter in my hand. "I'll be damned. I hadn't seen you since you was not long out of a crib."

"You would be damned if I had any say in it."

Now, you've heard of staring a hole through somebody. Well, I could feel the breeze blowing through the one he'd bored in my cheeks. All the same, my fog of confusion was burning away. This fellow didn't cotton to me one iota.

He nudged the envelope closer to my side of the table.

It was unremarkable stationary. Cream colored with a frilly, navy blue border. Here. Take a look for yourself. I keep it in this drawer right here. Hand me my specs, will you?

"Honey, I have been feeling poorly, and I believe that we will not be seeing each other again in this side of life. There is something that I most rightly should have let you know thirty-four years past. For some reason, I never could push myself to do it, though. I did not wish to be a burden on you. But now I do feel in my heart that I made a mistake and must set it right. My boy Felix who you knew when he was a little nipper is your boy, honey. There were so many times when you'd come to visit that I sent him off to stay with friends since I just knew in my bones that there was no mistaking the sight of you in his eyes and chin and his gait. He ambles just like you. The longer the secret got held, the more it set me in my ways, so I kept it from the both of you. I know now that it was wrong on account of how he has come to feel about you, but I hope that you can work it out between you. Felix has promised me true that he would bring you this letter, and I pray that the both of you can come to forgive me in time. It is my moment to rest so I must close. Your long time friend. Pearl."

My cheeks hurt me that day just like they do now. I tried to look Felix in the eye, but he had moved on to staring into a tree that sat out my window.

"When did she tell you?" I asked him.

"Not till after she wrote that letter."

"Did she say anything about her and me? It weren't your mama what gave a bad impression was it?"

His jaws pulsed real tight, and he went back to watching the tree.

"Well, I didn't know. If I..."

He cut me off quick.

"Don't feed me full of White man's shit. I know how you are, all of you. I've seen it my whole goddamned life. Using us up. Digging your ditches and being your whores. Well, we ain't Amos and Andy. Those are goddamned actors, playing your stereotypes and getting rich off it. My mama wasn't no whore, old man. She was a good, fine woman."

It took the wind out of my sails, that speech did. It was likely with a wee little voice that told him I always felt Pearl was a good, fine woman since the week I first met her, but Felix wasn't having none of it.

"Did you ever tell her you loved her?" he asked. Snapped it at me like a wet towel, as if to make his point.

I sat there and looked at him. Looked at him a long time. There was no need to think about it even a fraction of a second other than to let the lump settle back down out of my throat to wherever those things go. The answer was no. Not once had I told Pearl that easy little phrase, even when we was laying together, snuggled under a rumpled sheet with the hot city blowing through an open window, and us the only two people in it.

I knew the answer to my boy's question on account of it haunting me all those years. Hell, it wasn't my rules. I hated it. But it sure wasn't easy for White folks and Black folks to love one another, to be together, at least in 1920 something. Even in some high-balling gangster town like Chicago.

On top of that, I didn't live in Chicago. I was following my dream, no matter how meager the dream may look to you or anybody else. Still, I could have tried harder. All those years I thought I'd swum against the tide of society's norms, I'd barely made a ripple in the ocean. I know that now.

You know how much I love my Jenny. She was the greatest woman there was, better than anything I deserved. But here's the thing: so was Pearl, and I damn sure knew it.

You know, son, some folks believe that everybody has a perfect match walking around the Earth someplace, and that fate will lead their paths to cross. Do you feel that way? Personally, I call that bullshit. Ridiculous, deep piled B.S.. We have several true loves if we live long enough and are open to it. We ourselves are several different people in life, the product of our accumulated experience, so why shouldn't each of our selves be entitled to a true love?

And while I'm at it, no match is perfect. My Jenny used to fart in her sleep. Pop pop pop pop. I thought I was hearing gun fire the first time she did it. I was fixing to dive for cover on the floor until the odor of rancid turnips come wafting up through the blankets.

I wasn't so philosophical that day with Mr. Felix Rogers staring at me across my little dining table. I couldn't find any words at all, in fact. After what seemed like ten minutes, he stood up, left the letter on the table and walked out the door. He must have figured he'd done what he promised, and he didn't want to spend any more words on it neither.

I reckon up to that point, if I'd given it much thought, I would've liked to think that Pearl knew that I loved her. I hope she felt that when we were sharing all of our secret thoughts, cause there was nothing I couldn't tell her. I thought she felt the same way about me, but having a secret kid knock on your door pretty much busted the living shit out of that one, didn't it.

That bombshell coincided with me moving to Houston. It was serendipity him mentioning that he lived there of all places. I was just about to retirement age, but Gabe Paul and Tal Smith was leaving the Reds to move to Houston to start a brand new franchise. I don't know what come over me, but I had a thought surface in my thick noggin that I might go with them. Even if he hated me now, he was still my only living kin. Pearl's child down there wasn't mine in any sense other than a squirt of good swimmers, but I thought that maybe I might get to know him just the same.

I went to see Mr. Paul and said I was interested in tagging along on his new adventure. I'm not sure he thought much of the idea, but eventually they offered me an assistant clubhouse and jack of all trades job with the new Colt .45s. I took a Greyhound south out of Cincinnati in October 1960. Just over the bridge at West Memphis, I studied the empty fields and pretended I could see as far as Lee County. As luck would have it, the Reds won the National League pennant the same year I left.

HOUSTON

Chapter Eleven

Somehow big cities develop a personality same as we do, and like a human, that personality evolves over time. At least it did for the four metropolises that I called home.

Memphis in the World War I years was like an old whore gone to seed. Her manner and her perfume could be cloying in the extreme, but there was no denying her sneaky charm.

New York always put up a good front of disinterest, but that wasn't necessarily true. The city was bipolar. Sometimes you were as lonely as the skunk at breakfast, other times your neighbor was right there for you, though he likely complained about it. The old New Yorkers will tell you that there's something new to learn on every corner, but if you were laying bloody in the gutter, you were usually waiting quite a while to learn if anybody would stop to help you up.

I think of Cincinnati in those days as a ward level politician. She'd glad hand you, sit down and eat sausage with you, and even loan you her good hammer. Most of the time, she tended her own garden and hung American flags on her front porch. But when it come time to pay the piper, she never hesitated to remind you exactly how long you'd been holding on to her damned hammer.

Now Houston in 1960, well, that was the border collie who was smart enough to fetch her own leash and tell you it was time to go for a walk. I've never seen a place more hopeful.

Houston was a big spread out city, even when I moved down here. It didn't have as many people as New York, of course, but it was almost twice as big as Cincinnati, and boy, could you drive for miles and never leave. Not that I drove.

Most of my life, I'd lived pretty close to where I worked. If I needed to go anyplace, I made friends with the bus.

The thing that struck me most about Houston was how so much of it was new. And more new things coming every day. You'd leave for lunch, and there'd be a new neighborhood spring up before you got home. Folks were friendly as all get out. Your older towns had spent enough time to develop nooks and crannies, so living there was sort of like buttering an English muffin. People didn't give a shit about the butter that fell into somebody else's hole. But Houston was still young and smooth and shiny, and I reckon that people saw things as an adventure that we were all in together. I liked it right off.

The big wigs with the new club got houses. These low slung brick ranch jobbies with swimming pools and swing sets in neighborhoods with big lawns not far from the new ballpark. A furniture store, with the urging of ownership, even handed out living room sets.

Me? Well, I lived in a brick fourplex on Sul Ross Street. There was a Minimax grocery less than 600 yards away. A washer and clothes line in a little shed out behind my building. There were five strip centers within an easy eight blocks, so if I ever needed a watch shop, used dresses, vinyl records, easy credit, or genuine handmade cowboy boots, I was in good shape. I could also stroll for Mexican food or drug store cheeseburgers. A body could ask for no more.

I drank my cold beers at the Rich-Man Ice House that was located at the corner of Richmond and Mandell Streets. Odd name, ice house, but it's a Houston thing, I reckon. That's what those little neighborhood beer joints started out as. They sold blocks of ice and some small groceries, but mostly, it was a neighborhood spot to shoot the breeze and sip the coldest beer around. They had roll up garage doors on the front and a couple of picnic tables scattered about. On days that it wasn't raining or hot enough to hard boil an egg in your undershorts, you soaked up the sunshine and let the passing traffic carry your troubles away. The one I chose even had a horseshoe and washer pit in the side yard if you felt athletic.

The owner of the Rich-Man was a roundish fellow named Dutch Hadicek. A third generation Texan who still sported a Czech and drawl accent that was not so rare in these parts back then. Dutch had a slight limp that he picked up during the war, though nobody claimed to have ever heard the story. He had a yeasty smelling sister, Karen, who worked at the Rainbo Bakery, but made her own kolaches as a side business. I'm still hooked on the cream cheese or the apricot, though I've never found any that taste quite the same as hers did.

One slow afternoon at the ice house, I borrowed the bar phone book from Dutch while I was sipping on cold bottles of Grand Prize. I hunted up Felix Rogers. He was listed. He had him a nice little house at 2509 Cleburne Street. Though I rehearsed in my head just exactly how the conversation would go before I dropped the nickel in the phone, it did not go well.

"Hello?"

It was a woman answering, so that was the first deviation from the script.

"Could I speak to Mr. Felix Rogers, please?"

"Yessss. Could I ask who's calling?" I imagine a strange voice being all formal like that made her suspicious.

"Well, ma'am. I guess I'm his daddy."

Even through the phone wires, I could feel the shit hit the wall almost as soon as the words escaped my mouth. Though I couldn't make out the conversation exactly, I heard her voice raised, then his gradually headed up that direction. Finally, I heard a hand picking up the receiver, then her voice loud and clear, even though she was not talking to me.

"Well, you'd best figure it out."

"Who is this?"

A dollar and a quarter's worth of Grand Prize was slipping down the tubes.

"Felix, this is Rube Wingo. I was just thinking..."

"What do you want?"

The tone was not exactly good to hear from you.

"I was calling to let you know that I have moved to Houston. I am working for the new ball club."

I can only imagine in hindsight the dumbfounded expression on his face during the long pause that followed. When he spoke again, his voice was less angry and more determined.

"Lucky for me, it's a big city. I have nothing for you, and I don't expect to be hearing from you again."

With that he hung up. A quiet click rather than a slam, I noted. You find your hope where you can.

I ran into an old Cincinnati friend not too long after I arrived in town. I was standing on Shepherd Street, waiting on a bus. I had Roy Orbison stuck in my head. "Only the Lonely" was high on the charts, and being alone at the stop, I may have gone from humming to singing. Of course, there was no way I'd ever hit the high parts. My voice broke like a pimply teenager.

The bus pulled up right at that moment, the driver tugged the lever, and the skinny sliding doors moved back.

'Hello, Rabbit," I said.

For there was Rabbit Pink who was now a bus driver back in his hometown. Had him half a college degree, and the best job he could get was driving a city bus. Don't get me wrong, it's very respectable work, though Dennis Hopper and that fellow chauffeuring Rosa Parks didn't do the profession any favors.

My errands were nothing that couldn't be put off, so I plopped down in the front left bench and chatted to Rabbit while trying not to distract him too much. I done most of the talking, filling him in on the last few years with the Reds, supplying whatever gossip come to mind until his shift ended.

The bus barn was on Milby Street, and one of the best burger stands in the city happened to be nearby. Champ Burger, it was. Big, cheesy burger wrapped in paper. The kind that required extra napkins to wipe your elbows. They'd serve Rabbit, but we were obliged to sit on the curb a little ways down to eat them and drink our Coca-Colas.

Like I said before, there was no city in these United States where a Black person was treated the same as a White one, but Houston in those days was more blatant about it than the places up north I'd grown accustomed to. It wasn't as bad as the casual hate that I'd seen back in Memphis, but people of color in 1960 Houston were still expected to know their place. The ball clubs might have gotten things integrated, but that didn't mean the common folks were used to the change.

I say all that to point out that here I was with my first old friend in my new town, and the places we could go were rather limited. I do recollect one nice outing during those first few months, and not surprisingly, it had to do with our shared interest in music. The live music clubs were still segregated, and that goes for the Black ones, as well as the White.

There had been a nationally famous Black nightclub called the Bronze Peacock in the Fifth Ward. It was tied into Duke Peacock Records that produced some of the best rhythm and blues music ever made. That's the truth. But by the time I come to town, that club was a recording studio, so I never got to see it, even though I'd have been pushed to side entrance and a separate White section.

City Auditorium, though, was a bit looser. A select number of city buildings had been integrated some years earlier, to a certain extent, so Rabbit and I could sit together for a concert even though we'd be harder pressed to find the right diner to grab a club sandwich afterwards.

Picturing that night, I should mention that people were still wearing suits and ties when they went out someplace, though I can't say that all the suits got cleaned all that regular. I had two suits and three ties, and they were not even the best that Sears had to offer. Rabbit was spiffier. He knew a tailor on Dowling Street, and he was sporting a shiny forest green number. It's called sharkskin, though it was really made from wool, which was another of my life's disappointments.

The show I was excited to see was B.B. King, and he had a couple of local residents opening for him. Gatemouth Brown and Big Mama Thornton. One of the radio DJs was the promoter, and though he was on what everyone knew as a Negro station, I'd reckon that over a third of the audience was White. It restored my faith in both music and hypocrisy.

I reckon even youngsters like you might know B.B. King, but he was already a big star by 1960. Gatemouth was a fine guitarist, too. Big Mama Thornton, well, she was the one who made "Hound Dog" a famous song, way before Elvis. The original version was about some snaky good time man, and there ain't no rabbit anywhere in there. I would have loved to meet them. B.B. King had him a place on Beale Street in Memphis that I longed to talk about, but we didn't even have a baseball team yet, so I was just John Q. Old Guy, and there was no backstage in my future that evening.

I'd been in this whole segregation situation so often before, but now, things was different, wasn't they? It was impossible to experience without being reminded of my own son. My journey into self-examination had just backed out of the driveway, more or less. I would like to say that I'd always prided myself on being open minded about race, but that would be a lie. There was no pride involved. It was just the right thing to do. Still, I'd spent 60 years rolling with the punches and never stirring up a fuss. Now that I had a more personal stake in the fight, you might think I'd have changed my approach, but I can't say that I did.

I wrestled with myself over whether to even call my boy anymore. It was plain that he never wanted to hear from me, and accepting that would sure have been the easiest path. On top of it, I had no desire for me to be the source of his marital trouble. His missus sure hadn't sounded gleeful when she answered my phone call that day. Some months passed by while I did my cowardly mulling.

Then there was a little bit of kismet, or at least I thought so at the time. I'd taken the bus downtown in search of a new shirt. There was a wide range of stores along Main Street. The specialty men's places were well beyond my need or my wallet, but I had a whole day to kill. Chances were damn good that my new shirt would end up coming from the sales rack at Foley's, but first I planned to meander through Kress' and see what they had on offer. It was their Jubilee of Values, and I needed a couple of 40-watt bulbs. No telling what other bargains might be had. Plus, they offered a superior grilled cheese at the lunch counter.

Now, I want to mention to you that even during the worst of segregation, White and Black could pretty well shop at any store they wanted to. Owners were never looking to turn away money, but there was rules. Top of the list being that a

Negro was not allowed to try anything on or use the changing rooms whatsoever. If they got home, and the item didn't fit, that was just bad beans because you sure as Christmas couldn't return it. A White person could, but a Black customer just better be a good guesser about size.

That's a little context for you. Stores was well underway to being integrated in Houston in 1961, mind you, but trying on clothing was still another matter. You see, I noticed a Black fellow at a display a little ways off in the men's department. It was far from the best selection in town, but they had the basics in casual wear. He was facing away from me, but I could tell he was glancing about. Kind of furtive, it seemed to me. It slowed me at first because I thought he was fixing to lift something, but he was just wanting to hold a golf shirt up to his chest and gauge the fit.

I was three racks over, I suppose, looking at a marked down short-sleeved shirt. Green check. When the fellow I was watching turned and gave me a little more than profile, it was like somebody had punched me in the chest. It was my own boy Felix. The whole thing froze me like a spotlighted deer.

I stood there mindlessly fingering my potential purchase until a pinch-faced saleswoman pretty much told me to either take it to the register or skedaddle. She reckoned that another minute of that, and I'd have worn a hole plumb through the placket. My mind was in such a far off place that she scared me, truth be told. It wasn't very manly, but I blurted out a noise that was half alarm and half apology. That was when Felix looked up and saw me. It's not as if we'd been around each other much, so it took a fair moment for him to realize who I was. You could see the thought process pass across his face, and when he put it all together, it was easy to see that he didn't cotton to the idea at all. He slowly folded up the shirt and laid it back onto the table.

It was like scaring off a songbird at a feeder, though the songbird won't generally shoot you such a hateful gaze. Felix ambled off into the crowd while I stood there. I hung the green shirt back on the rack and headed to the exit. The saleslady was likely asking me something, but I didn't hear her. I was just about to the Main Street doors before I realized I'd yet to get my grilled cheese.

There was another old friend I looked up, and that was Gus Mancuso. He was always the easy going type back in my Giants days, and he still was. Gus was out of a baseball job for the first time in 40 years when I called him up, and working for a moving company. I was happy to tell Gabe Paul that they should latch on to him. Not that he needed my help, you understand. People in Houston loved him, and it wasn't long before he was working as a part time scout.

Gus was a family man, but we did meet up for lunch on occasion, and he and I sat at the bar at Joe Matranga's Spaghetti House a few times to sip wine and laugh about the old days. It was the sort of Italian joint you find in the immigrant neighborhoods everywhere. Paintings of home on the walls. Old wine bottles with no labels squirreled away here and there. Overripe women who used their brassiere as a purse. I learned never to ask for a Kleenex in an Italian restaurant.

A passel of guys from Matranga's cooked spaghetti and meatballs at a Catholic church every Thursday to raise money for the Sacred Heart Society. I went once. The food was delicious, and the welcome was warm, but it reminded me too much of the church hall in Manhattan and the night that Jenny got sick. I never went back.

I did meet a new buddy that day, though, courtesy of Gus. He introduced me to a younger fellow, middle 30s, name of Jimmy Leoni. Jimmy was from a semi-pro baseball family. Now there's a topic that doesn't get enough play. I mentioned it about Gus himself a while back, but there were thousands of players making notable money playing semi-pro ball. That was dying out by the start of the '60s, but some of the most knowledgeable baseball folk you found were from that semi-pro tradition.

Jimmy Leoni's uncle had been a big hoop-te-doo around town as an infielder and manager, and that same uncle plus Jimmy's daddy had owned a semi-pro Black ball team. For a brief while, they ran an all-Mexican team that barnstormed across Texas and Northern Mexico. Jimmy himself had played a bit of college ball at University of Houston and then was a semi-pro first baseman for a team sponsored by a printing and lithography company. The team was never worth a damn, but their lineup cards looked amazing.

I enjoyed shooting the breeze with Jimmy, as I would continue to do over the years, and even when he got a 12-pack in him, he never claimed any baseball glory or cried about rough breaks. That included that very first day when I mistakenly ate half of his fried ravioli. Damn it, I thought the owner had just sent it over to be nice.

Chapter Twelve

With no ball club for 1961, you're probably wondering just what on Earth my job entailed. Well, sir, I was stapling scouting reports, leafing through equipment catalogs, and doing a lot of walking around the construction site over at the edge of town. They had put Tal Smith as the club liaison over the construction, and they were basically building two ballparks at once. Colt Stadium was to be a temporary thing while the Domed Stadium was rising to the sky right next door.

Our main focus was on the expansion draft, of course, then there was the Rule 5 draft after that. The expansion one came up in October, but there just wasn't all that much meat on the bone. Paul Richards had taken over for Gabe Paul as general manager, and I liked the fellow, but he picked two guys by mistake. I swear it's true. I don't know if the challenge was reading or cocktails or the Tampico Trots, but he selected Jesse Hickman when he meant to draft Jim Hickman, and got confused and took Paul Roof when he wanted his brother Phil. Neither one of those picks ever made the big leagues.

A couple of the picks worked out just fine with Bobby Aspromonte being top of the list. He was the Colts most popular guy in those early days. Turk Farrell was the best player and provided a hell of a lot of good copy for the newspaper boys. He was our first All-Star, and might be the only 20 game loser to get that honor. I don't know. I mostly remember him shooting rattlesnakes with a pistol during spring training.

There were two other picks that caught my eye the day of the draft. To tell you the truth, Dick Drott scared me on account of his name. It sounded like something awful that you could pick up in the showers. I know it's silly, but every time he pitched for those first two years, I sprinkled the living shit out of the Gold Bond Powder in every corner of the clubhouse. Can't be too careful.

The other intriguing name to me was Toothpick Sam Jones. Now that was a nickname. I was sad that Toothpick never put on one of those six shooter uniforms. He had the toothpick in his mouth, he mumbled and snorted like a hayfeverish pony, had a shambling gait. With all that going for him, the man would've been a great cowboy.

The other expansion team, the Mets, loaded up on the old guys, but still, we had a few. Bobby Shantz, Billy Goodman, Hal Smith. My favorite was Jim Pendleton who had been with me at Cincinnati in 1959. He was just a nice man who freely shared his vices. Jim spent the bulk of his paychecks in bars and was never hesitant to stand a friend to a round or two. He also loved the company of happy women and could eat his weight in White Castle cheeseburgers. When he was young, his path to the big time was blocked first by Pee Wee Reese and then by Henry Aaron who was his roommate with the Braves for a time. He was about the last WWII veteran still playing ball. I don't know if that's what gave him perspective and gentleness, but for a fellow who was only with the team for a season, he was thought of as a leader.

Shantz started Opening Day for us. His arm was so shot that they put hot packs on it between innings, but he got the first win. Then he pitched for another three years, just not for Houston. The club had sent him along to St. Louis within two months. Bob Cerv and Billy Goodman both retired after 1962. Goodman was a hell of an underrated infielder, played for more than a decade with Ted Williams, and was the source of many a lively tale. Went back to his home town in North Carolina and for the rest of his life never wore anything besides silk pajamas. Bought a dozen pairs in a variety of colors. Trimming the tree or driving to the bank, chances were he was in those damned silk pajamas.

We stunk louder than a Colombian skunk that first year, but there were two teams worse. A high point for me was that I managed a big league ball club for the only time in my life, and it wasn't even the one I worked for. We had a Friday double header in New York against the Mets. I'd asked the club if I could tag along on that long trip to take a look see at my old haunts, and they obliged. It had been forty years since I'd first come to the Polo Grounds, and every turn down those back hallways stirred the memories. My old bedroom was filled with metal barricades and four wheel dollies.

You'll recollect that Casey Stengel had been on the Giants team when I first moved to up there. Between games, I tapped on the home manager's door. He was as friendly and gregarious as ever. We laughed about him being in that tightass McGraw's office and how the knowledge that somebody as loosey-goosey as Casey was sitting in his chair would have popped a couple a vessels in the old Napoleon's red nose. We spent maybe fifteen minutes catching up on the whereabouts of various suspects, then Casey give me a crooked grin.

"Wingo, I usually catch 40 winks when we have a doubleheader. Would you mind doing me a big favor and managing the first couple of innings?"

With that he give me a little ticky mouth noise and a big wink before he tipped his chair back and closed his eyes. Naturally, I figured he was joking, but then I remembered that Casey was more than a decade older than me which made him 72 at that time. I finally managed to let loose with a pretty coherent "uhhhh."

"We ain't worth a shit, so you won't have to say much. I got a spare uniform on the hanger." With that, he started snoring.

I still had some of the prankster in me, so I suited up.

The look on some of the Mets' faces was actually less confused than you might think, even though my arms and legs were sticking out of that uni like Little Abner. I reckon they had already seen a few head scratchers with Casey. The only person I had to talk down was Bob Miller, the starting pitcher, when he come strolling in from the bullpen. He was in the midst of a 1 and 12 season, so in all fairness, he might have been on edge before I sat down. I told him I was temporarily filling in for Casey as part of an exchange program, then I patted him once on the ass and told to get out there and throw strikes. He went through Al Spangler, Joey Almalfitano, and Roman Mejias 1-2-3. Probably the best half inning he had that whole year. I do recall that Norm Larker sure busted a gut when he looked into the Mets dugout at the bottom of the inning.

Houston had lost the first game, but we blasted them in that second one 16-3. Afterwards, I reminded Casey that the Colts hadn't put up a single run under my watch, and he allowed as how that was good enough for a late dinner on him. I'd always wanted to coach, but this was even better. That was a real bucket list item for me.

Before the World Series was even over that year, the country was in the Cuban Missile Crisis. It scared a bunch of people, but the truth was everyone had been hearing air raid sirens and climbing under their school desks for ten solid years. That's the Americans, though.

We had a kid in the minor leagues in late '62, a 17-year old named Flaco Escamilla, who had defected from Cuba. Since he had no place to go home to for the off season, the club put him up in an apartment and had various folks checking in on him. He was a lost soul that month, young Flaco. He'd already been away from home for six or seven months, but in October, he was suddenly without baseball. Those daily call times when he had to be in the cages, well, that was structure that kept his mind off of everything back in Cuba, and that was top of news.

I tried my best to drop by, and it could be that my rambling about the days I'd spent on that island soothed him a mite. I don't know. The main trouble was that he had this loopy uncle who used to be a low level bagman for Batista. Collected payoffs from pineapple farms in Ciego de Avila. This old man was calling up poor Flaco every morning and telling him that the Russkies were getting ready to bomb the whole island to take out their own missiles, and that Cubans in Miami were forming another army to invade Havana. Said they were drilling at a jai alai fronton up in Hialeah. The poor boy was convinced that his homeland would be ground zero before he could gobble his next plantain. Got the boy stirred up beyond reason. Shit, ninety percent of that talk was coming from a bunch of pungent old farts who already fled their country once while clutching satchels of greenbacks. The only place they were fixing to invade was a Calle Ocho wine bar, and even that would've been with a walking cane and a day nurse.

So, me and a handful of the local Colts people tried to keep him calm. Today, a ball club would have a whole raft of players and front office folks who spoke Spanish, but that wasn't the case back then. Roman Mejias had left town and wasn't coming back. We had young Ivan Murrell with us in 1963, but that off season, we had two announcers doing the Spanish broadcast. Other than those fellows, the organization was as monolingual as a wood duck.

Flaco had plenty of Mexicans to talk to, but they didn't entirely trust Cubans. His countrymen were scarce in Houston at that time, but he finally found a fellow who had been kicked off the island and was working as a cook over on Fairview. This was all unbeknownst to us, and unfortunately for me, it was discovered after I stopped by for a visit and found out from the tipsy old lady next door that Flaco had been M.I.A. for over 36 hours. Paul Richards was none too thrilled to get my phone call, though he proved to be rather understanding. Perhaps he recalled that he had drafted the wrong player twice. Still, he strongly suggested that I locate our prospect.

In hindsight, part of the difficulty in my task was that this Cuban cook worked at a Chinese restaurant. After another two days, I heard a rumor making the rounds about ropa vieja egg rolls. Little suckers were damn tasty. And sure as shooting, Flaco was sitting at a back booth sipping tea and leafing through a girly calendar. It was certainly much less dramatic than my search for Eustis Esterbrook back in Detroit. This one had a happier ending, too.

The young man ended up moving in with the cook, who was named Gordo, interestingly enough. It turned out that a major portion of Flaco's instability was not over big Soviet missiles, but Gordo's little one. Everything clicked into place for the boy once he got a handle on his sexual identity. He stuck around the minors for about three years, I recollect. Worked his way up to half a season at Oklahoma City but never could break the final tape. The two of them ended up opening their own restaurant after that, in Dallas of all places. Fewer expectations for Tex Mex on the menu, I reckon. I stopped in there one time, and Flaco said he was glad to see me. They comped my order of egg rolls.

We had mosquitoes at Colt Stadium the size of an Italian car. Outfielders' socks would be bright red with blood by the end of the ballgame from swatting those behemoths. They sold 6-12 repellant lotion at the concession stands. The Houston old-timers poopooed that as second rate. They said that in the minor league days, a Flit vendor wandered the stands at Buff Stadium charging a nickel for three squirts directed anyplace you please.

There were a few owners of that Houston ball club, but the one everyone remembers is Roy Hofheinz. He would be the first to tell you that's the way it ought to be, but the fact is that Hofheinz was a pure showman the likes of which few had ever seen. He grew up loving the circus and sought to create one wherever he went. He had slicked down hair like most every man in those days. He wore thick glasses, and a big fat cigar was never far from his hand. He was like P.T. Barnum without the midgets.

Colt Stadium had Hollywood Western themes every which way you looked. The signage, the 100-yard bar they put up in an overgrown trailer. Even the parking lot had signs like Matt Dillon Way and Roy Rogers Territory so you could remember where you left your car or your stagecoach. The parking attendants were dressed up like Tom Mix, and when the mercury on that asphalt topped 110, they dropped like rocks. But they made a good first impression. Every promotion I'd ever seen in the game up to that time brought you in to watch baseball, but Judge Hofheinz was selling an experience, even though that idea had not even been invented yet.

Hofheinz bought all the players and even the announcers these powder blue cowboy suits to wear on road trips. He'd fine you if you didn't dress up. Big Stetson and leather boots included. Some of the fellows groused about the whole thing, but man, I was disappointed that the clubbies never got one. Swear to Jesus that if they had give me one of those suits, I'd have added spurs, bought a pony and ridden to every ice house south of downtown. That was high living.

I tried to see Felix again. In spite of the withering look he'd given me at Kress', I was reinspired by it somehow. My letters were being ignored, not that I was shocked, mind you. I reckoned that if I could just get a chance to sit down with him, he'd come to understand that I wasn't the devil. I finally formulated a plan. It seemed to me that if I could bring a big league ball player into the mix, then Felix would be less inclined to send me away out of hand.

Not being a driver, I tried several of the fellows, but only collected polite deferrals. They was all busy with their own lives. A couple of them seemed ready but became less thrilled with the whole idea when they found out what part of town we'd be going to. Even some young, strong ballplayers were not immune to the notion that if a White person drove through a Black part of town, they'd be dragged from their car and switchbladed to pieces. They couldn't fathom why I'd want to go there in the first place. I had not exactly spread the word that I had a Negro son.

I hooked up with J.C. Hartman out of pure luck really. He overheard me asking around, and volunteered. He was a very nice man, J.C.. He'd played at the end of the Negro Leagues, after they'd lost their significance, and then spent some time with the Buffaloes, Houston's minor league team. After he retired from baseball, he become a Houston cop. I think he was one of the ones who meant it.

I had given J.C. a bare minimum of talk and information by the time we pulled up at Felix's house. Still, I imagine he was a smart enough fellow to figure out the lay of the land.

"Do you want me to wait in the car?" he asked me.

"No. I'd rather you walk up with me. I don't figure there'll be any gunplay."

It took a long time before Felix opened the front door, at least it seemed that way. He threw a nasty look at me, and then one at J.C..

"Are you one of his bastard children, too?"

J.C. looked like he'd been cut with a knife.

"No, Mr. Rogers, I'm J.C. Hartman, and I play shortstop for the Colts."

That knocked the wind out of Felix, for sure. First time I'd ever seen him without his chest puffed out. He sputtered some noises, and when words emerged, they were almost civil. As I recall the moment, I had that flicker of hope again.

"Okay. What do you want?" Felix give me a challenging look in the eyes.

"Son, I just want you to hear me out. You got to understand the times back then. It's not that I had the wrong answer. Back in those days, none of us even realized there was a question."

He stared at J.C. then looked back at me. He was thinking there for a minute. Finally, he wet his lips and pointed his chin a little higher.

"I told you not to call me son. It was nice to meet you, Mr. Hartman,"

With that, he walked back inside his house and firmly shut the front door. A rustle of the window drapery was as close as I got to meeting the rest of his family. My family.

There have been lots of stories written about the Colts' first spring training in Apache Junction, but we were back there again in 1963. People get the feeling that the first year out there was nothing but misfits and castoffs out of control in the desert. There was some of that. Turk Farrell filling Aspromonte's convertible with reptiles or putting a live rattlesnake in Walt Bond's street pants. Those things happened.

The next year was totally different. Almost none of the same position players were on the roster. Aspromonte and Warwick who had been the kids in year one were now the middle aged guys. Tal Smith as the farm director was getting more of a say. We had promising youngsters in the system, but the biggest change was that we had bonus babies, or as close to it as Houston ever got. There was no draft in those days, so clubs would get into bidding wars, tossing out a few thousand in signing bonuses. Rusty Staub and Ernie Fazio were our young phenoms, as they say. Both lit up the Cactus League that spring. Fazio was a California kid, straight out of the College World Series, but Staub was naïve 19-year old from New Orleans. He'd been in Durham the year before, a B league college town, so throwing him into the deep end with partiers the likes of Farrell, Nottebart, and Drott was like tossing a raccoon out of a bird's nest and expecting him to fly.

I don't think it did young Rusty any favors when they installed him in the clean up hole either. A righteous living teenager. He was the first rookie to ever hit clean up in an opening day lineup, did you know that? Yesiree. Harry Craft, our manager, was putting the pressure on him right from the git go, and the veterans give him short shrift. Part of it was that they had nothing in common, but the other thing was that nobody wanted to get blamed for breaking the teams prized kiddo either.

The spring training home the franchise had constructed was Geronimo Park, and early in the spring, we had a game cancelled on account of a sandstorm. I was busy trying to throw plastic over everything. I found out the hard way that those little grains have an unfettered path to every crevice whether inanimate or alive. A week later I was still finding grit in the most personal places every time I showered.

The expansion clubs like Houston got a raw deal filling out a roster, so the Colts signed better than 100 free agents before that spring. They figured if you threw enough worms against a wall, a few wigglers might evolve into big leaguers. There were exactly two new oldsters who stuck, with Pete Runnels being the main one. He lived in Houston already, and he was the reigning American League batting champ. With Houston, he didn't get within 70 points of his total from the previous year. The other veteran was Johnny Temple who'd been a mainstay of the Reds teams I worked for. He'd actually come over for the last month of '62, though I'm not sure what the club hoped to accomplish.

The rest of the new faces that spring were not even old enough to order a near beer. A handful of those become solid players later – Jerry Grote, Sonny Jackson, Jimmy Wynn, Staub, of course, and Little Joe Morgan who overachieved his way to the Hall of Fame. The lion's share of those kids fell into the "other" category, though.

The name I recollect the most was Reese McCoy. He was a strapping right fielder out of Pfiefer, Kansas. One of our scouts had seen him playing Legion ball in Hays, and swore up and down that the kid had one of the prettiest left-handed power strokes you'd ever laid eyes on. So, there he was at Apache Junction.

I reckon that McCoy was like your typical farm or ranch boy. Polite and helpful most of the time, but ready to go to fist city at the first hint of a personal slight. He looked all right in the cages and sure enough sent some balls on a ride in the late days of February, but damned if he didn't call attention to himself for the worst reasons. Since his non-baseball hours were spent wearing a sweat-stained straw cowboy hat, and his cheeks were baboon butt red, the poor fellow might as well have worn a neon sweatshirt saying "I'm gullible, have at me."

Sure enough, about a week after we arrived, Farrell and Drott come trotting into Geronimo Park on a pair of tall appaloosas, and right behind them, on a mangy donkey, is Reese McCoy loaded up with two golf bags as if Sancho Panza ever decided to caddy at Pebble Beach. We all got a damn fine laugh out of it, I'll give them that, but when the little equestrian parade started to tear up part of the third base line along the main diamond, Harry Craft and the entire grounds crew started getting a little hot under the collar. Since it was McCoy who the two vets had sent to rent horses, a lot of the shit slid down hill to him. That included the two literal piles that he was told to shovel out of the on deck circle. Here he was thinking he was taking part in a hysterical little prank, and he ended up being the proverbial butt of the joke.

Now, my guess is that if young Cowboy Reese had faced this situation back in Kansas, he would've slugged about six people in the kisser prior to picking up that shovel, but he was hoping to make a professional baseball club. That embarrassment and a few more were shirked off with a silent grinding of teeth and a flame of the eye. That is until he stepped into the left-handed batter's box against Dick Drott in one of his first intrasquad games.

Dave Adlesh was behind the plate, another one of the 19-year old brigade, and he called for Dick to bring a fastball inside. Drott shot a little smile toward the dish. He only had two pitches – a hard fastball and a curve – and if he had better control of them, the Cubs would've never let him go. He unleashed a corker, and it knocked poor Cowboy Reese flat on his ass. Everybody has their last straw, and I reckon that was McCoy's.

The lad jumped to his feet and took off for the mound. There may have been a second or two where he was the only one in the whole ballpark who was moving since everybody else was pretty much stunned. This was spring training after all, and the pitcher was on the same damn team. Drott snapped to right before impact, but McCoy took him down. I have no doubt that if he'd had a rope, the boy would've hogtied that pitcher and raised his hands for the judges. As it was, the club brass took a dim view of a would be rookie on a short term contract taking down their possible bullpen ace with a flying tackle.

Before he got unceremoniously sent home to the prairie, though, a fine thing happened to Reese McCoy. About three weeks earlier, a yellow cur pup just missed getting runned over up on the highway. McCoy and a couple of the other younguns snatched him away from danger and took to feeding him, but there was no doubt who that puppy latched onto. The last I saw of Cowboy Reese was him tossing his big duffel bag into the bottom of a Greyhound and slipping the driver two bucks to ignore the little dog he was carrying. I like to think that mongrel lived another decade or better as the happiest ranch dog in Kansas.

Chapter Thirteen

During those days the Astrodome was getting as much buzz as the Colt .45s. We were watching it rise every day. As bad as the mosquitoes were before, they got even bigger once they dug a giant water filled hole in the ground. After a good rain, it was a 40-foot deep stagnant pond. I heard tell of mosquitoes that got big enough to carry off a beetle. Not the bug, the Volkswagen. In spite of those minor annoyances, and the fact that we were anything but a contender, folks around the ball club were excited for things to come.

At the start of July 1964, my phone rang one afternoon. The team was on the road, so I was puttering around my apartment. I should mention, in case any youngsters ever listen to these recordings, that a phone at that time was a relatively substantial contraption permanently plugged into the wall that worked okay for talking but took no messages, had no camera, and never showed pictures of cats riding a vacuum. Mine was mounted upright near the kitchen light switch. It was also still a bit of a thing to call long distance since it meant someone thought you was worth spending money on. A low grade occasion, I reckon you'd consider it.

It didn't take more than four syllables to recognize the voice at the other end as my old New York running buddy, Eddie Ardoin. It was a moment that made your voice get louder and could've raised your mood in a funeral service.

"Eddie! How the hell are you? Your rich wife ain't kicked you out after all these years, has she?"

"Non, she still tolerates me."

I swear to Jesus his accent had gotten even thicker.

"Arthur," he said. "It is not good, the reason I call."

He always said my name like R-tour. I grunted, and he continued.

"I telephone to tell you that I am consumed by the cancer, I am afraid. I did not want to pass from this world without talking to one of the best friends I could ever have. Perhaps you have some time to shoot the shit, as we used to say?"

After he filled me in on every drop of heartache that the doctors had poured over him, we rehashed old times for better than two hours. Long distance be damned. He sounded like he still hadn't quite gotten over us running off and leaving him dangling from that traffic light.

After not hearing from each other for probably 15 years, we had two more phone calls over the next month or so. Each time, I could hear his voice getting weaker. The third time, Mary Lynn made the call. Eddie was in the hospital, and she thought hearing an old buddy might bring him some cheer. She handed him the phone, but after a soft little "Hello, Arthur," he fell asleep. She eventually come back on and apologized for potentially having let me ramble too long, but hell, it's something I'm good at.

My old friend passed over two days later at a fancy cancer hospital in New York City. Lord knows that sometimes even your money can't save you, though it is surely the thing that gives you a fighting chance.

I didn't get to see him again, but I prefer picturing him in a smoking jacket and enjoying a cocktail anyway. The night Eddie Ardoin died was the first time in my life I ever felt old.

What's that? I've never mentioned my real name before now? Well, I'll be jiggered. Yep. It's Arthur, but nobody excepting Eddie called me that once my mama died. Even my childhood buddies, Tommy and Sam and them called me Wingo.

Well, son, I got the name Rube when I was still with the Yankees. Fact is that I went longer than most without a nickname. Everybody gets one. Baseball's funny that way, though.

Anyhow, I think it was Bill Dickey, my fellow Arkansan, decided that I needed a nickname. We were all sitting around during a rain delay. The boys were playing cards, even though McCarthy, our new manager, hated that. I was starching some jocks for Frank Crosetti.

So Big Bill points at me and says, "Prune Danish."

That was a code the guys used when they wanted me to get them a breakfast pastry. So, I drop Frankie's jock, Bill had seniority see, and I started to run up to this little bakery on 163rd street. Just as I get to the clubhouse door, George Pipgras says, "Hey, Sparky, hold on a minute."

Well, a couple of the guys tittered. They allowed as to how they think Sparky would be a good nickname for me. Several of the guys were partial to Three Fingered Wingo, but nobody was strong enough to hold me down. They finally settled on Rube as a compromise.

Barbeque is a big thing in Houston, and there was a joint I used to go to up off Shepherd Drive called John's. Rabbit had turned me on to it, and you could get there on his 47 bus. Old fellow that ran it cooked up a beef rib the likes of which you'd only seen on the Flintstones. In fact, since John Davis come first, I'm not sure that Hanna or Barbera or somebody hadn't eaten there. The smoked flavor watered your eyes, and the meat was tender like a pot roast with a handle. I can damn near taste them now.

For something so simple on the face of it, smoking meat is an art form. A pitmaster will swear by his mix of wood, and his slow cook time, how much air to circulate through and even how many times you flip the meat. Old John used to scrape the grill leavings into his pinto beans, and those were delectable, too.

It was one of my favorite spots to eat, and I always reckoned it was lucky for me on top of everything else. Twice I found a dollar in the gravel parking lot. Once a stranger ordering in front of me paid for my lunch. I picked up five or six stray cats there and managed to find homes for all of them, though I got a little scratched up smuggling them onto the bus under my shirt. It seemed like the natural place to go grab my to go lunch before I headed to the Astrodome for opening night in April 1965. That was to be a monumentous occasion, and I wanted fortune on my side.

Naturally, the clubhouse staff had crossed all the Ts weeks prior. We'd been working out in there for a good while, so we knew there'd be no surprises on our end. Still, I was at the ballpark by 11:30 with two chopped beef sandwiches and a cup of pintos.

As much as we knew the building, we had never seen it with people. When those plush theatre seats started to fill more than an hour before first pitch, well, son, I've never seen such excitement at a ball yard. You could literally hear the ooh and aahs down on the field. Most folks were dressed to the nines, with the exception of the drool coming from their slack jaws. Throughout the whole ball game, over half of them were watching the roof or generally looking around. Nowadays, it's not uncommon for someone at a sports stadium to be staring at the scoreboard instead of the field of play, but in 1965, it was unheard of.

It was my second time to open a brand new ball park. Yankee Stadium had offered a certain measure of awe in 1923, but it was nothing like the spectacle of the Dome, a phenomenon that would last years, as it turned out. The other thing that become evident was how much of a pitchers park the Astrodome would really turn out to be. We suspected it, of course, but until the fellows are really and truly trying to bear down and win a game, you can't be certain. It was going to take a lot of Ovaltine to muscle one out of our new yard.

I met LBJ on that opening night at the Astrodome. The Secret Service pulled his little motorcade up to Gate 5, the entrance over by Judge Hofheinz's office. They had already done a sweep through those lower concourses, and about a dozen of us had come to stand in that little lobby where the club executives worked. It ain't every day you get to see the President of the United States, you know.

The Judge was there to meet his old friend, and though he was no little man himself, LBJ stood half a head taller. He was big as me. Even from a distance, I'll wager the whole assemblage felt like the president was looking them straight in the eye. I couldn't help but like him.

It wasn't no big crowd hollering, mind you. We were barely fifteen feet away, but still everybody was saying hello or welcome, and LBJ, who was a handshaker, was pressing the flesh. For some dumb reason, per my usual, I blurted out the first thing that popped into my noggin.

"Give those dogs of yours a good scratch for me, Mr. President. I sure do like seeing them when they come on TV."

That stopped him in his tracks. His grin got a little bigger.

'What's your name?"

"Rube Wingo. I'm an assistant clubhouse man here."You have dogs?"

"Yes, sir. Had dogs my whole life. Right now, I've got a real good boy. He walked straight up to me out front of a Mexican restaurant and told me he was ready to come home."

"I couldn't live without them. We still got Him and Blanco, but I sure do miss little Her."

You could see a cloud of grief pass over the man's face, or maybe I was projecting.

"I was awful sorry to hear about Her dying, Mr. President. There are few things make a man sadder than losing a faithful dog."

He took a couple steps closer until we was breath to breath. You could almost hear the butts pucker on the Secret Service boys. But Mr. Johnson just stepped over and gave me a big, firm handshake for a second time.

"Maybe when I'm done with this job, I can get you to bring your dog up the ranch. There's a cool stream to splash in and more cow shit than a pooch can sniff."

"I'd like that. It sounds like dog heaven."

"It is, Rube. It is."

With that, the boys in suits closed around him and the Judge, and they all kept walking around toward the elevators. He was my second president, you know. Both of them impressed me as being real people.

Back around August of 1965, least I know it was when the Dome was still shinier than a debutante's eyes, I went with some of the fellows one night to a strip joint. Now normally, I don't fancy such window shopping, but one of the young players was having his 21st birthday, and a whole passel of folks was headed to the Crystal Pistol just down the road from the ball park to wind down after our flight from Milwaukee. And truth be told, once our eyes adjusted to the light, I had to admit there was something to be said for a beehive hairdo, a pert bosom, and a Wilson Pickett song.

The Crystal Pistol was chock full of gals with shapely legs, smoky voices, rode hard faces, and properly bleached hair, but the best thing about the place was one of the swingiest neon signs this side of Vegas. It was a fifteen foot tall beckoning, big-haired cowgirl that I could have stared at for hours. That night however, we all went inside.

The boys was having a large time, and the girls couldn't have welcomed the Sheik of Araby any better than they was welcoming those ballplayers. There was titties every which way you turned. The sad part was that even these young ladies, who for all their trips around the world was still lacking in cosmopolitan knowledge, could tell at a glance that I was no ballplayer.

I was off to one side, enjoying my whiskey and view when one of the larger people I ever seen pulled up a booth next to me. He had to weigh 450 if he was a pound. The back of his neck had more rolls than Rainbo Bakery, and there was great dark circles under his eyes, like they were permanently blacked for right field.

It turns out the man was a local bookie, a sort of fellow I'd seen for as long as I'd been around professional ball. His real name was Jesse, but everybody called him Sweet Jello. I could only figure that was because every time he moved, most of him jiggled for the next half hour.

Sweet Jello considered himself to be quite the ladies' man, and I'll be damned if he didn't have him a pair of little skinny girls flanking him. As big as he was, there might have been a couple more lost under his armpits. I just couldn't tell you.

As notable as his appearance might have been, Sweet Jello's voice was even more memorable. You'd expect that he'd have pipes like Barry White or even Louis Armstrong, but instead he opened his mouth and out flowed a clear, silky tenor. Sounded like Dennis Day from the old Jack Benny Show.

"How you doing this fine night, Mr. Rube?" Jello asked me. Obviously, I looked surprised as hell. I'd never met this big man in my life, as far as I remembered. He shook his head and give me this little three-part chuckle.

"Hehehe. Yes, I know who you are. Hehe. Sports are my business, Mr. Rube. And someone like you is worth knowing."

"Well, that's something I don't get told a lot."

"Hehe. Sugar, bring another whiskey to Mr. Rube," he hollered to a waitress. "You know I am a season ticket holder for your ball club. Section 122, Row BB, Seat 1."

My first thought was that the unluckiest fellow in the Dome must be the one scrunched into seat 2.

"It's near the chute to the concession stands. I've got to maintain my svelte physique, you know, Mr. Rube."

Hell, that one made me go hehe. Sweet Jello had a certain charm about him at that.

"Mr. Rube, I hear tell that Mr. Robin Roberts is set to make a start on tomorrow evening."

The Orioles had just released Roberts, and sure enough, we picked him up, but he hadn't thrown yet.

"What you hear about his right wing?"

Jello winked at me. Now, I know you're not supposed to consort with gamblers, but to be honest, I was never sure what consorting really was. Far as I was concerned, I wasn't planning on doing any consorting that night.

"Skinny is he's hankering to pitch," I said.

Immediately, I wondered if he'd take me saying "skinny" as an insult, but Jello just give me a slow nod, like a dashboard Chihuahua on wavy asphalt.

"That's fine. That's fine."

From what I heard later, Sweet Jello made a bundle and a half on Robin Roberts the rest of that season, and believe you me, picking the right time to bet for the Astros that year took some doing.

Considering the weak, overpriced drinks, the Crystal Pistol wasn't that bad a joint. I'm just now remembering this one girl who worked there and really had her cap set for ballplayers. She went by the name of Bare E. Mason. Used to dance to the theme music from the old TV program that was popular then.

Duuuum. Dum, Dum. Glove went flying.

Duuuum. Dum. Dum. Dum. High heel hit some guy in the eye. It was sexy as hell, quite frankly.

Chapter Fourteen

My lifelong buddy Paul Flinkenberg retired from his job at the start of February 1966, and decided to move to Houston. He said it sounded like as good a place as any. He had divorced his fourth wife about a year prior, and per usual, she had gotten the house. Paul always said that you go into a marriage with a moving van, but when it ends, all you need is the trunk of your car.

He had done real well for himself. Bought him a little house on Ferndale Street that was walking distance from my apartment. He got him a charcoal grill and metal patio furniture and commenced to flirting with every neighbor woman he could get a peek at. A natural convert to the suburban lifestyle, he was.

Paul also decided he needed a hobby, and he settled on playing the guitar. He went to Evans music store on University Boulevard and found himself a used Kay archtop. Pretty mahogany thing. With heavy strings, that son of gun was loud. It was a good thing he had a house cause that was a guitar that would've got him tossed out of any respectable apartment house. I'd known Paul for better than 40 years, and somehow I'd missed that he had played guitar back in Indiana as a kid.

I'd drop by his place during the off season and listen to him practice. We'd drink until we fooled ourselves into singing. Most of the popular music back then had notes higher than we could hit, so we'd croon out some Jim Reeves or Johnny Cash. I've no doubt it was pitiful, but it amused us.

It turns out Paul Flinkenberg was not the only old man who liked to play music. Gradually, through conversations here and there at some bar or record store, I think maybe a note left on a bulletin board, a few of these old geezers started meeting up for what I reckon you'd call a picking party. Then one night, their youngest member, a 54-year old pediatrician named Sheldon Brooks, showed up at Paul's house all atwitter. He had found the group a gig. Well, the rest of the fellows didn't realize they ever wanted one, but they agreed to hear Dr. Shelly out.

It seems the doc was a member of the American Legion post on Waugh Drive, and the band they had hired for some Friday night shindig had canceled on them. That's the way musicians operate sometimes. If they can hustle an extra five bucks across town, off they go. The doc said there wouldn't be nothing to it. They'd play two 45-minute sets, and the pay was ten bucks a man plus drinks and cheeseburgers.

Son, I'd reckon there were wartime decisions made in the bowels of the Pentagon that didn't summon up as much discussion as whether or not these six old gaffers ought to take a paying job as a band. They hashed and rehashed equipment, instrumentation, seating arrangement, and whether this meant that they needed to invest in matching embroidered jumpsuits. The answer to that last one was no, at least for the moment.

A few of the questions were fair ones to ask. For starters, they totaled things up and imagined that they knew maybe 37 minutes worth of music. Dr. Shelly used his best bedside manner to assure them that the Legionnaires, being members of a private club, would be drinking hi-balls at a rapid rate, and there was no way on God's green Earth that they would recollect by the second set what the band played in the first. The next thing that I admit was a little problem was that at these picking parties, there were five guitars and one mandolin. That was played by an octogenarian who went by the name of Kentucky Dan.

As it turned out, one of the fellows had a trap kit stowed in his attic, and he agreed to become the drummer, and after much haggling, the rest of the fellows convinced Dr. Shelly to switch to playing bass. They told him that whether he went with a full upright or an electric with an amp, he was the only guy who could still carry the rig. That's also how I ended up in the band in spite of the fact that I couldn't draw a note from a player piano. Three of those old gents all realized at once that I was an equipment man. Shit, they said, I carried things for a living. They cut me a deal whereby Paul and the Doc each forfeited three dollars of their pay for the following Friday, and they promised to buy me an instrument I could handle. And that's how the Legion post ended up with three guitars, a mandolin, electric bass, one snare drum, and an egg shaker.

If you thought those negotiations were something else, the last order of business was to choose a name. Either the Schlitz or the Pearl did the talking on that subject for about half an hour, then we finally all agreed that the name should be something befitting to our advancing experience in life. Kentucky Dan was fond of The Senile Playboys. Geezy Wheels got some consideration, and two of the fellows were very fond of Cowboy Fossils. In the end, the most votes were for The Broken Pokes.

Our debut gig was surprisingly well received. The third time that old Dan sang "Act Naturally" the post commander told him he sounded exactly like Buck Owens. The fourth time around, he told Dan it was even better. We decided not to point out that by then we were done playing, and the voice coming out of the jukebox actually was Buck Owens.

The Astros were a young team those first few years at the Dome, not counting crusty old-timers like Nellie Fox and Eddie Mathews sprinkled on the roster here and there. I've heard people who claim to know baseball talk about how young guys are just happy to be there. Now that's a bigger load than your grandson's britches. Every major leaguer who ever lived is competitive. They wouldn't have got there otherwise. I knew fellows who would fist fight you over a game of hopscotch, but still there are different kinds of competitive, I reckon.

There were the paycheckers who went out and gave it their best, but who knew the team was going nowhere. Then there were the ponies. At least that's what I called them. They were the ones who thought there was lightning in the bottle every spring, and guys would somehow come together to make a magic greater than their parts. It's like the little girl who walked into a room full of shit and just knew she was getting a pony. But you know, the beauty of baseball is that sometimes the magic did happen. You don't think the '69 Mets figured in April that they'd be world champions, do you? Or my old 1921 Memphis Chicks.

In 1966, the Civil Rights Act notwithstanding, the little places in Houston was about 60 or 70 percent integrated, I'd say. Of course, that depends on your perspective, I reckon. The city had been out in front of some others in the South, but the white business owners sure didn't all simultaneously open their doors with a smile. The government places and big venues had been open to Blacks for quite a spell, but I'd wager most of the smaller bars and restaurants were still giving a rough reception to would-be customers who seemed less than lily white.

I was still a regular at the Rich-Man ice house, of course, but I didn't necessarily limit myself. I had kept inviting Rabbit to let me buy him a beer there, but he kept deferring, so I'd never put things to the test, and I'd never seen any other Black customer in there, neither. Not that I stayed there 24/7, but I was sure there often enough to make an educated judgment.

There was a place I went from time to time out by Dowling and Polk. It was called the T&H Drive In on account of at one time it was owned by two Mexican gents name of Tony and Hector. The story I come to hear in drips and drabs was that Hector got caught after closing time one night standing real close behind a woman named Wilma who happened to be bent over the jukebox with her skirt hiked up under her armpits. Wilma might not have been the biggest prize in the carnie booth, estimates was she topped the scales at 240, but she had a husband who was pretty proud of her.

The husband come up there about 12:45 that particular night, peering through the greasy garage door windows, and seen his beloved dancing the fleshy mambo. He walked around to the back door, of the building that is, and let himself and his .38 inside. Shot Hector in flagrante, as they say. The bullet went right through Hector's ass and lodged in Wilma's. I believe that was the very moment that Hector decided to leave the bar business.

As for Wilma, she turned around to her husband and started yelling, "Ay! Papi! Me duele!"

That's Spanish for letting him know that her rear end hurt. It was more of a scolding, really, and, duly chastised, she and the mister went on home and patched everything up. So, by the time I knew the joint, there was only Tony, but the H remained in honor of Hector's rear.

I liked old Tony a great deal. He had been born in Houston, over to the East End. His folks had run from the Mexican Revolution, and Tony liked to show off a picture of his daddy all decked out in a big sombrero standing next to Pancho Villa, Emiliano Zapata, and a couple of other moustachioed dudes. Tony kept that wrinkled photo in his wallet, and rare was the time that a new face at the T&H didn't get to see it. His daddy was still around, and most days he'd be sitting at a porcelain-topped table listening to Mexican music on his transistor radio.

The T&H was open to anybody who had a quarter for a beer. Tony used to tell me that a lot of the Mexican folk didn't cotton much to "Naygros", as he called them with his Tex-Mex accent, but that he was second generation and therefore open minded. He was very proud of that.

Rabbit and me was sitting in there one Sunday afternoon, just a shooting the breeze. Most likely solving world problems, we was, when I asked Rabbit the time.

He looked past me. "Oh, I'm guessing about a quarter to shit," he answered.

My boy Felix had just pulled up out front.

If he had spotted me, he would have surely spun on his heel, got back into that Fairlane and drove off. Me not having a car to scope out from the parking lot, though, he was halfway into the place and therefore committed. His pride demanded that he keep walking up to the bar with head held high.

Rabbit gave me the wary eye.

"Let it go, Rube. A scene in here ain't going to change any minds."

I tried. I sure did. The two of us sat there, but I could sense my boy, Felix, someplace behind me. I didn't hear his voice, and in that little bar, I knew that meant he had either grabbed a stool or was alone at a little table. My buddy did his best to keep me occupied with conversation, but in the end, it took me slightly less than ten minutes before my unreasonable expectations overtook my better judgment. I excused myself and went and plopped down at the two top across from Felix.

"Nothing's changed. Got nothing for you."

He didn't even look up when he said it. Sounded like a disinterested cop working a minor traffic accident.

"I just figured I might have a word or two. I'm taking the fact that you stayed to be a glimmer of hope," I told him.

"I'm only sitting here to finish this beer so I don't look like an asshole walking out. You go no power to run me off from no place."

"Then we might as well use those last few swallows for good effect, don't you think?"

Felix was keeping his voice low enough, but that knife edge was still there.

"You lost your chance to say anything worth hearing a long time ago. I grew up not knowing who my daddy was. I got comfortable with that burden. But when I become a grown man, I started to realize why my mama stared out the kitchen window with that pining look. That pained me. You had years and years where you could have shown up with something to say. But that time is long past, old man."

"I didn't even know you existed, son."

He pointed his finger and made a short buzzing noise at my use of the word, but I wasn't going to back down now. I had him talking.

"A different path just never occurred to me, Felix. If I'd known, then things might have been poles apart."

"Bullshit!" Felix's volume had inched up just enough that I could sense a couple of neighboring ears perking up.

The power of it recoiled me, but he was not finished by a long shot.

"If you had bothered to come around more than every few years when it suited you, when you got your hard on or bored or whatever drove you, then you'd have known about things just fine. You never had one inkling to do the right thing, kid or no kid. You're a coward, God damn it. You can talk about how times was, how things still is, all you want. Fact is that you never made the move to stand up, and that is just as bad as if you were wearing a Klan hood, at least as far as it concerns me. Say whatever makes you sleep nights, but none of it puts a daddy into our little apartment. And I damn sure don't have to listen to you. Now, git."

He folded his hands neatly around the almost empty Pearl bottle in front of him. The old hate was still in his eyes, but so was disappointment. I was struggling to keep my voice lower than Buck Owens singing "Think of Me" on the juke.

"Look, Felix. How many times can I say I'm sorry? I'm happy to go on saying it. I'm sad and hurt for my family, but I can't go back and change things. I can't understand how you feel because I can't be you. All I can do is try to be better."

He opened his mouth a little to say something, but it was just a suck of air. He stared at me then decided to get up without a word. Not that he was a regular, I suppose, but that was the last time I ever saw Felix in the T&H.

One night in late December, I turned the corner onto my block after some colder than the outside temperature beers at the Rich-Man, and I noticed a brand new Olds Toronado idling at the curb. As I glanced over, the power window rolled down, and there, with the driver's seat pushed damn near back to the trunk, was Sweet Jello.

"Evening, Mr. Rube."

It was out of context, but there was no mistaking the incredible bulk of Sweet Jello.

"My grandmamma got a little carried away making her Christmas tamales, and I figured that you were a man who could use some good food."

"Thanks, Sweet Jello. Please tell her that's very kind."

I knew that half of those homemade tamales wouldn't live through the hour.

"As long as I'm here, Mr. Rube, I was wondering if you were going to be working the clubhouse for the Oilers this next year."

"No, why would I be doing that?" I asked, though I already suspected where he was headed.

"Oh, no reason. I heard tell that Mr. Adams and Mr. Hofheinz had a phone call the other night about them moving to the Dome for 1967. If that took place, and I'm not saying it will, those Oilers would be stupid not to have a man like you in the locker room."

"Well, that's the first I've heard about it."

"No problem, Mr. Rube. You have a Happy Christmas. I'll give my grand-mamma your best."

I stood there for a minute watching him drive off in that fancy new car wondering how the world's biggest Mexican knew about the private phone conversations of two millionaires, but I could feel those tamales still hot through the foil. They were damn good.

The Astrodome was the biggest thing in sports, of course, and they had all manner of things going on in there most every night. Motorcycle jumps, Boy Scout Jamborees, bull fights, crazy preachers, but the best of the lot was the three Muhammad Ali title fights. The one I recollect most was the middle one. Ali versus the number two heavyweight in the world, Big Ernie Terrell, on Monday night, February 6, 1967. Yes, sir. I still know the date.

Angelo Dundee was Ali's trainer and corner man, and he had his guys, of course, but two nights before the fight, his junior man went and got himself drunk enough to sucker punch a police sergeant outside the Dome Shadows club. The popo was not going to let that young man out of jail. Dundee's phone calls eventually led him to Doc Ewell, our trainer, but Doc had bought tickets for him and the missus and their kids to vacation in Acapulco, Mexico. People in Houston considered it very avant garde, but there you were. And that's how I found myself ringside for the Ali – Terrell fight.

Dundee made it very clear that my duties included sticking the spit bucket under Ali's chin when needed and removing all towels, bandages and other para-phernalia that become saturated with a bodily fluid. That was it he told me. Don't touch anything else, and don't talk to nobody.

That fight was a show I'd never forget. Ali dancing on his toes, floating like a butterfly just like he said, while Terrell just stood there, plodding like a Franklin Parish mule. Half the floor of the Dome could hear Ali chirping.

"You an Uncle Tom."

Then he'd throw a flurry of punches.

"What's my name? What's my name?"

Terrell's answer was this long left hand, so powerful I thought I could feel the breeze.

Those fights were spectacles, and nothing showed the glitz of the new Astrodome better than they did. Naturally, you had your celebrities there, and I sneaked a peek every so often. My stool was right down from Howard Cosell, who I also watched slug down vodka in a coffee cup that got refreshed at least twice within an hour. What took me by surprise was when Joe DiMaggio sat down with Cosell as they were getting ready to start the 12th round. He was about eight feet away with Cosell between us. I hadn't seen him in better than 20 years.

"Joe. Hey. It's me. Rube Wingo from the Yankees clubhouse."

"Hey," Joe told me.

"I work for the Astros now, but one of the corner men got arrested, so they eventually got down to me."

Cosell leaned away from the mic, and his breath darn near curled my lashes.

"Pally, we are on live television."

"I know, I just wanted to say hey to Joe since I was the one who tricked Bill Essick into signing him back when he was with the Seals."

Joe may have been starting to get a flicker of recognition.

"Oh, Wingo. Now I remember."

Looking at his eyes, though, I don't think he knew me from any other soul in the whole stadium. The one thing I was certain of is that Cosell was getting pissed. In spite of the air conditioning, he was also sweating like a Presbyterian with the dinner check.

"If you two could perhaps postpone your rapprochement until after the commercial break, America would be grateful," Cosell said in that voice of his.

"I just hadn't seen him in, I'll bet it's 25 years."

"Clearly the moniker Rube was awarded with foresight."

Out of my other ear, I heard Dundee scream, "Bucket!"

"Sorry, Joe, Ali's got to spit up."

I reached over in time for Ali to hock a mouthful of something in the pail, and that was followed by a couple of sweat soaked rags. I could've plucked a clean one, I reckon, but for some reason I fished out the top one and handed it to Cosell.

"You need a sweat towel, Mr. Cosell?" I asked him.

He made a couple of big circles on his face before that queasy drunk look overwhelmed him. He made eye contact with me for just a half second before he whispered, "Bucket."

After he tossed his dinner into my metal pail, I tossed him a clean towel and a nod, and then I heard Ali over my shoulder.

"I'm still prettier than you, Cosell."

With that the bell rang, just like it was a movie. I never did catch up with DiMaggio, but that just means I didn't get stuck with the drink tab.

Chapter Fifteen

Right at the very tail of the 1967 season, I met a woman at the ice house, and I saw her for a bit. Don't fret, son, I won't tell you any more about the sex, but even old folks need companionship. Not that 66 was old, mind you. That was half a century ago, for crying out loud.

She was a looker for her age. Puffy hair dyed a tasteful shade of copper, set off by sparkly eye shadow in a robin's egg blue. She wore cat eyed glasses with twinkling rhinestones and a chain that held them around her neck when we wanted to smooch.

Oh, there were drawbacks. She was a pessimist, if ever I met one. Had three cats, which is never a good sign to begin with, but even then I think she was expecting the worst out of them felines. She'd named them Nat Turner, Denmark Vesey, and Spartacus. Every time I knocked on her door, I half anticipated finding her severed head on top of a carpeted post.

Her name was Judith, and I tend to distrust folks who refuse to go by nicknames. Should have been a warning.

She was divorced from some muckety banker and ended up with a fine house over toward the art museum and enough of a settlement that she never hesitated to buy me some little trinkets, even when I told her to knock it off. Her paying for the dinners at some fancy seafood or steak place didn't bother me one bit, though. I couldn't swing two dozen oysters at Angelo's by myself. No doubt she was slumming when she come to the Rich-Man.

My first red flag was walking in my front door just before lunch one day to find the phone ringing. Back then, long before the days of cell phones, you left your keys dangling and hot-footed it to snatch up the receiver before the caller hung up. I was out of breath by the time I said hello.

"Where've you been?" Judith was asking from the other end of the line.

Now, I'm an independent old bastard when it comes to things like that, but she had caught me off guard.

"I went to browse the record shop up on Westheimer, and treated myself to an ice cream cone on the way back."

That was during my used records phase. Finger's Furniture was giving a big ass discount to team employees as part of their sponsorship, and I had dropped almost $200 of my savings on a Zenith console stereo and hi-fi. It was a humdinger. I kept that baby for over 35 years, so I'd say I got my money's worth.

Judith's game was subtle at first. I didn't even notice that she was a jealous lunatic. She was smart enough to follow up her questions with something good. That day, before I got a chance to even register the first sentence, she told me that she wanted to take me to Sonny Look's for steak dinner. The drool probably started immediately.

Over the next couple months, though, her tricks wore off. She was wanting to keep tabs on my every move, and her tone was like a flat ass accusation. If I got out of bed to take a leak at night, I'd wager the little devil in her brain was asking who I had stashed in the can. I know her husband had kept a stable of floozies big enough to fill the gate at the Derby, but that didn't mean that I did.

Her jealousy got to the point that I started pushing back. More than a couple of times, I deliberately forgot to call her when I said I would. Then one Saturday afternoon, she come storming into the Rich-Man when there was a good crowd watching Southwest Conference football.

"Where have you been? You were supposed to call me last night."

No doubt I could have been more diplomatic, but the first words that popped into my noggin was something my old buddy Brody used to say at the Licky back in Cincinnati.

"Damn, woman. You ain't washing my drawers."

That got a giant laugh from the assembled throng, and clearly increased her embarrassment. Those were the last words that ever passed between us. She left the ice house, and my mouth to God's ear, she was married to some other sap inside of two months. On my end, my diet went from prime rib and shrimp cocktails back to lots of salami and Velveeta, frozen fish sticks, and golden tubes.

Still, I've always believed that we take something from everyone we cross paths with, some lesson. She is the one who taught me that it's imperative to have the cheese next to the mustard side of a good sandwich. I think of her often at lunch.

I would see my old buddy Rabbit Pink about every month or thereabouts. He was a friend to me, but as I mentioned, also an acquaintance of Felix. Now, Rabbit was a good man, and not at all a gossip. Once he found out the situation between the two of us, he made a decision to stay clean out of it. What he knew about Felix, he mostly kept to himself, and I can only figure that he done the same when it come to sharing any of my tales with Felix.

We had been especially long at the T&H one night, though, when Rabbit slipped up and dropped a bombshell he didn't mean to. He said something in passing about having seen my boy a couple of nights previous. It turned out that Felix and him was on the same P.T.A.. Blackshear Elementary School in Third Ward. That's how I learned that Felix had kids which meant I was a grandpa. Now that's a sobering thought if there ever was one.

Rabbit knew he'd thrown it in the fire, but he didn't try to backpedal. He said there was two little girls, and from what he heard, Mrs. Felix, who I'd never met, mind you, was close to popping with her third baby.

Actually, most of what I knew about Felix and his family come from Rabbit, though inadvertently in little snippets here and there. If I asked a straight question, he'd look me in the eye and tell me the truth, but I could tell he wasn't looking to be in the middle.

Among other things, I'd learned that Felix and Mrs. Felix had met in Chicago, but she was from Houston originally. Her daddy owned a rug and upholstery store on Scott Street over in Third Ward, and when she and Felix got married, the decision was made for them to move south and join the family business. From what I gathered, it suited my boy.

Believe it or not, the Pokes was playing about two gigs a month around that time. I could only join them during the offseason or nights when the ball club was out of town. I'd quit traveling at all by then. That meant, more or less, that I was doing a fair amount of egg shaking. Someone had also gifted me a tambourine someplace along the line. Though it made my old muscles feel it the next morning, I continued to haul the little PA system, too.

Someplace along the line, we had acquired a good musician. The other fellows were passable, don't get me wrong. If there was enough background noise to smooth off the edges, we sounded rather spiffy. This new guy, though, was a real professional. His name was Clifford Wilkerson, and he loved baseball. That's how we found him. I got to talking sports with him one night when he wandered into the Rich-Man, and as the conversation unfolded, we edged over into music.

It turned out that Cliff had been playing lead guitar since he was 14 years old and in a Louisville blue grass band. At one point, he and his compadres had their own 20-minute radio show across the river in New Albany. His big claim to fame was being a studio musician on two Spade Cooley albums. Now he said he was mostly retired, but that if I was willing to slide him some free Astros tickets at least once a homestand, and as long as we never asked him to rehearse, he'd be happy to sit in with the Broken Pokes. Being just north of 70, he fit right in.

With Cliff laying down some of the jazziest country lead lines you've ever heard, we started to get the occasional booking in the B level nightclubs. We played Bill Mraz a couple of times. We even did a turn at Dance Town USA opening for Larry Butler. That was our big shining moment, and I'll tell you, it was at least two steps up from the usual. I kid you not, in 1967 alone we played not one but three filling station openings.

When word got around that I had a musical career on the side, a couple of the fellows from the ball club dropped by for an offseason show from time to time. Few of them enjoyed country or western music, but some did. I still preferred R&B myself, but those Western Swing tunes were truly growing on me.

One particularly memorable night was at a spot on Spencer Highway out in Pasadena called Shelly's. Big old barn of a place with beer bottles always clinking and a fist fight roughly every half hour. Not surprisingly it was Doc Shelly's favorite place to play, though I don't think he ever convinced more than a handful of his patients that he owned the place, even the five-year olds.

That night was a cold one. A blue norther had just blown through. Late January most likely 'cause I hadn't yet started thinking about compiling the gear to head off to Astrotown for Spring Training. People were wearing coats and stocking caps even indoors because Shelly's at that time did not have anything resembling central heat. Hell, it had only had walls for a couple of years. The bartenders had brought in a space heater, but the rest of the audience, and there were not that many of them when we hit the stage to fulfill our opening part of the program, were bundled up and pounding beer, hoping to get numb enough that their teeth stopped chattering.

One of the guitar players I hadn't mentioned was a retired refinery man name of Wesley Hamm. He was a sinewy fellow, not large but still muscled up from all those years of physical labor. Everyone in the group wore cowboy hats, of course. How else would they know we were a country band? Underneath that hat, Wes Hamm's head was as shiny as a hundred year old newel post, but when he was wearing his beat-to-shit used Stetson, he was probably the most virile looking amongst us.

About halfway into the set, Wes started to fall out of time. Happened maybe three songs in a row, and the boys were fixing to get annoyed. Normally you'd put that down to drinking, but we were the damned opening act and it wasn't even nine thirty yet. My place on stage was next to his, and I noticed him staring into the audience. When I followed his gaze, I could just make out a beehive-haired woman back about four rows of tables. She was looking straight at Wesley and flashing him. Wasn't a solitary garment between her green double-breasted coat and her ample chesticles. The jacket was wool, and I remember thinking that must have itched something fierce. Every once in a while, she give those things a big shake. Now my egg playing was off rhythm, too.

By the time we finished the set, every one of the Broken Pokes had figured out the cause of the disturbance, even if they didn't have the sight lines me and Wes did. Well, son, when we hit the final note of "Mama Tried," Wes threw his guitar into the case and beelined back to his generous admirer. They was getting all flirty, and things were humming along just like you might imagine until Wesley made the mistake of taking off his hat. Naturally, we were all looking in that direction out of curiosity, and we could see the beehive straighten up and take a step back. Wes realized it immediately, slapped the Stetson back on his pate and started buying beers like it was last call.

We had a big laugh then forgot all about him. Those of us who stayed behind were watching the Sunnyland Cowboys. They had them an accordion and put out a nice polka. After better than an hour, Paul come back from the can just a howling. He walked me back past the last pool table, and there was Miss Beehive, wool coat wide open and leaning against the wall, but all we could see at chest level was the back of Wesley Hamm's bald head.

It just so happened that one of the couples nearby had brought a Polaroid Swinger, and we had the young lady snap a quick picture of Paul, the doc, Cliff, and me. The camera flash made the beehive woman scream out loud. That was the end of Wesley's Pasadena revelry, but after the photo slowly came to life, perfectly placed in the background of us four smiling bandmates was a crouching man's bald head half wrapped in a green wool coat.

The Pokes laughed about that photo for the rest of our time together. Two weeks later, Wes' wife made him quit the band. We replaced him with a 68-year old fiddle player.

I didn't party with the ball players like I did back in my New York days. I was the same age as their grandpappies, and they just weren't in any hurry to get to know me beyond asking for more towels. Their assumption was that dragging an old man along would be a real fun sponge. From my point of view, I was a lot tamer and wiser than in the days when I couldn't tell cotton from corn, so why on God's green Earth would I want to watch 20-year olds act the fool. But every so often, things wound up coming together. In very small doses, it could make a body feel younger.

I don't recollect what prompted it, but when a bunch of the fellows was headed to the Crystal Pistol on a Friday night at the end of May, they asked if I wanted to tag along. We had started the '68 season four and oh before young Nolan Ryan of the Mets beat Dierker. By the end of May, we was still hanging in there. Cuellar and Dierk were throwing good. We wrapped up a trip to Atlanta with an 11-0 shutout, and then Dierk outdueled Fergie Jenkins on our first game back at the Dome. That was the night in question. The record was almost back to .500, and the mood was dandy.

I can't tell you precisely who all went, but I know one of them was Big John Bateman. He had doubled in a couple and won the game for us. It was unfamiliar territory for John much of the time. He'd had an injury-prone, up and down career coming off a rough dang upbringing, so you rooted for the guy. His big hit was all the sweeter because he had done it in front of a boyhood pal of his from back up in Oklahoma.

Now, like I told you, the girls at the Pistol were well acquainted with the Astros, but they didn't know Big John's friend from Shinola. I wasn't riding in the same car, so I don't know who come up with the idea, but by the time Bateman and his buddy and some of the others piled out of Wade Blasingame's Buick Riviera, Bateman's friend Joey was blind. Not for real, mind you. But they had come up with the notion that it would be a hoot and a holler if they let the dancers believe it was so.

It was a funny visual from the get go. Big John at 6 foot 3 with a face like a caliche cart path, and Joey about five seven and looking like Geronimo's grandson wearing a dark pair of Ray-Bans. He was hanging onto the arms of a couple of the boys, and they proceeded to deposit him on a stool at the bar and ask Gruber the drink slinger to keep watch over their blind friend while they went to the front to enjoy the girlie show.

Joey might as well have been wearing magnet coveralls. Those girls flocked to him like seagulls to Wonder Bread. While Gruber was filling him full of free drinks, two, three dancers at a time were cooing and rubbing all over the boy. Turns out they all wanted to show off their stuff, but tactile-like. They was putting Joey's hands on every part of their bare bodies and making sure he got in a good squeeze.

"Oh, Joey. You don't want to miss these."

"Here, Joey. Do you like that?"

He grinned and groped and pretended to look off in the wrong direction. Every once in a while, he'd growl out some low noise to remind them that he appreciated it all.

For all the times that topless dancers were just in it for the money, that one moment, they were proudly sharing their assets. They were bringing some joy to someone they believed was less fortunate. Joey, of course, felt like he was the most fortunate man alive that night. The best part of it was that not a single fellow from the team ever let on to the girls that the story wasn't 100percent true. After a couple of hours of drinking and laughing, Bateman come back to the bar, and his friend grabbed his arm, and the two of them strolled on out to the car. Oh me. If he's still living, I'd wager Joey from Oklahoma is still boring all the old dudes at his local tavern with the story of his trip to the Crystal Pistol.

Nineteen sixty-nine spring training was interesting. We were back at As-trotown in Cocoa, Florida. The Judge christened it that back when the club changed names, figuring it would have the cachet of Dodgertown, but it never did. That might be because the Dodgers seemed all Hollywood and glamorous. The Houston facilities were excellent, though. Four fenced practice fields. There was laundry and dry cleaning that I didn't even have to do. The club put in a game room with pool tables and ping pong, a television, and there was a cafeteria open during meals. They also had a soft drink machine.

You might note that none of those amenities sound like they'd tempt a 25-year old male of an evening, do they. The City of Cocoa had carved our spring home out of swamps and woods. And don't go confusing Cocoa with Cocoa Beach. That famous burg with bikinis and astronauts was 17 miles distant. If you were an established big leaguer, you could set up housekeeping in a hotel or rental on the seashore, but if you were either single or, Lord help you, in the minors, it was a cinder block dormitory. A handful of the larger party hounds tended to get a tad disgruntled come nightfall.

Those days were also the birth of Black Power as far as the rest of the world knew. The two guys at the Olympics the year before had stirred up a shitstorm in the world of sports. It was also empowering to a lot of the young generation of African American kids, and we had some of them coming through our farm system. Of course, the NAACP had been about Black Power for two generations, but it was not always the thing that made it into the news, I reckon.

There was a young fellow in big league camp that year from Bremerton, Washington name of Dwayne Austin. His daddy had been a mess steward at the Navy Yard there. I'm not sure if that was where Dwayne had that big chip land on his shoulder, but I can tell you that none of the later winds that guided his life had blown that thing off.

I took a liking to another of the youngsters, Cliff Johnson, out of San Antonio. He had bounced around the rookie leagues for a couple years already on account of him being Bam Bam with the bat but Dino with the glove. He was struggling with it I think, and I tried to make him feel welcome and bond with him about music.

One afternoon, as I was picking up equipment from the fields, and Cliff had just finished a session of catching instruction that was no doubt wasted time, I fell in with him walking back to the clubhouse.

"Are you a R&B fan?" I asked him.

"Oh, yeah. Retha Franklin, Marvin Gaye, the Isley Brothers."

"I just found a new album in town last night. Green is Blues by a fellow named Al Green. It's a good one."

Cliff gave me a very skeptical look.

"That's really your kind of music? Not Merle Haggard or Johnny Cash or something?"

"Oh, I like good country and western if it swings. I even dabble in a country band, but my heart has always been with the blues and jazz."

Cliff shook his head a little.

"I'll be damned."

By then, Dwayne Austin, who had yet to say a word to me all camp up to that point, had fallen in behind us. He had even been ignoring me when I dropped fresh towels or picked up his dirty uni, so I tried to hook him in, you see.

"Dwayne, how about you? This Al Green does a version of Summertime that is soulful as all get out."

I had turned to look back at him, and Dwayne bobbed his head a couple of times before he answered.

"Okay, okay. You may have gotten on fine with that music shit when you worked with Stepin Fetchit back in horse and buggy days. Maybe you had common ground. But you and I don't, old man. Get it straight. Learning our music ain't fooling me. It's a new world out there. I ain't gonna give you 'I'm just glad to be here' or 'It's all in the hands of the Lord.'"

My knee jerk reaction was to tell him that I'd seen him in the batting cages, and him having to say that he was glad to be there wouldn't be a problem. Even Cliff threw his eyes open wide wondering where that sudden gout of hate come from.

But truth was that little outburst hurt me deeply. He was looking for the affirmation that he felt he deserved, of course, but I just thought back on my good friends like Herbie and Sam Estill. I wanted to tell him that I'd partied with one of the greatest Negro League teams of all time and smoked reefer with Louis Armstrong, but I didn't. It all had that too familiar ring to it. Truth was that he wouldn't care about my journey, and I didn't know much about his, either. I put it down to youthful anger, and we all three walked on in that uneasy silence.

None of that kind of talk fit the natural flow of our manager at the time. That year it was Harry Walker, as much of an Alabama cracker that ever sullied a dugout floor with chaw. His brother, Dixie, had been with the Yankees for a couple of my seasons, then I knew him as the star hitter of the rival Dodgers in the early 40s.

Folks nowadays know Dixie's name because he was the ringleader against them signing Jackie Robinson, and I'll just say the worst you hear was true. My dealings was with Harry, though.

The fact that he ordered all the unmarried players to be locked in the Cocoa Beach dorms at midnight, and that every player had to run a six-minute mile first thing in the morning did not sit well with anybody. He fined them. He yelled at them in front of everybody else. And when he wasn't being an asshole, he was back slapping to be their buddy.

Harry liked me on account of my Yankees days. He swore he'd met me in 1931 during his older brother's rookie year when he made the trip north and got to hang around the clubhouse with the Babe and Gehrig and all the stars. The guys were always bringing in kids or younger brothers, and the fact is that I likely did meet young Harry, but he didn't make an impression. He was twitchy as all get out as a player, and hyped up like an over-caffeinated spider monkey during his manager days. If he was anything like that as a youngster, I probably put it out of my mind deliberately. When I did know him, of course was with the Reds for half a season in 1949. I gave the man close to a dozen caps in just four months because he wore them plum out fidgeting with the things.

Nowadays you still find people who think like Walker, but at the end of the 1960s, he was most white Americans. He'd earned a Bronze Star in the war, but anything that didn't fit into Harry's American textbook was to be feared or ridiculed. Women shouldn't work, everyone ought to speak English, God damn it, and Blacks were lazy. In those days, he might have been from Boston or Chicago, but his people was Alabama and Mississippi. And that didn't help.

One story I heard was that Harry encouraged young Bob Gibson at St. Louis when Solly Hemus rode his ass all year long, and that may be true. I know for a fact that his coaching turned Bill White around at the plate. He made up for it all in Houston, though. It was not so much any open name calling as it was just different treatment. A Black player had to live up to a higher standard, like Harry was testing him, trying to provoke a reaction. He belittled Don Wilson so bad on a road trip that Little Joe Morgan had to hold Wilson back from beating the dog snot out of the manager. Later Harry thanked Joe for saving him, and Joe basically told him, you dumbass, I didn't do it for you.

The clubs all had Black players, of course, but most of baseball management expected them to be quiet about it. In Harry's world, there was the White way and no other. He might not have used the worst language to player's faces, but "you people" was never far from his mindset.

Jimmy Wynn had grown up in Cincinnati just down the street from Crosley Field. His father was a garbage man that may have picked up my very own trash. The Reds were scouting him in high school the last year or two I was up there. I'd like to say I remembered him as a kid, but I didn't. In that regard, he was no different than me remembering Harry Walker.

Wynn was a power hitter, the best the Astros had ever had up to that time. His swing already had the sweetest groove on the team, and Harry Walker wanted him to choke up and slap at the ball just like Harry had. It was loony. Harry got after Morgan's swing the same way, but he never said boo about the swings of the established White hitters.

There's no doubt that Harry ragged Jimmy harder than anyone else on the team. If there was a general ass-chewing that Harry figured needed to be handed down to the whole club, he singled out the players of color. Most every time, that included Jimmy Wynn.

I was real sympathetic with Wynn and Morgan and Wilson. Hell, Jimmy was one of the nicest people you ever met. I've always considered myself a good person, you understand. My daddy, in his way, brought me up to be kind to all folks, and that's the hard part. Harry could be a friendly enough fellow about 85 percent of the time. He talked non-damn-stop. Larry Dierker said that Harry was the only fellow alive who would keep jawing right through his own golf swing. I'd known people like Harry Walker my whole life, but never give them too much thought. It could've been any one of them that started to open my eyes a little, but it wasn't.

We had some really good players on those Astros teams. A few years later, they could have filled out a whole All-Star squad with players that drooling fool Spec

Richardson traded away. He will go down in history as the worst general manager ever in the game. Not everyone got along, though. Like any other group of 25 adults, they formed cliques of close friends, and part of what kept the little groups apart was the damned manager. Harry was fine for those who didn't have racism as part of their world, but he made it very difficult for the other players to get comfortable. Makes a body wonder what could have been, don't it?

There's a famous saying that all it takes for bad things to happen is for good men to do nothing. That ain't it exact, of course, but that's the gist of it. How long had I been looking the other way when things didn't affect me personally? Water off a duck's butt, as Babe used to say. Few of us will ever change the world, son, but I reckon justice is everybody's job.

Years later, when I'd reflected and ruminated, the timing of my life lined up a little better in my brain. It become clear to me that there was a correlation between the times I had another depressing run in with Felix and the home stands where I'd watch Harry go after some of the Black players. I'd sure as hell be lying if I failed to admit that my troubles with my own son didn't make me hate Harry Walker just a couple layers deeper.

Chapter Sixteen

There was one of the biggest events in history that took place around then, of course. You wouldn't recollect it, but July 20, 1969 is when man first landed on the Moon. Americans ain't worth a flying shit when it comes to attention span, so they lost interest a few years later, but in the late 60s, everything was all about outer space. It was something. Every little boy in America had a model Saturn rocket, and every pair of eyes in the world was tuned to Houston.

As far as me personally, it was during the All-Star Break. Dierker and Menke were the club's representatives in D.C. where the ballgame was, and the rest of us were left to our own devices. The landing was on a Sunday afternoon, and Paul come by in his new Ford LTD to pick me up. It was a sort of metallic lime color with a black vinyl top. It had hidden headlights that made it look like the grill was squinting into the sun. We stopped at the corner store and grabbed driving around beers, safely slipped into their little brown paper sleeves. Our plan was to find someplace special that befitted the occasion, but after a quarter tank of gas, which did not take you very far in a '69 LTD, we still couldn't decide, so we pulled into the Rich-Man.

It was typical Houston July, as hot and sticky as Totie Field's thigh. The rolling doors were open, but it wasn't helping. You'd get stronger breezes from your snoring grandma. With sweat dripping down every crack, we was all crowded around a black & white Zenith that sat atop a piece of carpeted plywood up over the cash register.

There was this cranky old Cajun freight hauler who hung out there named Jeff Dubuclet. He was a set-up man, as opposed to beer. Canadian Club and

Seven-Up. I'm saying that back in those days before liquor by the drink, you could bring your own bottle of hooch and pay the bar for a soda and a glass full of ice. Someone had gifted Cajun Jeff, as we cleverly called him, a carrying case for his whiskey that was in the shape of a miniature golf bag. Some of the regulars would jack with him by stealing the tees off the outside which prompted loud cussing in two languages.

Cajun Jeff was on his fourth bottle of Seven-Up, and as it was nearing time for Neil Armstrong to poke his head through the hatch, he started asking to change the channel. Since this was the biggest thing that had ever happened before, the Moon landing was the only option except for this lone UHF outlet that did reruns and wrestling. He was whining because he was going to miss an episode of Topper. He had the major hots for Anne Jeffreys, you see. Or more precisely, for her character, Marion Kerby.

Now, people everywhere were kind of holding their breath. We'd never been to the Moon, and as much as your heart was brimming with American pride, there was this tiny fear in the back of your mind that some green-antennaed alien was going to jump from behind a boulder and snatch Buzz's helmet off. The world was trying to concentrate, but Jeff kept getting louder.

I'd quote him, but all we could make out in that Cajun slur was Marion, cher and ghost titties. I was getting a little hoarse from telling him to shut up. That's when Paul started laughing, one of those laughing fits where you can't stop. About the time that Jeff got up and tried to stagger around the bar to switch over to Topper, I caught the giggles, too. A couple of the huskier women in the joint hopped up from a picnic table and tackled Cajun Jeff as he was trying to hop high enough to reach the TV knobs. When his pants fell down and the three of them tumbled into a heap on the concrete, I got to tell you that it was the last thing that registered.

Paul and I were still guffawing and wiping our eyes when the magic first step was long over. The only person who had stayed glued to the screen was Old Man Sakowitz. He wore a patch over one eye and a Coke bottle lens on the other, and he was deaf as a fence post. Not surprisingly, he had misheard everything.

"One tall mannequin," he kept hollering. "The astronaut said that was 'one tall mannequin'. What did he mean by that? Did somebody else beat us up there? I think somebody beat us up there."

It may have been the first moon landing conspiracy theory. Crazy bastards. But I'll never forget where I was, that's for certain.

It was a good year all in all – 1969. That was the first time the Houston ball club was ever in what you might consider, well, I wouldn't call it a pennant race, exactly, but we was in damn good shape late in the season. We started September winning 6 out of 7. We pounded the yak snot out of Don Sutton on a Wednesday night to pull 10 games over .500. It tied us with the Dodgers, and we was only two lousy games out of first place. Two games. It was rarified air in that no Astros team had ever been there before.

If you'd have heard that prediction back in April, you wouldn't have believed it. Spec Richardson, who still gets my vote for the ass end worst general manager in the history of the game, had virtually given away our best hitter and one of our starting pitchers over the offseason. The others guys stepped it up, though. Dierker, Don Wilson, Tom Griffin, and Denny Lemaster. The Dome was a pitchers park, of course, but they set the all-time National League strikeout record. We were unhittable at home. The trouble was that on the road, well, they couldn't have won the clap at a Hanoi whorehouse. The slide started the very next night. The Dodgers and Claude Osteen outdueled Don Wilson 1-0, then we went 1 for 900 on a road trip, and that was that. The boys had never been there before and didn't know how to act, I reckon. You get the tuxedo on, but you can't work the cumberbund.

Into the middle of that here come Jim Bouton working on his book. Ball Four, I'm talking about. It was famous. I'd catch him a time or two talking into a little tape recorder after most guys had cleared the locker room. Couldn't make out what he was saying, though. I got no personal quibbles about anything he wrote, though I was never mentioned then, was I? Some of the guys thought it was all funny, and some got their noses out of joint. Joe Morgan was one of the fellows who felt betrayed by the whole thing. It made others of them famous, whether they'd ever admit that to themselves or not.

You know, between us and the Seattle club, Bouton pitched more than 120 innings that year. More than he'd done in four seasons. And he'd thrown 73 more in 1970 before he decided the cold shoulders from those inside baseball might not be worth bucking, especially when your coaches and managers didn't believe in you anyhow. But putting aside all the knotholes cut into dugout walls so the guys could ogle up a woman's skirt, it was a really book about the anxieties of trying to hang on to a fading career, wasn't it? It's hell to be an old man at 30, to be washed up in your chosen profession, to know that the fans, who you sometimes loved and sometimes hated, would never scream for you again. I watched it happen a thousand times, you know. Sure, it made me sad, and I kept thanking myself that such a thing never happened to equipment managers.

Birthdays and age have never meant much to me. As I told you at the outset, January 1 is a lousy time for a kid to have a birthday, so maybe that's the sticking point. But there I was about to turn 70, and I still had some notion that I ought to be with somebody. Share my life, as they say. I think it was as much or more for the sake of convention as it was any personal emptiness, but then what do I know. Most men of the early 20th century were not known for being in touch with their emotional needs.

I reckon what I'm saying was that I still had a dating mindset, a traditional idea that I needed to go through the whole tap dance of meeting for dinner or movies and trying to impress one another. From time to time, a circumstance would present itself whereupon I would find myself in an enjoyable conversation with an available woman, and as a given mutual laugh subsided, I'd find myself suggesting we meet up for dinner sometime. And that right there would be the first step on the inevitable road to disappointment and shared disgust. Sounds a mite negative, but it's true.

Between Thanksgiving and Christmas that year I found myself sitting at the bar of a spot called the Marquis Lounge on West Gray. It was in a strip shopping center next to the toniest neighborhood in Houston, but I didn't hold that against it. The bartenders were nice, and they poured generous drinks. In my many previous stops in there I'd found the snooty folks would leave you alone and the genuine ones might offer up some delightful bar banter.

That's how I felt when a trim lady who appeared to be about my age climbed up on the stool one over from mine. I could tell by the way she dressed that she likely belonged to one of those fancy sprawls of a two-story house around there, so I made no move other than to give her a smile and a nod. She was probably ten minutes into her first drink before she said a word.

"I have always thought rye whiskey was made for a chill night like this."

It's still one of the finest opening lines I ever heard. You find out right off what kind of drinker you're talking to. It's the same strategy that complimenting the pork sausage sandwich is a great way to weed out any vegetarians.

I told her I agreed with her, and we proceeded to visit for nigh on two hours before I realized it. We just talked about stuff. Things. Movies. Favorite buildings that were no longer there. I hadn't learned much of anything about her personally beyond that she was a widow who could hold her liquor. Somewhere along the way we made plans for a date the next night, and I was happy to let her chose the place.

The lady wanted to go to Farrell's ice cream parlor in the new Galleria. Now I am not lactose intolerant or anything, but at age 70, or close to it, after approximately a half gallon of cherry vanilla, a person's gut gets a titch uncomfortable. It's a worry that the elderly might carry in the back of their mind. When we got there, she decided to order something called a Zoo. I reckon it got that name for one of two reasons - either because it would feed a cage full of baked monkeys or the smell you'd leave in your bathroom the next morning would be reminiscent of the elephant enclosure.

In case you're wondering, the Zoo started with three full bananas, then it was piled with 12 big scoops of ice cream, five flavors of topping, several dollops of whipped cream, a gorilla-sized fistful of chopped nuts, those maraschino cherries that I love so much, and 3 or 4 toy animals. I'm unclear on whether Farrell's was insured against an 8-year old swallowing a plastic hyena.

As we ate our ice cream, I couldn't shake the feeling that this woman was giving me a cold, judgmental eye. Nothing very outward, but a little pinch of the lips at how I handled my napkin. A gentle lift of the eyebrow over the way an old broken finger made me hold my spoon. We weren't drinking, and in the bright glare of sobriety the easy flow of conversation we'd had the previous night was nowhere to be seen. We were both trying, mind you, but the questions would loose a one or two word answer, and that, in turn, would bring a nod or a facial expression that you hoped didn't look fake.

The one that left me speechless was from one of my attempts. I summoned up my most caring tone of voice.

"So, if I might ask, when did your husband pass away?"

"Thursday."

It was fine, probably, but I did have a small fear that she'd want me to be her plus one for the man's funeral. I'd certainly had worse experiences, but I imagine that was the moment when I disappeared from what I'd call the dating world. I started to value the notion of companionship, and companionship is supposed to be a warm, breezy current, the way I figure it. It's what I enjoyed with Jenny or Pearl, of course. Part of what I enjoyed. I wasn't expecting anything that snug to come along again, but I decided right then that I was tired of working so dang hard to impress a woman. I've no doubt I was late to the party with that one, but I would have to say it come to me about the time I wiped strawberry topping off my chin and excused myself for the men's room at the Houston Galleria. It was a satisfactory bus ride home.

"Good evening, Mr. Rube."

It startled me, though how I could have missed a man so heavy that he was making his open top convertible list like a racing catamaran, I couldn't tell you.

"Why don't you let me give you a lift home tonight? You can take a night off from the bus."

It was late September of 1971. I had just walked out the loading dock at the Dome, and hung a left to where I caught the bus over on Fannin. There was something about Sweet Jello's tone, sitting there at the curb, that stopped me from asking any questions. Besides, I can't deny that I just wanted to ride in his car. It was a brand new Cadillac Eldorado convertible. The '72s had only been out about a week, but here it was - long, sleek, and pewter grey with a red interior that felt like sitting in whipped cream.

Jello let me get my oohing and aahing out of the way before he got to the point. Finally, as we crossed over the Braes Bayou Bridge, he commenced.

"Mr. Rube, I was hoping that you might let me help you with something."

I was confused since I didn't have any idea that I had problems.

"I hate to be the bringer of bad news, but your oldest granddaughter got arrested tonight."

It brought a physical reaction. The whole thing caught me off guard. It took me a minute to realize what it was. I'd never really had a parental responsibility before. Shit, I was past 70 years old, and I'd never had much in the way of responsibility at all. After a time, I regained myself and asked him what happened.

"Oh, it's nothing serious. She was part of some high school kids that got caught up in a Vietnam War shindig. Somebody took the occasion to break into a TV store, and HPD rounded up a bunch of protestors. They got no imagination."

"Jello, how did you know I had a granddaughter? I've never even met the girl. And she's only 15 or something."

"She's a good girl, Mr. Rube. Not anyone like I run around with, so don't you worry about that. I just hear things is all. You're my friend, Mr. Rube, even if we ain't exactly drinking buddies. You're still my friend."

"You said you could help?"

Sweet Jello laughed.

"Yeah. I got this client who is a desk sergeant at Reisner Street. He pictures himself being kinda hard boiled, but he don't know shit about college football. Chinga. Baylor." He laughed to himself. "I imagine it won't take much to get a favor."

The conversation was throwing me a lot of curve balls, as they say.

"I really appreciate it, Jello. I really do."

"You probably don't know my neighborhood, Mr. Rube, but it's called Denver Harbor. Did you know that, as far as per capitas, more Mexicans have got drafted into the Army than anyone? There are five or six of my homeboys from growing up who have lost sons in this pinche war. It breaks my heart. I just figured that your granddaughter might be the type who wants to go to college someday, and she don't need this kind of shit on no permanent record. Besides, I think protesting something ought to be a badge of honor, not an arrest."

Of course, I agreed with that, but the why of it was still marinating. I said the first thing that come to mind.

"That's a mighty hopeful sentiment."

Sweet Jello laughed again.

"Hopeful people are my business, Mr. Rube. All those hopeful people."

"And I'd be happy to have a drink with you someday, Jello."

"Yeah. That'd be cool. Some night I'll stop by the Rich-Man."

Chapter Seventeen

I had become a fixture at some of my haunts by then. I'd been a Houstonian for over a decade, and just being around Southerners again made me feel comfortable. I reckon I never knew I missed it, but people down here are just friendlier. Leastwise when they ain't trying to kill you.

I knew a lady in those days name of Mary Garcia, hairdresser by trade, but a real look at me type. Always posing and injecting a touch of drama into an evening. Rumor around the T&H was that she was married to some old slob who had lost interest, but I can't confirm or deny, as they say. She hit all the different beer joints within several miles, and likely would run off with any guy who bought her drinks, but from what I'd heard tell from the youngsters in their 40s and 50s, she didn't put out that much. Still, it was a total crap shoot on your bar tab. We called it throwing a Hell Mary.

Even though it was just an ice house, Mary liked to dance to the jukebox. I think she could close her eyes and feel like she was someplace fancier. She longed for that. It was a pleasant distraction to the fellow, too. Mary was shapely and soft. That might have been a product of her diet, though I have no idea what that entailed since she steadfastly refused to eat in public. During times when everyone else was enjoying burgers or brisket from the rusty old grill that sat out back of every ice house, she had nary a nibble. A group of us would stagger down to One's a Meal after last call at midnight, but she never come along. She was still walking and breathing, but how was a mystery.

One slow night at the Rich-Man, we was shooting the shit at the bar, and some Patsy Cline come on the juke. Mary asked me if I wanted to dance. Now I was 70 years old, and she was maybe 45, but I was still of a mind to enjoy the touch of a woman. We was slow dancing, or maybe sort of drunkenly hugging to music, in a wide spot between the tables, when I kept hearing little noises. It took me two thirds of "Walking After Midnight" to recognize a fart. Well, more than one. Her butt sounded like the Jetson's car. High toned and musical, really. I guess that's why I couldn't place it at first. It blended right in like a tiny steel guitar.

It also was a revelation. When you're young, a partner ripping cheese on a dance floor would be petrifying, but when you're 70, it ain't necessarily a deal breaker. In fact, the dancing was good enough that I bought her two more cans of Schlitz.

My apartment was only four blocks away, and it was a nice night, but Mary insisted on giving me a ride. She'd had the same Buick Skylark since I'd known anything about her, but she said she wanted to show me her car.

I'll be damned if she hadn't decided to give the old man a go. We pulled up in front of my little building, and before I could find the door handle, she slid over and stuck her tongue in my mouth. Hell, I would gladly have invited her up, but she was intent on doing it right there in the car. She pulled her little miniskirt up and hopped on top of me, fumbling at my sansabelt. I was trying my best to cooperate, but right about the time some fellow strolled by with a French Bulldog on a leash, I got the worst cramp in the back of my thigh. Not surprisingly, she mistook my moaning and writhing for something romantic, but I swear to you that the only passion I had right then was for getting her off me and stretching my leg out. It was quite the wrestling match and lasted well longer than I desired. By the time she faked something loud and dramatic, I was damn near dead from pain, and the dude with the dog was totally winded.

I continued seeing Hell Mary at the various ice houses for several years, and occasionally, she'd snag me for dancing, but that night in the Skylark was never repeated. As for all the regulars who speculated over cold beer that Mary never put out, I knew them to be damned liars.

As far as the ball club was concerned, they replaced Harry Walker with Leo Durocher, of all people. He had been a pretty good manager back in New York, at least as far as results went. By the time he got back into the game with the Cubbies, you had players that were making good money. Rumors of something like free agency was coming. There were better athletes who had the options to make real dough on the basketball court or football field, and, unlike in the 1940s, they were TV stars. All of that meant that they were not going to put up with Durocher's assholian ways. He durn near come to blows with Ron Santo, and that chippiness in the clubhouse might have been one reason he managed to blow a nine game lead at the end of 1969. That was a negative swing of 17 games to the Mets, who was not near as good a ball club from where I was sitting.

You remember that story about the Babe beating the living shit out of Leo Durocher because he was convinced that the little bastard stole his watch? I sure hadn't forgot that in 1972. It was the first thing that come to mind when they signed "the Lip" as manager of the ball club. Now, I'd see him all the time when he was managing the Giants and then during his comeback with the Cubs, but I always had the feeling that he couldn't quite put his finger on where he knew me from. That's the plus of dealing with a self-absorbed shitheel, I suppose. A few times over the years, I'd catch him staring my direction with a mixture of question and stink eye. Like he knew he didn't like me but wasn't sure why.

From my end, there were a lot of reasons to dislike that son of a bitch. He was dishonest, mean-spirited, a show boat, and wouldn't know a real sense of humor if it was a snapping turtle hanging off his nut sack. When the Cubs would come through town a few years previous, Wayne Chandler and the boys up in the big electronic scoreboard would play those cartoons just hoping to make Durocher go off. It was not a long trip.

He complained about the playing surface, and the scoreboard boys mocked him. He ripped the phone off the dugout wall, and the Judge sent him a bill. It was so easy getting in his craw and so much fun. Then Spec Richardson, I reckon just to underscore what a dumbass he was, goes and hires Durocher to come to Houston and manage.

I'll tell you right up front, that it run through my mind that my time in baseball was at an end, that he'd peg me for sure as one of the Babe's gophers, and see me escorted to the clubhouse door. He never did, though.

I can't swear that I've ever used the term self-improvement, or even thought about it, but I will admit that this was about the time I made a concerted effort to expand my horizons a touch. That year, 1972, was the year that the fancy new Hyatt Regency opened in downtown Houston. I may have let drop to you that I've always had a fascination for elevators. Simple man, I reckon. Those elevators were humdingers, though. They had a glass wall so you could see a show while you were going up or down. It was a magical thing, and I'd sometimes take the bus down there with elevator riding being part of my agenda. It's important to take your fun where you find it.

It was a good year for music. Folk and R&B and rock and country, you'd find all of those things in the top 40 charts. My favorite new discovery that year was Jackson Browne. Something about him. He had a bluesy spirit to that folk rock. I bought his first album at the Record Rack on Shepherd by my apartment, and I damn near wore it out.

That was a fine little store. There was a bigger, fancier one over on Westheimer and Kirby, but I liked the one that was a little scruffier. The kids in there knew their music. It's not like today where you go to a book store and none of the clerks seem to have every read one. The people at the Record Rack sought the job for the 20percent employee discount.

There was a long-haired kid named Derek who I recollect. Owned two sets of clothes, as far as I could tell. Navy t-shirt with navy pants and brown t-shirt with brown pants. He also wore sandals, even on those rare days the temperature dipped into the 30s. But I knew I could ask Derek what was good, and he'd turn me onto something. By the same token, he genuinely appreciated some of the old blues singers I related to him. One day there was a knock on my front door. When I opened it, there stood Derek. It was a navy day, and he was on his way to work, but just wanted to say thanks in person for telling him about Mississippi John

Hurt. He said he'd hunted down a single of "You Got to Walk That Lonesome Valley," and it made him smile and cry. That Derek was a man beyond his years, he was.

I also started watching birds. One day I was walking home from the Minimax, I saw the prettiest blue bird I'd ever spied in my life. Blue that was bright enough to put your eye out. I found out later, after asking around, that it was an indigo bunting. Seek one out if you've never been so blessed. It brought to mind my long-lost Cincinnati drinking buddy Brody Bryne.

That bird prompted me to find the bus route to Memorial Park. It was in the middle of the city, but it was the biggest expanse of wilderness we had. There were a few open places down a bank by the bayou where you could sit on a log and feel like you were really out in the woods. It would recharge a body, if you needed it.

Our next manager for the club was Preston Gomez, one of those great examples of how a fellow can have a job for life just by being a good baseball man, whatever that might mean. Gomez was from Cuba where they hold baseball closer than a Croat woman and her rosary beads. He sure didn't get there on account of being a star player. He played in eight games for the Washington Senators in 1944. Now that's eight big league games more than me, mind you, but 1944 was in the middle of the war. Shit, they were signing midgets and guys with one arm.

No, sir. I reckon Gomez stuck around because he was one hell of a nice guy. He coached for good teams and bad ones, in Canada, Mexico, Cuba, and all over the damn place. When the ball club decided to wash the stink of that asshole Durocher off of them, Gomez was the perfect choice. We was .500 his first year, though that was the season he pinch hit for Don Wilson while he was in the eighth inning of a no-hitter. In spite of what Don said, I don't think that one ever wore off. It would have put him with Koufax as the only National Leaguers to ever throw three or more. Tough gristle to swallow.

Of course, poor Don died in the off season. He never saw that third one, and I think he might have had it in him, too. He sure had all the talent. His first no hitter against the Braves back in '67 was some of the best throwing I ever witnessed. All fastball and slider, moving all over the damned zone. Ended the thing by blowing one by Henry Aaron.

Don was generous, bitter, open, moody, friendly, and sometimes overwhelmed. Like a lot of people, I suppose. His end was as much a tragedy as you run across in baseball, but sad to say, not unique.

When we showed up to spring training down in Cocoa and saw the black uniform patch with number 40 on it, a little wind fell from guys' sails. Couple that with the ownership kerfuffle, and, well, it wasn't good. There was some young talent on that team, but nobody put much of anything together in 1975. One of the worst years the ball team ever had, and Gomez never made it to September, neither.

There was one high point from Florida that year, as I recollect. It's the tale of Ronnie Bingle, the hippie squatter. That wasn't his real name, mind you. It was just the name that Rader give him the morning that he found the guy standing nekkid in his kitchen making eggs.

See Doug Rader and Tom Gottlieb, two of the older guys at 30, had rented them a house for a couple of months. Dierker or Joe Niekro, one of them fellows was supposed to be with them, too, but at the last minute, whichever one it was decided to let his wife come over. It left Rader and Tommy with a spare bedroom.

I don't reckon I've mentioned Gottlieb. Never made much of a splash with the ball club, but he stuck around as an extra outfield bat for four or five seasons, and that is a long time to be a bench player. The rest of the guys loved him, because he was both good hearted and crazy as a one-eyed capybara.

Tommy Gottlieb earned himself the nickname of Oxtail around the Astros clubhouse. You know what boning a bat is, don't you? Hell, son, how'd you miss that? Nowadays, most big leaguers use maple bats, but when I was in the clubhouses, they were ash, and an ash bat needs to be boned. Least that is the tradition.

Ash wood is flexible, let's a body whip the bat through the zone, but it is also soft. So, some genius back a century and a half past, come up with the notion that rubbing a big heavy bone up and down the barrel would make the wood denser, make the bat last longer and give you more pop. The preferred bone is a cow femur. Thigh bone. About the biggest thing available, and something you can grab hold of and bear down. After 80-plus years in hardball equipment, I still can't swear that it works, but everybody thinks it does, so that's good enough for me.

Most of the time, the bat boy gets the job of boning new bats. It's right there in his job title, ain't it? Some guys, though, are natural born do-it-yourselfers. Tommy Gottlieb was one of those.

There wasn't much danger of Gottlieb cracking the Astros starting outfield. Cesar Cedeno, who was one of the most talented players I ever saw, had a spot wrapped up. Early 70s, so did Bob Watson and Jimmy Wynn. Wynn got traded, and Jose Cruz come right in behind him. Watson moved to first, and a young phenom named Greg Gross come along. So, Tommy Gottlieb cracked his jokes and bided his time for a situational at bat now and again.

Not long after Gottlieb come over as the throw-in part of a trade with the Braves at the start of the '73 season, he discovered a soul food joint named This Is It. Ate there three times a week, and maybe more. Round along mid-July, he come hot-footin' into the clubhouse with a greasy sack full of late lunch from the steam table at that fine establishment. He spread everything out in front of his locker and while he slowly got dressed, he was slurping down oxtails and candied yams and boudin balls, and generally annoying everyone else by giving them hunger pangs. Those This Is It yams always reminded me of you know who.

About halfway through this meal, the bat boy comes over with four new Louisville Sluggers with Tom Gottlieb cut into the barrel. Tommy gets all excited, announces he's going to get an RBI with his new bat, and without taking another breath commences to rubbing that piece of lumber down with an oxtail. Trouble was he hadn't finished eating them. So, he'd rub for a bit, gnaw a little, suck some marrow out, and go back to rubbing. In between, he's using a sanitary sock to wipe off juice. Half the boys were doubled over laughing, and half were staring slack-jawed like they just wandered up on a fresh train derailment. The show must have gone on for 45 minutes, I'd bet you. When it was through, Gottlieb looked his work over and pronounced himself satisfied, even though the bat had gained a rich mahogany sheen and a small swarm of houseflies. When the bat boy carried it out to the dugout rack, he was careful to keep it at arm's length.

Sure enough, leading off the bottom of the 10th, Durocher calls down to Gottlieb to pinch hit for Jerry Reuss. Oxtail, as the fellows are already calling him, yanks his new meat stick out of the rack and heads to the plate. Bill Williams was the umpire back there that night, and he starts eyeballing that bat, wondering if Gottlieb had soaked the whole damn thing in pine tar. Billy was finally satisfied, and points out to Mike Marshall on the mound for the Expos. Down to his last strike, Tommy fouled off a two-seam slider, and I swear to Jesus a vertical spray of gravy wiped across the faces of the catcher and ump. It looked like a soul food crime scene. Jimmy Wynn was on deck, and I reckon he let go a little squirt of pee from laughing so hard. As much as Wynn was the Toy Cannon and Rader was the Rooster, Tommy Gottlieb was nothing but Oxtail ever after.

But back to that spring of 1975. Now, finding a stranger in their birthday suit comes in stride to a lot of ballplayers, though it was normally a stewardess and not some long-haired dude with a spatula. For a guy like the Rooster, though, whose idea of a good time was shitting on birthday cakes, you roll with the punches.

Rader opened with the obvious question.

"Who the hell are you?"

Now this was the 1970s, when folks was busy getting in touch with their consciousness, and those who considered themselves more enlightened would cut some slack for the hippies. It was also back in the reasonable days when ballplayers, or anybody, for that matter, didn't have automatic rifles laying around on the couch.

"I have been called Ronnie, I think, but the owl is most definitely named Teeter," the hippie told Rooster.

Sure as shooting, there was a barred owl perched on the back of a kitchen chair just looking at Rader big as you please. Normally, a body would notice that first, but a six and a half foot nekkid hippie with a skillet will tend to distract you.

"We've moved into your spare room, man. How do like your eggs?"

"Hold on there, chief," Rooster said. "Does the owl bite?"

It turned out that Teeter the owl had his wing hurt real bad when a tree in which he was perching got struck by lightning, and Ronnie rescued him. Fed him, nursed on him, and for his part, the owl followed the big guy around like a puppy. He couldn't fly, but he hopped along behind Ronnie just as close as if he'd been on a leash.

The last name come about cause of Ronnie insisting that last names were bourgeois. Rooster looked the guy up and down and said, "Well, that sure ain't a home run pecker, so we'll call you Ronnie Bingle."

Though there never was any explanation as to how the man found out about the spare room, the boys let him stay all spring. When it was time to break camp and head on back to Houston, Ronnie baked a big box of oatmeal cookies and waved the boys goodbye. For all I know, he might be 75 years old and still there, sleeping in somebody's guest bed.

The best way I can describe him is kind of like a hippie Jethro Bodine. Rader was a big man at 6'3", and Ronnie Bingle had him by a good three inches. Part of the agreement letting him stay was that he do the cooking and start wearing pants. He met the boys half way, sporting a pair of blue jean cut offs and green suspenders. He had him a big bushy beard with a tiny red ribbon tied into the bottom of it.

One day, Oxtail decided they needed to get Ronnie a date. It was likely more of an experiment to see what Ronnie did on a date, really, and I must say as far as entertainment value, he didn't disappoint.

The fellows had run into three women from the local NOW chapter at the ball yard who coerced them into going out for a few cocktails, and they was all too willing to say that they would bring along the most famous pitcher on the team,

Ronnie Bingle, who was a shy lad poised to get a very rich contract. The hook was baited.

They went home and dressed Ronnie after they made sure he showered and whatnot. Though he was reluctant to leave the house, fearing it was a ruse to change the lock or something, he agreed after they said he could bring Teeter. What they didn't realize until later was that Big Ronnie had comforted himself by licking a few squares of LSD just about the time they got to the lounge, which was in some kind of upscale Chinese restaurant.

Things was humming along pretty copacetic for two rounds of drinks until they decided to move over to the restaurant side of this establishment. The acid kicked in about the same time as the Crab Rangoon. The Rolling Stones were playing on the jukebox when Mick Jagger interrupted his lyrics to speak directly to Ronnie, telling him that he, and he alone, could spread the gospel of world peace.

Ronnie started with the other five people at the table. Oxtail and Rooster, of course, just leaned back and egged him on. This was proving to be even better than they'd hoped.

When Ronnie, with Teeter hopping along behind him, started going from table to table suggesting that the diners take a minute to end all wars and hug each other, well, let's say they was less receptive than Oxtail and Rooster had been.

Ronnie realized at once that he needed to really grab everyone's attention. He did what he did best. Stripped down buck nekkid. His Texas leaguer johnson bobbing as it pleased. Climbing up on top of the giant Buddha was a new twist, though, and when the barred owl jumped up on his shoulder, I'd wager it made for one of the weirdest totem poles that the central Florida coast had ever witnessed.

The manager had a hell of a time getting them out the door on account of Rooster kept saying that this was perfectly acceptable behavior in Ronnie's country.

Chapter Eighteen

The Broken Pokes had pretty much run their course by the middle of the '70s. One of the fellows died, and another had his kids move him into a nursing home and take away his car keys. Then Cliff, our lone talent, got married of all things, and he and the new missus moved to a house on Lake Livingston. He said he might even learn to water ski. All that meant that we ended up back in the shit gigs where we started out.

We did manage one great hoorah on the way out of show business, such as it was. There was a fellow out in Baytown, other side of the San Jacinto River and halfway to Beaumont, who retired from oil field work and bought him an ice house. Now, my belief is that if you run a comfortable place and charge a fair price for extra cold beer, customers will come in. This gent, however, reckoned that he needed to add music.

We'd played there once before, and it happened to standing room only. It had nothing to do with us, mind you. Our two sets followed the high school football game. In spite of the visual clue that all 80 people in the joint happened to be dressed in maroon and gray, the doofus that owned the place put it into his head that the Broken Pokes were a draw. We were happy to take the back slaps and another round of beers.

When he booked us the second time, it was a Saturday, not a Friday, and it was rainy. The pay was the same – fifteen bucks a man plus the bar tab – and in the end, it was still an ice house in Baytown, Texas. Unbeknownst to us at the time, though, the owner's expectations were higher than a helium duck. He just knew that our gig would cover his weekly nut.

Let me say that until I was hoisted onto the lowest rung of the music business, I always figured that baseball owners were the cheapest bastards on Earth. I'd watched them cut a player's salary after he knocked in 80 runs, but compared to bar owners, the Charlie Comiskeys of the world were rank amateurs. It reminds me of the old joke where a man at the grocery store comes upon a little boy whose face is turning red from choking. The kid's mother is screaming for help, and this here fellow calmly kneel down in front of the lad, grabs him by the scrotum, and starts to squeeze as hard as he can. Finally, the kiddo coughs up a nickel, which the man drops into his own pocket.

"Thank you so much! You saved my son's life. Are you a doctor?" the mother asks him.

"No. Divorce lawyer."

That's the kind of nickel and dime thinking that a bar owner employs every time they hire some band.

I don't even need to tell you that we played three sets that night for about ten or twelve of the bar's regulars. When it come time to settle up, after I'd hauled our little PA and amps out to the various car trunks, Paul went to the owner. I was still holding onto my own little canvas carryall, but I was gassed, so I plopped onto a bar stool and ordered a cold Schlitz to revive my spirits.

The bossman laid four sawbucks on the bar top, straightened his posture, and looked at Paul.

"Nobody showed up, so you'll have to pay for your beers."

Paul was careful to put the bills into his pocket before he said anything, and I instinctively gulped down the rest of my cold beer. Once the Hamiltons were stowed safely into his Haggar's, Paul leaned close to the bar.

"The bar tab is half our pay. Now give me the other twenty dollars."

Aside from some shaky math, I thought my buddy came across as pretty menacing for a guy in his mid-70s wearing a shirt with embroidered yellow roses.

"You said you were a draw, and I advertised you on the sign."

I peered out through the drizzle toward the road.

"Even if people did know us by name, how the hell is 'Live Band' supposed to tell them we're here?"

I'm pretty sure Dr. Shelly, who's supposed to be all calm and soothing, was the first to break the cuss word barrier when he called the owner a cheap son of a bitch. I definitely recall the new fiddle player, a half-crazed ex-Navy chief who went by Mingo, being the one who first brought up evening the score. He reasoned that if we were getting short changed, we'd just cause twenty smackers worth of damage. He started by pawing a big jar of pickled wieners onto the floor like a degenerate cat.

At that time of night, the band outnumbered the customers 6 to 3 plus the owner and his wife. In the brawl that ensued, there was not a punch thrown by anyone who was not eligible for Social Security. It was mostly slow moving and tame. A table did get knocked over, but it was largely because a fat, drunk beer drinker lost his balance. Kentucky Dan tripped another poor slob with his cane. It sure wasn't like some movie Western where chairs got busted over cowboy's backs because nobody there could lift one.

I've never liked fighting, and probably the last meaningful fisticuffs I was a part of was when Herbie and me got our asses tanned in a Memphis alley, but I'd be lying if I said I didn't get some satisfaction out of socking that cheap sonofabitch owner on the noggin with my tambourine. Dented the instrument beyond playable, but damned if it didn't leave a fine mark. The best part is that the devilish bastard couldn't very well share the true story with anyone either. "You should've seen the tambourine player" just doesn't strike fear in the hearts of men.

You know, one of the great things in life is when young people can learn an important lesson while they still have years ahead to enjoy it. Most every young athlete you see, no matter how humble the talk, harbors the notion that they are on the verge of stardom. I know I contradicted this earlier, but every so often, though, you get one that really and truly is just happy to be there. That situation arose in 1976.

We had a fellow in the organization name of Louis Glendenning, utility man. I never thought he was good enough to break the bigs, but evidently someone disagreed with me cause Louis got him a September call up. As it turned out, young Louis had the same opinion of his talents that I did.

Truth was that Glendenning was nerdier than that boy back in Lee County who collected Boer War trading cards, but he was determined to make the best of his time up in the National League. He had him a little Kodak camera, and he had teammates snapping pictures of him and everybody else. Cedeno, Dierk, Cabell, Cruz, you name it, they all posed with Louis Glendenning. Opposing teams, too. I personally snapped four dozen of the things, including one with both Niekro brothers. I also looked the other way when I noticed him sneaking little things from undershirts to cups out of the building in his gym bag.

Like I told you, Glendenning understood that he was never going to stick in Houston. He never even got an at bat that September, but the way he sealed his fate was unique. He wore his uniform out to a disco. Somehow he got out of the Dome without ever changing into his civvies. Maybe it was raining and he put on a long coat or something with the notion to get some strange tail and go out in a blaze of glory.

His thinking was that all of the hot women would fawn over the chance to bed down with a real live professional ballplayer. But him walking around in a smelly polyester rainbow uniform proved to not at all be the chick magnet he expected. After getting a mix of stink eye and blatant flame outs from some 30 or 40 women, Louis just started doing his own thing. By that I mean knocking back over a dozen Tequila Sunrises at the neon-lit bar.

The evening concluded with his arrest and handcuffing after he refused to stop doing hook slides on the dance floor. The management might have just asked him to leave, except that his cleats were scratching the woodwork pretty bad. The last straw come when he accidentally spiked some bottle blonde in her leggings. Tal had no choice but to give him his unconditional release.

It's easy to be sad over the end of the road, but Louis Glendenning went out happy as a nine-legged spider. He can live the rest of his life knowing that he made it to a Major League clubhouse, and that's something to be proud of. Hell, it'd take me half a day to count all the guys I overheard making that claim falsely. They were signed by the Cubs but threw out their arm, something like that. There was one fellow who cornered me in a bar when I was with the Reds and talked my left ear bloody about how he played four months with the '33 Yankees. I try hard to let these guys have their pretenses, knowing I'll never see them again, but I finally had to set that record straight out of pure self-preservation. Glendenning, though, he'll be the real McCoy, and he has photos of him and Biff Pocoroba to prove it.

Chapter Nineteen

I found out in October of 1979 that Felix had died, about 20 years after his mother. Rabbit Pink gave a ring one afternoon with the news. He'd had a heart attack at work, right in the middle of the rug department. Rabbit said it was quick, so that he didn't suffer. Hell, the customer looking over the sculptured orange shag thought at first that Felix was suddenly demonstrating its pleasant smell.

It was a strange feeling, I'll tell you. I was sad not for the loss of my own boy. Hell, I never knew him other than to be yelled at, lectured, or given the bum's rush. But I suppose I still carried the idea that I had me a son, and the death of that idea made me maudlin.

I reflected on it, and eventually I decided to go to the funeral. I hate funerals more than just about anything I can think of. I'd rather have a horsefly enema. But I went to that one just to say goodbye. It was a goodbye to Pearl as much as anything else, though that thought hadn't quite congealed in my brain yet, I don't reckon.

The service was at the McCoy Funeral Home over in Third Ward. I rode straight down Wheeler Avenue staring out the window, the best dressed person on the bus. Though segregation was supposed to be behind us, it was still a pretty Black part of town back in 1979. I had a haunt or two over that way where people knew me, but to most of the mourners, I figured I would be a tad conspicuous. Thing is though, that the crowd was more mixed than I'd imagined. They must have been people that Felix worked with, I reckon, but there was at least two dozen

White folks and Mexican folks who thought well enough of him to come share a final goodbye.

Did you ever sit in the back row at a funeral? It's a sad but informative show. People mourn in many different ways, and certain folks' passing hits them harder on account of where they might be in their own life, releasing their own stored up troubles. Sure, there were some ladies that are born to be criers. Blubbering and leaking more water than a single-wide's toilet. There were a few of the "amen" folks scattered about in there. And there was some who stared at their shoes or the ceiling. Maybe making sure they looked grim enough, maybe replaying some favorite moment with the departed, or maybe just not wanting to forget the grocery list for the drive home.

I can't tell you why I had expectations that day. I didn't know a damned thing about Felix Rogers. And yet, I was still surprised when a half dozen people stood up to say what a loving daddy and uncle and fishing buddy he was. Even the preacher sounded as if he genuinely liked the man.

When folks finished talking and said a final prayer, I skittered on out the back door. I knew how Felix felt about me, and I sure as shooting wasn't there to bring no hurt and anger. A few had no doubt noticed me and wondered who I was, sitting all alone back there. You know, the trouble with riding the bus is that a quick, clean getaway is about as rare as a lavender fart, especially for a man of 78 years. I shuffled out toward the street and all of half a block away, and there I stood for 15 minutes. Alone in the hot Houston sun, everything I had on glued to me with sweat. Anyone who'd been curious about me sure got an eyeful.

You know what I was feeling riding back on that bus, son? Fear. Yes, sir. I was damned near 80 years old, and though I had a whole passel of folks I called friends, they were really acquaintances, weren't they? Except for Paul. I was an old man in a big city with not a speck of family one. How many of the guys at the ball club or drinking buddies down at the ice house were gonna take me in if I ever needed such a thing? If I come to a juncture where I was unable to take care of myself, well, then what? I sure wasn't rich. There wasn't no private nurse coming to sponge me off at 10, 2, and 4. Nosirree. I was facing the dark unknown all by my lonesome. Those were some quiet nights of drinking down at the Rich-Man.

Two weeks after Felix's funeral, I got the best surprise of my life. No doubt about it. It was a whole déjà vu thing, but different. Two good-looking girls, one about college age, the other a little younger, come to my door. They favored one another around the eyes, maybe the shape of their nose, too, but one was more of a hot tea and cream complexion, and the other was a bright chocolate. They were my granddaughters, and I had memorized their faces from the back of the funeral chapel.

It didn't take me but 15 or 20 seconds to work out that the dark one had more than a passing resemblance to Pearl. It's tough to be honest in hindsight sometimes, but more than likely, I stared at them a little fearful, wondering what kind of scolding I had coming my way this time. Nevertheless, I invited the ladies in. There was a moment or two of awkwardness, but I figured out straight away that my fretting was for naught. Within five minutes they was giving me a hug, and they was just a laughing and giggling like college girls are prone to do.

It is not often in life that a body gets instant karma. My granddaughter's words, not mine. Yet that is what that doorbell was for me. It was as if I'd asked the postman to deliver a mail order family, and he had come through. The youngest one was still in school, seventh grade, and these two thought that she might be too young for this first meeting. Still, Olivia and Natalie, the ones standing before me, didn't want to wait any longer.

I'm not sure if they spotted me at the back of the funeral home that day or not. One or two of them will tell you today that they did, but I think part of that might be revisionist history, as they call it. What I do know, or come to find out, is that there was a carpet installer from Felix's work who knew all about me. Had known about me for years. See, he had never even known who his daddy was, this fellow, and the story goes that one night him and Felix drank about a hundred beers and compared notes. Airing instead of drowning their sorrows, you could say. Estimating which was worse, that your deadbeat father was some no account cracker with a case of jungle fever or that he was just the faceless notion of a drunk or junkie.

All those years later, as he leaned over his dinner plate after the service, this buddy of Felix's overheard one of the relatives asking about that mysterious old white man while he was eating potato salad or green bean casserole. I never even knew his name, but that's who I have to thank for my greatest fortune. In a moment of charity, he figured that with Felix gone there wasn't no harm in telling the tale. As far as he was concerned, the girls deserved the truth.

Now, that might have been the end of it before it started. Sure, it piqued their interest, finding out who their granddaddy was, but I ain't at all sure that it would have made them hunt me down. But then the other shoe dropped, as the saying goes. Or shoe box in this case. As they were cleaning out their dad's house, they'd found a whole passel of letters in their daddy's stuff. Letters from me. For some unknown reason, my boy Felix had saved everything I ever sent him. Part of me likes to think that he wanted to answer one or two of them but never worked up the courage or never decided what to say. A bigger part of me reckons that they were just a touchstone for his hatred, something he could go to if he ever needed to stoke the fires of his resolve. Most of me knows that since he never answered one word I wrote him, there ain't no use in wasting time sorting it out. I never ran into a "coulda" that mattered worth a damn.

It took me a long time, I'll bet two or three years, before I mustered up the courage to ask my granddaughters why they really decided to look at me different than their daddy had. I'd been afraid to bring it up. It's like when a fawn comes out of the woods, and you just stand stock still so it won't run away. There were two of them come to my place for dinner one evening, and I said I wanted to know why they took a chance on me.

It was Natalie that answered. She was the school teacher, you know.

"That was my idea, Pawpaw," she said. "I told everybody straight out that I wanted to know your intentions. We all read those letters, and it was easy to know that the way you treated Grandma Pearl was not right. You'd told our daddy that you were sorry, but I think we wanted to know what was in your heart. It's easy to find hurt, but you don't have to keep it, and you don't have to let it define you. The first time we came to your apartment, it didn't take but 10 minutes to discover that you were a kind man."

My jaw line locked up, and couldn't even answer. But she give me a big hug nonetheless.

Did I tell you I have 5 great-grandchildren, and there are already 10 great-greats? Each one a slightly different hue than the next, too. It's reassuring to me that people come in different shades. If they didn't, it would sure be the world's shittiest box of crayons.

I'll tell you, the different colors of all those young ones reminded me of a comment that Sam Estill made back in the late 30s but never explained. He told me that there were eight or ten players in the big leagues that were passing. He never named names, and I never did get over the idle curiosity.

The 1980 Astros team was the first championship that I'd been involved in for many a year. With the Reds, I'd come too late for 1939 and left too early for 1961. It had been all the way back in 1937 since I'd been part of a post season anything. The twin shitters was that the team almost blew it, and it all happened on the road with me not there.

They went to Los Angeles to close out the season with a three game lead, and for the first time ever in the twenty year history of the ball club, the guys were cocky. We had added the great Nolan Ryan and got Joe Morgan back. But cocky ain't always good, is it? They lost all three. It brought on a tiebreaker, but Knucksie made it a non-issue. It was a 7-1 beat down. I didn't get a locker room squirting with champagne, and the whole drama and sad story of J.R. Richard was never far from our minds, but I've still got to tell you that it felt good.

Of course, I'm sure you've read about the NLCS against the Phillies. I can tell you, son, that out of all the World Series I'd been a part of in New York, that league series in 1980 was the most exciting by a long shot. The last four games went extra innings. There was some clueless umpire shit, timely hitting, clutch pitching, close plays at the plate, and two or three clubhouse tables splintered by pissed off ballplayers wielding Louisville Sluggers. I stayed up all night between Games 4 and 5 since they had to convert the Dome from baseball to football then back to baseball. And through the three games in Houston, it was the loudest I ever heard a baseball park. Losing stung, of course, but damn, that was some series.

The following year, in 1981, the Astros had a scout run off on them. Seems he had a few too many nips off the flask during a twi-night double header at El Campo High School. He hooked up with a like-minded divorcee during the fifth inning, and one of them got the bright idea to hijack the mascot's uniform while the poor kid inside of it took a bathroom break. When the school authorities found the scout, he was busy trying to rear mount a six-foot tall ricebird in an equipment shed. From what I heard, it was the woman screaming "Not that hole!" which called attention to them. He must have been overwhelmed by the embarrassment 'cause the team never heard a squawk out of him again.

I'm sure they must have made 30 or 40 unsuccessful phone calls before they finally asked me if I'd be willing to take over for a month or two. I don't have to remind you that I'd been telling everybody who'd listen that I could scout ball players for better than 50 years. Well, sir, I jumped at the chance quick as a cheetah fart. I'd seen almost everything there was to see in baseball, and I figured that made me the perfect man to evaluate talent.

I needed a driver to get around, of course, and it just so happened that a downstairs neighbor of mine had a son that had just got out of juvie. The boy had smoked a bunch of weed and led a mall cop on a very low speed chase that ended up with him crashing his skateboard into a Whitman's Candylicious store. Between the boy, the mall cop, and a display of cherry cordials, the apprehension of the said criminal took over 45 minutes.

His name was Wallace Spoonheaver, and once I heard that story, I figured he was just my style. Nobody could get hurt with him driving. He had him a beat-to-shit Nash Rambler, mint green with white trim. At some point he had taken the back seat out and replaced it with a folding cot, likely for nefarious purposes, and then he promptly forgot where he left the back seat. We looked like a rolling hospital ward, but it got us where we had to go.

My territory was to be the little towns to the south of Houston, covered about 300 miles or more down to the Rio Grande Valley and Laredo. It should have been good turf for me, but for the first time in my life, I came to understand that a head full of experience might be a double-edged sword, as they say.

I'd go out to look at a good player, and see a little bit of Ty Cobb in the way he held his hands, some Ted Williams in the tilt of his head. Same time, the point of his front foot would look just like my Uncle Stump Dibrell, and that foot wasn't even Uncle Stump's. My daddy always figured that foot had started life as a cedar scratching post since the little knot where his index toe should have been used to itch him something fierce.

Do you follow what I'm trying to tell you? There was too many memories in this old head of mine. Old worn out memories, as Willie said. My time for concentrating had done gone. Turns out mine was a young man's dream. Or at least younger than 80.

On top of that, moving from place to place just didn't hold the appeal it had once. My folding chair by the clubhouse door had a pad on it, and the years had shaped it to my butt bones like it was a just right pair of jeans. In less than three weeks I'd figured out that traveling ought to be done by someone who had less baggage. So, I retired from scouting.

I can see that shocks you. The question you want to ask is: Why in this grand world would I finally reach one of my goals and then chuck it all in? Well, let me tell you something about getting old. One of the hardest things to come to grips with is recognizing when your opportunity has arrived too late. Dirty Harry was right. A man's got to know his limitations.

I'm sure you've heard the old saying that you're only as old as you feel. Well, that's a bunch of horse shit. Don't get me wrong. You go through the vast majority of life looking at the young girl and thinking you still have a shot or figuring that one of these days soon you'll get a chance to finish your novel or take up oil painting. Eventually, though, your old hands won't let you hold the brush steady.

There's things that have been on my mind for many years that I know I'll never get to do, and it makes me sad. I'll never get to Australia to see kangaroos and penguins. That was one of my big imaginings, riding in an open jeep with kangaroos hopping alongside, sun on my face and red dust in my mouth. I pictured them smelling like a big sheep dog, and thought if I sat real still, one might come close enough for me to get a whiff.

Silly things. Playing the accordion. Scuba diving. I always wanted to learn how to bake an éclair. Boy, do I love those things. Well, I reckon you can't do it all.

Interesting postscript to the story of my retirement, though. I was only an Astros scout for the grand total of eighteen days, but I did sign me a player. It was way down in the Rio Grande Valley, a little town called Lyford, Texas. After you crossed the King Ranch and the Yturria and maybe another one, you popped out into irrigated green country, and Lyford was maybe five miles past that. The only landmarks in the whole damn town were a water tower and a cotton gin. Maybe a Fina station, if I recollect.

I was headed to Harlingen to see a big pitcher, left-hander, but we were a day early, and as we passed through Lyford, there was a ball game on the field just off the highway, so I told Wallace to pull in. The Bulldogs were playing the Port Isabel Tarpons, and it was the top of the third.

There wasn't no charge, so we clambered up a bleacher down the first base line, and I let that warm Valley sun heat up my bones. That's a thing about getting old. Most days you just can't get warm enough, so it was nice out there. Certain odors were in the air, too. I found it kind of pleasant. One of them I identified as fresh onions, a field full of them. It wasn't till later that I figured out the other was insecticide from crop dusters. Surprisingly not stinky, but I wouldn't wear it as cologne.

That might have been what cast a spell over me, the onions, not the crop dusters. It was one of those times like I mentioned a minute ago, where my imagination took me back. In this case, I was all the way back to 1918 and a trip

I made with the Chicks to play the Little Rock Travelers. I talked my way into tagging along so I could hop off the train at Forrest City and say hey to my folks who had rode up for the occasion.

I did that when I got a chance, ride with the ball club back then. It was the Choctaw Route of the Rock Island Railroad that run west from Memphis all the way to Tucumcari, New Mexico, a lyrical and mysterious name for a place if ever there was one. That particular train also held a special significance for me at that time since I knew that if a body had the money, he might ride the Choctaw Route to McAlester, Oklahoma, the town where my boyhood hero Joe McGinnity would be puttering around the iron factory during the off season.

But back to Little Rock. In 1918, the Travelers played at Kavanaugh Field. That was on the west edge of town in them days. Today the football stadium for the famous Central High School sits on that very spot. That's the school where the little Black girls had to be protected by the Army, but they sat down in desks next to those Arkansas rednecks, and they earned their diplomas. A good story, that one is.

Well, just the other side of Kavanaugh Field ran a railroad track, and I recollect getting a big unexpected whiff of what must have been a box car full of onions rolling past on a hot day that summer. Interesting team the Travelers had in 1918. Kid Elberfeld was their player manager. You ever hear of him?

The Kid was in his 40s by then, and that would be his last year doing any playing, but he was as scrappy and cantankerous as ever. In his earlier days, his own teammates disliked him something fierce, and the opponents he spiked and baited even more so. On top of that, the man was a bench jockeying fool, so when you played the Kid's teams, you expected to hear a heap of invective about your mama or your tiny manhood. Maybe both. The Kid wasn't exactly Mark Twain.

Like most minor league clubs back in those days, there was a mix of old and young. At least a couple of the boys, Ham Hyatt and Herbie Moran, had seen time up in the show. I noted Herbie right off since he had the same name as my buddy at the rooming house back in Memphis.

Amongst the youngsters was Oscar Tuero, the pudding fiend who I'd come to be friendly with a couple of years hence, and a 19-year old kid at first name of Charlie Grimm. Yep, the same Jolly Cholly who I'd know during my time in Cincinnati. Ain't that something how small a world baseball can be?

You remember I told you about Charlie and some of the Cubs having them a string band? Well, before one of the games on that road trip, he and another fellow was ripping off a few tunes for the early arrivals in the grandstand. They was good, too. I think they were belting a version of *The Cubanola Glide* when Elberfeld made them knock it off. I don't think I ever mentioned that to him. I should have. He was a fun-loving fellow, Old Charlie. More than that, he was a hellacious first baseman, too.

I'd played first base myself, you know, just a year or two prior to the days I'm talking about, so I paid particular attention to the position. Charlie Grimm, though only a couple of years older than I was, put on some kind of show fielding his position that series. He said that he'd learned some of it from the great Hal Chase when he was a ballpark peanut vendor as a kid in St. Louis and Chase passed through to play the Brownies. But some of it was just improvised. I know he snagged at least two wide throws with his bare hands, and that's what the onion scent brought to mind.

See, Lyford had a big first baseman called Ricky Mendoza, and I'll be straight up damned if he didn't make the same reach with his bare right hand on a low throw from third. A real zinger coming in about knee high. His palm made almost the same popping noise that his mitt would have. It woke me up from my sunny slumber, I tell you what.

I just couldn't stop watching Ricky Mendoza. Damn near every move he made in the field was reminding me of Charlie Grimm. And he weren't no slouch with the stick either. He went three for three that first day, two doubles and a single. Good contact.

I went on down to Harlingen to see that pitcher I come for in the first place, but the kid had a blister that made him miss a start. So, we headed back to Lyford,

Wallace and me, where I stuck around for a while and saw Ricky two or three more games. Met his family even.

You did that when you scouted a kid. It's not just how they play, you got to know if they can behave themselves in the clubhouse and hotel, too. You don't want to find out after you sign him that everybody in his family carries on like a hopped-up nutria rat, swinging from chandeliers and chewing up the furniture.

The Mendozas was right nice folks. His grandmother, Irene, was a looker, too, in a Mexican Ethel Merman sort of way. Of course, that could be my cataracts talking. I do know that the last day I was there she brought me leftover chorizo tacos rolled up in foil, and one of them had her phone number tucked inside of it. Or at least six digits with a big orange grease spot in the middle. And that's a score when you're my age.

Well, sir, I come back to Houston talking Ricky up as a solid young first sacker, and on the day before the 1982 draft, none other than Al Rosen's personal assistant called and invited me to come down to the Dome to watch. It was one of the proudest moments of my life, or at least I felt so at the time. In the 31st round, the club took Ricky Mendoza, high school first baseman from Lyford, Texas.

Ricky had a decent year at Auburn, New York, then moved up to A ball with the Asheville Tourists where he broke his thumb in July trying to bare hand a hard throw in the dirt. That offseason, the club tried to make him a player to be named later in the deal that brought Mike Scott to the Astros. He failed his physical, limited movement in that thumb, and the Mets didn't want him. When Houston released him later that winter, he'd had enough. He decided that he'd rather stick his hand up a heifer's coochie instead of riding any more buses in the low minors. So, he went back to school to become a large animal veterinarian. Yes, he did.

Here's the thing with that story. Seeing as how he was the only ballplayer I ever had a hand in signing, I kept up with Ricky. His grandmother might have had a little to do with it. I tried sparking after her for a time, but a long-distance relationship just don't work when you're over 80 and can't drive. Hell, at that age, there are times when the bathroom is too far away, let alone the durn Valley.

Anyhoo, Ricky stopped in to pay me a visit one day about 1986, and that's when he met my youngest granddaughter, Angeline, a newly minted school teacher following in her sister's footsteps. Took a bit of a shine to her, I reckon. Least ways they've been married for 29 years now. I sometimes think back to my son Felix and wonder how he'd feel if he knew a child of his mixed-race daughter married a Mexican. And one that she met through me, at that. Makes me chuckle.

The ball club gave me a gold pass so as I could go see a ball game any time I please. First ten or fifteen years, I missed nary a one. Or close to it. I bought Angeline her first legal beer at the Dome. Once I got up around 100 years of age, some nagging something would keep me home now and then, watching on the TV. I still make a few, though not as many as I used to. Hard to get around. Once you get past 105 years of age, things start giving out on you.

Chapter Twenty

Do I have any regrets? Hell, you've heard my life story. I made plenty of mistakes, but I always tried to follow my mother's advice to be kind and keep improving. I could've done a better job, but I guess I look at like this here: My granddaughters forgave me my transgressions, so who am I to disagree?

I'll say that's the kind of question that'll draw up a different answer every day you ask it, but at the moment, there is one thing comes to mind. Baseball had grounded me my whole life. When things went sour, I always had the game to crawl back into. It did a wonderful job of keeping me honest, and for 80-some odd years, if you'd ask me what I most needed in life, I'd have told you baseball. It turns out maybe I was wrong.

Well, son, I must admit that I have enjoyed talking with you more than I expected to when you first telephoned. It makes me feel downright young to go back over my baseball stories like that. Let me know how your little article comes out. Send me a copy if you get the time.

Sorry to hustle you out the door, but my great-granddaughter is supposed to pick me up at seven-thirty. She's a good one, and my personal driver, too. Leastwise, that's how our little joke goes. I never learned to drive an automobile. Did I tell you that? I often wonder if that whole set to with Bilbo Prewitt and Old Snack just put me off the idea. Could be.

We're going out for Vietnamese food. It's a favorite of mine. I ain't never been afraid to try something new to eat, and that Vietnamese really caught my fancy. I'm partial to the stuff you can roll up in a side of leaf lettuce and eat it like a hot dog. They even let you dip it in the mustard, if you feel like it. My wife probably would've never stood for that. Pearl might've, though. She sure might've.

AUTHOR'S NOTES

Just as I wrote in the notes for the first half of this duology, it's a tricky thing to include so many real people in a fictional setting. I'll repeat what I wrote then - my constant goal was to portray any real people in a manner that made sense given the available historical record. Bottom line, though, is that this is entirely a work of fiction. Many of the choices were made because I wanted a given episode to be funny. End of story. None of this should be taken seriously. Any actions on the part of real people are fictional.

There is one area, and one area only where that is not the case. Just as before, I tried to be precise with all game details. If one of Rube's teams played on a given day or a certain pitcher threw, that should be accurate all the way down to the final outcome and a specific player's line in the box score. If I made a mistake there, it was not my intention, and I apologize. In the midst of so much outrageous fictional behavior, I figured it was the least I could do.

Many of the locations are also real. A few are totally invented. Like New York and Memphis in the first book, I studied Cincinnati to get things right where needed. The Licky is fictional. So is the Rich-Man in Houston. I've written so much non-fiction about Houston history, that I know that place very well, even from the time when I was an infant and decades before. I tried not to overdo it on details, but the places Rube could walk from his apartment were all real, and he could indeed ride buses to the other places, too. So when Rube buys an album at the Record Rack or goes to McCoy Funeral Home on a bus down Wheeler

Avenue, those were things real people were doing at the time. Derek at the record store got his wardrobe courtesy of a French professor I had at University of Texas.

Since we baseball history folks and SABR types are nothing if not geeky, I need to say that the underlying cover photo in the orange is from Buff Stadium in Houston when there was an exhibition game against the Chicago White Sox in the 1930s. Wingo never worked there, but I always loved this photo, and it has the Houston history connection. We looked at a couple of Astrodome photos, but the ones affordably available just didn't work for me nearly as well. It was obtained from the Houston Metropolitan Research Center decades ago. That wonderful facility is now the Houston History Research Center, Houston Public Library. It is located in the amazing Julia Ideson Building in downtown Houston.

The top photos are both courtesy of a Creative Commons license and obtained from Wikimedia Commons, a great source for photos operated by fine and generous folks who are making the world better for creators of all types. The Ford Frick-era National League baseball is over the top of a 1950 image taken from the stands at Cincinnati's Crosley Field. This combination means that both cities in this second book are represented on the cover.

Books are not a one person operation. Even independent authors have a serious, if limited, team of people helping them out. There are various readers and editors putting some eyeballs on different aspects of the book. Hopefully, it makes the book better. Think of it as a cousin to the old maxim that any person who represents himself in court has a fool for a client.

The cover was designed by the super talented Marla Yadira Garcia. She did excellent covers for three of my non-fiction books, also the fist Wingo book, and has done the same good work for several other book projects I've been involved with through Night Heron Media. Expect to keep seeing Marla-designed covers on my future volumes.

Big thanks go to my beta readers – Jim Kreuz, Jay Trotsky, and Carl Faulkenberry. Those are the folks who first let the author know that you're not delusional and haven't wasted months simply amusing yourself. One other thing about Carl

Faulkenberry, he was kind enough to let me reprise one of his very funny jokes from the days we were both working the comedy clubs , the one about a divorced man fitting everything into the trunk of his car. Like everything in Carl's comedy act, it's a great one. Go see his show should you ever get the opportunity.

My longtime friend David Singleton answered a question or two about where Paul Flinkenberg might have bought his guitar. David was playing the Houston folk music circuit at the time.

I am also lucky enough to have gotten to know a few of the Astros ballplayers I watched as a kid and even a club executive who is one of the most knowledgeable and kind baseball people ever. Here and there, those good storytellers dropped a tale that may have served as small inspiration for something in the book. Jimmy Wynn was very candid in his autobiography, which he wrote with my pal Bill McCurdy. I read what was in the book, but Jimmy was kind enough to elaborate in person about his feelings for Harry Walker. Joe Morgan later confirmed it one afternoon. Morgan, by the way, believed that if Spec Richardson had not been such a horrible general manager, the Astros would have been World Series contenders at the start of the 1970s. It's not surprising that Rube holds the same opinion.

My beloved script writing partner, Marijane Miller, has supplied terrific support over the many years. Chris White, an excellent writer whom I've known even longer, has done the same with a heavy emphasis on the publishing industry. Both Chris and Marijane also read this book in an earlier form. Chris read it again in this form, as well.

My wonderful wife, Anne, takes time out of her own busy schedule to trudge upstairs to the Eagle's Nest office, as she calls it, and give me opinions on this or that. She also provides an excellent proof reading eye.

Thank you to all of them and others I've unintentionally omitted.

The Devil's Lease

a novel by Mike Vance

Coming in Fall 2024

The next offering from Mike Vance will mark the beginning of the Duckworth Historic Crime series of novels. Irascible Texas defense attorney J.B. Duckworth also has an innate sense of fairness, a quality which does not always set well with his peers in the legal community at the start of the 1900s. Duckworth sometimes takes clients who other lawyers ignore, and he generally does it with an eye toward what plays well in the press.

In The Devil's Lease, the first installment in the series, murder inserts itself into the already brutal convict leasing system. Find out what J.B. Duckworth, one of the most nuanced fictional attorneys ever, will do to find justice for his clients.

Please sign up for the newsletter at mikevancewriter.com to stay up to date on all of Mike's work, and be sure to follow @mikevancewriter on social media. Above all, if you enjoyed reading the Rube Wingo duology, please spread the word.
Thanks!